ANGEL TEETH ARCHIVES

Book One: Evolved Whispers

Brandy Lee Hunter

Copyright © 2024 by Brandy Lee Hunter

The moral right of the author has been asserted.
All rights reserved. No part of this publication may be reproduced, stored in a retrieval system, or transmitted, in any form or by any means, without the prior written permission of the copyright owner, nor be otherwise circulated in any form of binding or cover other than that in which it is published.

...itious, and any resemblance to real
...ly coincidental.

In Memory Of

Jackson William Walker
3 May 1998-1 June 2017

I want to thank my son, Joshua Walker, and my
daughter-in-law, Brittnie Robertson Walker,
for their endless encouragement throughout this first book,
for seeing the potential and for the many pep talks
they gave me when deciding to publish.
I would also like to thank my editor, Agatha Whitechapel
whose expertise, professionalism and patience were invaluable
during the editing of this project. I owe her a debt of gratitude.

Contents

Chapter 1: The Surface 1
Chapter 2: Madness or Sloughing? 13
Chapter 3: Pacing 26
Chapter 4: The Wait is Over 38
Chapter 5: Too Many People in My House! 48
Chapter 6: Sinking In 60
Chapter 7: Ripped Open 72
Chapter 8: How Big of a Freak am I? 82
Chapter 9: The Lost Ones 91
Chapter 10: The Hidden Outrage 102
Chapter 11: Stop Asking Questions! 112
Chapter 12: Not So Fast 121
Chapter 13: The New Toy 131
Chapter 14: Collation 141
Chapter 15: Sins of the Father 152
Chapter 16: Red Reign 162
Chapter 17: Unearthed 172
Chapter 18: Beneath the Wailing 183
Chapter 19: The Hits Just Keep on Comin' 196
Chapter 20: The Depths 206

Chapter 21: Resurgence...215
Chapter 22: Evols and Vampires and Leprechauns! Oh My!........225
Chapter 23: Lost in Purple...237
Chapter 24: Passing into Legend 249
Chapter 25: I Wasn't Alone..259
Chapter 26: Answers in Whispers...270

Chapter 1
The Surface

I fold my worries into paper planes and turn them into flying fucks.
—*Author Unknown*

I hear you, your wretched erratic breathing, only slightly drowned out by the sound of that primitive loud heart. *THUMP-THUMP, THUMP-THUMP*, the echoing drumbeat disrupting my peace. More than a mile in distance and yet I can feel your anxiousness, no doubt caused by the thoughts driving you into a state of panic as the drumbeat quickens. The scent of fear is almost as thick as your obnoxious cologne flowing toward me. No one should be in my woods tonight. You know that but you came anyway.

The ridiculous defiance of humans never ceases to amaze me. All the evocative legends swirling around my property and here you are, creeping in closer. I see you now in the darkness with my fierce penetrating eyes. Your brain blinds you to my presence, it cannot comprehend something like me. So easy it would be to dim your light, to remove you from your petty existence. In an instant I could shred you, body and soul. I am no monster read about in fairytales. I am not your sideshow. No longer human, however, not fully resigned to my new life or gifts. Trespass further and you will regret it. Your hair stands on the back of your neck but still you push forward, taking another step, and another. Idiot. Curiosity kills more than just cats.

Solitary creatures invent clever deadly ways to deter outsiders. What I have become has enabled me to eliminate any who venture too close. I will admit I have fallen into the temptation of abusing these gifts a time or two. Forever in internal debate, I must stay hidden and yet how glorious it would be to turn you inside out and fling you around, painting the sky a brilliant mosaic of crimson soul.

Luckily for you, I have to get my butt to the airport to catch a flight. Continue your hunt while I tear myself away from the desire to rid this boring world of another monotonous human. I am both newly born and ancient, which makes my attitude somewhat contradictory. My true nature and potential are limitless though, tread carefully. I went from human to infected remolded being, to something unexpected and unexplained by my new kindred. A mystery among the mysterious, you could say.

During that all-consuming rearrangement of physical matter, like something from the movie, *The Thing*, an unseen entity came to be and follows me now. Everywhere. No form, just a pair of beady creepy eyes. It's seemingly tethered, unable to escape. Now, on my plane, it's hiding in the corner. My creature sticks to me like glue. Anywhere, anytime, or anyplace, those eyes haunt me. That pathetic shadow has no choice and it's not happy to say the least. Although I now know what my creature is, I will continue to call it creature. I'm not sure it deserves much more than that. It doesn't belong to me anymore, yet it clings to me. By the end of this story you will know it's identity. By the end of this story you will know many things.

For two hundred years I haven't been able to get many answers about this new life of mine. Hell, with all this extra time I haven't been able to answer questions from my old life either. That significantly changed in recent days. An explosion of profound and heartbreaking knowledge came spilling out. So, I apologize for the interruptions; my mind goes in many directions after the events of the week, and I am most definitely more erratic and unhinged. The reason for my current mental confusion is due not just to acquiring *some* answers but millions of years of answers. Too much information for any one brain to handle, even a brain as advanced and otherworldly as mine. Anyway, I have much to do and a short time in which to do it. I had best write this down before I forget once more.

There is a danger it could all be erased. That I could be removed from this existence suddenly. I'm recording my story as I travel; from one airplane to the next. From one country to the next. I will try to keep the facts in the correct order. Again, I am a little all over the place lately. My incredible and frankly unbelievable journey spans many continents and breaks the concept of time itself. Traveling though folds in space influences your mind. Memories evaporate or become twisted into an altered reality.

I am not always clear if what's in my head is a human thought or a peek behind the curtain. Before all this, I was human. Humans are wont to do human things. Things that by now are not shocking. Nothing is new. They are doomed to repeat all of it, generation after generation, but what happens when humans are upgraded? If body and mind are rewired? Do they cease to be human? I'll let you be the judge of that. I'm not here to sway your opinions. In all honesty, I don't give a fuck about your judgments. They will not change the outcome.

My transformation tossed me into a side of human history we never knew. Some of our folklore and fairytales are true; just not exactly as you may have read them. My kind have been the best kept secret ever. Who we are gave rise to many fables, such as witches, vampires, and aliens but my life and who I am is no fable. Besides, there is no greater monster than a human in his natural state. I'll start my story off slow; with what brought me to my new existence. The physical rebirth of my body is as important as the journey I would embark upon. I assure you the excruciating trauma I survived was only the beginning of pain for the decades that followed. And I endured that unbelievable physical metamorphosis alone.

Most of our kind has had to transform in secret and solitude. The physical changes often trigger a deep madness. It was unbearably confusing with no one there to keep me sane through the process. I wouldn't be alone for long though. New people entered my life and I need you to keep in mind, I use the term 'people' loosely. You must get past the vocabulary I use as description does small justice to what we really are. It was with these new people that the true chaos and madness began. The relationships I cultivated, once reborn, would be some of the most important and most devastating I had ever experienced. Without them, however, my story would've floundered.

If you're hoping for hot, young, and sexy, you have come to the wrong place. My journey was one of gore and heartbreak rather than romance and glee. I have not yet put an end to it but what has transpired thus far must be recorded. Nothing in this world has been what it seems. Not even how humans think the earth was created is true. In fact, this world was never supposed to be as it currently is. There have been powerful forces surrounding our planet from the very moment it came into existence, and they have played us like a game of chess, a game humans cheat at constantly. You're losing, by the way. You can't successfully cheat at a game you don't actually know how to play. Remember that.

My name is Emma. To be official, I was born human in the year 1973 as Emma Jane Alexander. I was the mother of three children, a grandmother, divorced twice, and served in the military for twenty-two years as a medic; among many other things. I was an average-looking lady, I believe. Topping the charts at just five feet, five inches with shoulder-length blondish brown hair. Gray eyes with middle-of-the-road Irish skin, red blotches on my neck when my temper rose. I neither considered myself homely or beautiful. No makeup on a regular basis as I worked and sweat on my land quite a bit. Plus, I didn't feel the need to dress up for myself; sweatpants and T-shirts would do, flannels and jeans during the winter months. Two of my children, Joshua aged twenty-seven and June aged twenty-five, lived on the opposite side of the United States. My youngest passed away when he was only nineteen, several years earlier. Jake.

Prior to the beginning of my journey, I led a solitary life after retiring from the military. Withdrawn and grouchy at times, I was more comfortable talking to my cat than a friend at Walmart. My military service was both the best part of my life and the worst. I often hid my pain, which caused outbursts and bouts of anger. Uncle Sam thought it would be a good idea to deploy me to war nine times. Nine times I was shoved around like cattle from one demolished country to the next. As a surgical medic, people and blood were my job. Blood, mostly. Bodies covered in blood, torn to pieces, and at times thrown in different directions. Do you know what it's like to go searching for a twenty-year old's arm or leg? Gathering up what remains of a literally shattered soul? I do. Events like these rewire your brain in the worst ways.

I was, and still am, fairly sarcastic and cynical. I'm known by friends and family for having a dirty mouth. Cussing is my standard.

Fuck could be a preposition as far as I'm concerned. If that offends you, I don't care. My vocabulary is vast and my intellect above average, and cursing makes me smile. My grammar and writing skills leave much to be desired though. I'm more of a painter, not so much a writer. I have no particular religious preference and I feel strongly that, 'live and let live,' should be everyone's motto but it is not. Those are my basic attributes in a nutshell.

Now that introductions have been made, let us begin.

Three years after retiring and following the untimely death of my son Jake; I was broken. I had been in the process of moving to a mountain top home when my son suddenly died. The log cabin was not intended to be an isolated insane asylum but that is what it became. After I buried my child, I returned to my new home and hid. A shut-in. A completely self-sufficient, don't-fucking-talk-to-me, stay-off-my-property, crazy person. Retreating from everything and everyone who threatened my dwindling sanity.

The only regret was my remaining adult children lived very far away indeed. I didn't get to see them often. With technology being what it was, however, video calls and social media made my communications with them feel closer. It's still not the same and I would wonder if moving to the middle of nowhere was smart. Don't you worry about where or on what mountain I lived, that's not something I tell most people. All you need to know is that I was located on the East Coast of upper North America. My mountain was secluded and protected, my log cabin had only one way in or out. It was perfect. Surrounded by trees, animals, and a few far-off neighbors who kept to themselves, I blotted out the world and almost chucked the key. Every few weeks I would venture down to the small, local hick towns to shop, run errands, or go to the post office. I grouped together as many appointments as possible to ensure I got the most done in one day. You see, I have an aversion to people in general. Even before the death of my son. Between my abusive childhood and the military, I wasn't, am still not, a fan of the human race. I rate living alone forever over taking part in human society ever again.

I took immense pride in my property. I kept the lawn manicured and the flowerbeds spotless. I lived on my own little slice of quiet heaven for nearly six years. All was peaceful and settled. I suffered from multiple health issues that came from serving; some extremely painful. So much pain at times that I would wish a sudden death to make it stop. Days later I would be fine again and wouldn't think about dying anymore, not until the next episode. Though, over time, the episodes added up and wore me down. It was exhausting. All the more reason not to involve other people. It's why I stayed alone, caring only for my property and cat, Vader. That was all my body and brain could handle.

It was the winter of 2022 and I had just turned forty-nine years old. One night, just after dark, I was sitting on the back deck smoking a cigarette, scrolling through my phone, looking at Facebook and deciding which online game to play. A small group of deer were hanging out in the snow just steps from me. I was feeling low, having just recovered from a particularly bad episode of debilitating pain. That was the ongoing cycle of peace and pain, off and on, one day to the next. That night, however, there was a change. A life-altering event that snapped me from my self-pity.

A loud growl rumbled through the air. Not like a wolf or dog but a deep rolling, slow growl. It sounded much like a crocodile, which made the whole situation even more alarming. My head swung up from my phone to look in the direction of the deer, who had startled off, into the woods. As I searched for what had spooked them, I saw a man. He was standing at the edge of my deck to the right of me. He did not move.

"Who are you?" I asked as I jumped to my feet and raced to the sliding glass door.

Nothing was his reply.

I looked around but could see no footprints in the snow surrounding the deck. "How did you get here?" I barked.

Nothing again.

I opened the sliding door and stood half in and half out while looking him up and down. He was dressed warmly but not as warmly as most people would be that time of year. Tall, slender, dark hair, and a well-groomed beard. Olive skin and bright soft eyes. There was something calming about his presence. His stance was neither aggressive nor threatening. Nevertheless, I bolted inside, locked the door, and peered out. He slowly walked right up to the glass and, after I loudly demanded to know what he wanted, informed him I was calling the police. He remained unfazed as if my agitation just didn't exist.

Finally, he spoke, "You called to me. Why would you want me to leave?"

Okay, great, I thought. *A backwoods psychopath*. It took a few years but one of those bad horror movie inbreds had finally decided to make his move. I envisioned hearing a banjo playing off in the distance and me hogtied in the bed of a pickup truck. No one in six years had ever made a surprise visit to my property. Rarely did I have visitors of any kind, most certainly not in the middle of the night. The only conclusion I could come to was that he was crazy. Standing at my back door for nefarious purposes.

He bent down slightly so we were eye to eye with the pane of glass between us, and insisted again that I had requested his presence, "Emma, you called to me and I am here. Settle your mind and remember. I am here to help you. I will return in one month."

I was frozen, fixated on his eyes. They had too many colors, if that makes any sense. And the pupils moved a lot, contracting rapidly. The colors in his irises rolled into themselves like a dance, and I thought I might be experiencing a stroke or hallucination.

As he finished speaking, I blinked, and he was gone. And I mean, *gone*, gone. No gentlemanly retreat, just ... *THWIP!*

How did he do that? Oh crap, maybe he went around to the front of the house! I couldn't remember if I had locked all the doors. *What had he said?* Dammit, I sped through the house checking to ensure everything was secure. Windows, doors, and basement. I picked up Vader, and raced to my bedroom, locking the door behind us. I removed my gun from its case setting it next to me on the bed. My mind could not shake what he had said. *I called to him? Why did he say it like that?* It was weird, the whole thing was weird. I had been so focused on his eyes I felt like I was forgetting something ... but it was gone now, vanished as he did into the night. I tried to convince myself sleep would make things clearer in the morning. Calling the cops at this hour to report a strange man would not elicit much of a response due to my location. Cops up here were far and few between. They didn't do house calls in the middle of the night if nothing was actively happening at that moment. Kind of a Catch-22. I had to let it go.

I woke up early and fixed myself some coffee, looked outside to see if there were any signs of him. Nothing. I decided to get dressed and drive down to the police station to file a report. On the way there, I went through details of his description, the clothes he had been wearing. But the problem was, it was gone from my mind. *Poof!* Like smoke it had disappeared. *Dark hair? No, blond? Tall? Yes, he was tall but no, wait, was he closer to my height?* I pulled the car over and just sat for a while. I realized if I made a report about a man who had showed up out of nowhere during a snowstorm, who spoke to me face to face, and yet I couldn't give an accurate description of him; they would think I'd gone mad. Cabin fever is a real thing, after all.

I decided there was nothing for it, but to put it all out of my mind and my world moved on as normal over the weeks that followed. It was not much, that life of mine. Slow and unremarkable, I seemed to be suspended. I would get up each day, wander around the house, clean, do some chores, maybe paint a picture. Most days I would simply cuddle with Vader and watch TV or movies all day. Up until the move and Jake's death, my life had always been go, go, go. Oddly, I had been semi-social even though it never truly felt right. How I was living way up there on my own, was a waste, according to many. Most saw what I was doing as giving up or not contributing to society, blah, blah, blah. Screw them. Up there I was enveloped in peace, calm, and quiet, and it's what brought back my sanity. To a point anyway and about to be severely tested. The stranger I encountered would change much; my body, my reason, and my future.

A month had come and gone. The snow was falling again in what seemed like a never-ending winter. I loved sitting out back watching it float down. It was that special type of snow when the flakes clump together forming pure white, graceful feathers. That was my favorite. The deafening sound of silently falling snow was another benefit of my seclusion and it intoxicated me. Drowning out all painful thoughts, memories, and anxieties. It was an extraordinarily beautiful night, the kind most people only see in pictures. Then it all came crashing down. Fast.

My stranger was standing at the end of the deck again.

Startled, I shouted, "Jesus! Dammit, you scared me!" I began interrogating him. "What do you want from me? Are you a rapist? *Yeah, I know a rapist wouldn't confirm that.* "Are you Death?" was my next insight.

"Yes and no," he replied.

"Riddles? No! Fuck that. I'm not playing these games. What the fuck are you doing here and what do you want?" I snapped. I stood waiting for an answer.

He remained motionless but replied, "I am here to end this life and begin something new for you. I want to bestow on you a gift. One you have been subconsciously asking for," he proclaimed.

"So, you *are* Death," I mumbled and sat back down to light another cigarette. "All right. If this is happening, then it's happening." This was both to him and to myself, I ought to address everybody. I knew very well you can't outrun Death. Might as well roll with it. To tell you the truth, I was a little relieved. It was kind of a, neither here nor there, moment. I asked him to let me finish my cigarette and then I would change clothes.

He looked at me puzzled.

"I don't want to be found dead in my nightgown and robe!" I said.

He smiled but stayed silent as I sat with what I thought would be a thousand questions.

But only one came to mind. "Do you have a name? Does Death have another name?" I asked.

"Seth," he replied.

"SETH?" I let out a chuckle and even a snort. *Oh, the parody*. The whole night was ridiculous. Madness had consumed me, obviously. I finished my cigarette then walked to the door, planning on changing my clothes. In an instant Seth was there standing behind me. I felt a sharp breeze on my back which caused me to turn.

He carefully pushed me up against the glass and kissed me.

I was right, I thought, *a rapist local inbred*. I struggled at first until inexplicably I began leaning into him. Exhaustion and weakness enveloped my body. My mind wandered. *So, the kiss of Death is real? Too bad I won't get the chance to tell anyone that old saying is true.*

He stopped and instructed me, "You're very tired," he encouraged, "and you want to sleep now. Follow my directions and everything will be fine."

As I turned to close the door, he had vanished. Again. With no warning or sound of footsteps. My eyes stared outside, I was still in shock, and there was a red-hot anger in me for allowing it to happen. I'm a fighter. I would have never let anything like this happen … before. *Why now? How in the hell did I not try to stop him?* But the anger was lessening, something was distorting my vision. Eyes heavy and weepy. In a haze of confusion, I made my way to the bedroom. In my mouth I could taste something like copper.

I sat on my bed, and turned on the TV with the lights out. Lying in darkness and not really paying attention to the flickering glow, the copper mineral flavor lingered on my tongue. I had just let a creepy stranger, who I thought was Death, kiss me. Only two words came to mind before I drifted off to sleep. *I'm fucked.*

Chapter 2
Madness or Sloughing?

An image too blurry to be a person or an animal was holding me, rocking me back and forth and whispering static in my ear. *What is this? Where am I?* Frozen, but comforted by this thing, I wondered why I hadn't been here before. Just then, the ghostly night maid began to speak, forcing my eyes to open and it was no more.

I had slept until 10:30 a.m. the next morning. That never happened. I was usually awake by 6 a.m. My nights were fitful and often, I didn't sleep for more than an hour or two before giving up and going out to the living room. Nightmares are a story for another time. Sleeplessness and fatigue are a veteran's curse and penance. Anyway, last I remembered there was a coppery blood taste in my mouth, but it was gone. Maybe I was okay. Maybe everything would be okay. No worries. It wasn't real.

I got up, put my robe on, and headed to the kitchen for coffee. I couldn't tell anyone about what I thought had happened, they'd lock me away for sure. It was just a dream. A product of isolation. With coffee in hand, I proceeded to the back porch for a smoke. As I sat down, I reached into my bathrobe pocket for a lighter and felt something sharp and thin. It was business card. It occurred to me that Seth had put it there when he kissed me the night before. *Oh crap, time to worry.* It *was* real.

I flipped the card repeatedly. Feeling it between my fingers, my hand started to tremble as I read it aloud:

"If you tell others of our time together you will be eliminated." *Okay, that's harsh,* I thought. Upon turning the card over I gasped when I saw them. Directions: 1: Consume as much calcium-rich food and meat proteins as possible. 2: You will sleep well above average, this is normal. 3: Physical changes will come. 4: I will see you again in a year.

Faauukkk! I read it several times trying to rationalize an irrational event. I was in trouble. *So* much trouble. For the rest of the day and the weeks that followed I stressed about it. Relentlessly I researched strange encounters, even alien encounters but found nothing comparable to what I had experienced. *What was I going to change into? Was he Death? Am I dead right now in some kind of weird hell of my own making? Was there a car accident and I'm in a coma making all this up in my head to pass the time?* The card became frayed and worn. If I was in a horror movie it would be the most boring non-sexy one ever. This surely *had* to be real because I could've made up a better scenario if it was just in my head.

After the second month I began to relax and tried to put it from my mind. Gradually, I went back to doing normal regular life things. Nothing was going to happen. Too much time had gone by. That's what I told myself. Put the laptop and Internet searches to rest. My cozy quiet existence was back on track and I would never speak of what was possibly a cabin fever mini episode again, but normalcy was not to last much longer. Month three I awoke in pain, extreme stomach and body pain. Later that afternoon I threw up violently again and again. Most of what was coming up looked like blood and tar. This shit hit in a flash and turned on a dime.

I have the flu. That was what I said to myself while sweating buckets. *I have the flu. I have the flu. No need to panic. I have the flu.* This had NOTHING to do with that Seth guy, surely! It got worse when the same substances began coming out of my other end. Throwing up, then diarrhea. Over and over. Sometimes I found myself sitting on the toilet and puking into a trashcan. I brought a pillow and blanket to the bathroom. Curling up on the floor. It was the only way to sleep between episodes. I was exhausted from what felt like my guts liquefying. What the fuck was the sticky slime crap pouring out of every orifice? I could feel each of my organs as they moved, operated, or changed. Unsettling was not a strong enough word. Once while throwing up, a long string of soft bodily tissue appeared. Full of clotted blood and bile. I had to pull it from my throat before I choked to death. It looked exactly like the lining of a stomach. This was no flu! My innards were exiting my body!

Passing out between the bouts of heaving, retching, and crying, I wanted to go to the hospital. I needed to be examined by doctors but was concerned about the warning on the card. *That stupid fucking card.* Seth must have given me something like an STD or rare disease, I thought. Ebola? No, I would've been dead weeks ago. WebMD was no help with any of my symptoms. According to the website either I had nothing or I had everything! Cold sweats and near unbearable hot flashes. Zero food intake. I couldn't hold down a cracker. Eventually, I tried to resign myself to it. I was going to die right there in the bathroom. Soon enough, I welcomed it.

Yet it was not to be. Within two weeks all symptoms had begun to dissipate. Somehow surviving, I began to equalize. By the first day of the fourth month, I felt good but was craving sugar, chocolate ice cream. I had been starved for so long during the sickness, the hunger seemed primal. I took myself shopping and excitedly bought up loads of ice cream, cottage cheese, yogurt, cream cheese, milk, coffee creamer etc. And meat. Lots of meat of all kinds. It was as if I had never eaten before or ever experienced a grocery store. High as a kite and everything smelled so delicious. I spent a fortune that day on enough food to feed an army. After what I had just gone through, I didn't care; I was determined to buy myself whatever I wanted.

Throughout the fourth month I gradually recovered and ate like nobody's business. If someone on the outside was watching they'd think I was trying to gain 200 pounds and get diabetes on purpose. Neither of those things developed. Just me and my insatiable appetite. Isn't that everyone's dream? To eat anything and everything with zero consequences? A nagging feeling persisted that there would be consequences, though. A foreboding telling me that the next changes would top the last. My happiness would soon be replaced with new weirdness.

The turn came again. Severe fever dreams began, haunting me almost nightly. Dreams of my past war deployments. Some were so realistic I would wake on the floor under my bed, shaking and crying. Dreams of my children; of me leaving them for some reason but not knowing where I was going or why. Intense visions of running alongside animals. Sometimes next to panthers and wolves. Fighting in large stadiums with winged creatures I had never seen before, had no name for, and no clue as to why I was there. All the world was awash in bright purply colors draped in blood and chocolate. Some dreams I didn't want to end, even those that would send others screaming. While other dreams tore me in half and threw pieces of myself to the corners of the bedroom. A plague of nightmares consumed me for weeks. I would walk the house in a trance; sleep deprived and mentally unstable. Vader could do nothing but watch intently, not knowing what the hell was wrong with his mom. Then the waking visions started. The creeping madness. The small hiccups and ticks that jolt you out of this world and into another.

 I began seeing weird things when I was awake. I didn't know if it was because I hadn't been sleeping or if what I was seeing was in fact there. Tiny mite-like creatures on my skin. On the walls. On Vader! I was losing it or possibly whatever this illness was gave me super vision or mind control. I had to have a brain disease. That must be it. Hallucinations of ghosts and moving shadows. Hearing beetles talk to each other. It rained in my living room one night!

 You don't understand. I'm not explaining it right.

 Petting Vader one minute and the next he would walk into the room. I'd look down at my lap, confused because I had just been petting him but he was not there. What was happening? How long would this last? My body was twisting; remolding itself into what, I didn't know and now my mind was melting.

 Music was partly the reason I survived thus far. I had always credited music for helping me through difficult times ever since I was a young child. This transformation was no different. Whenever I began seeing shadows move or another strange pain in my body started nagging me, on went the music. I thoroughly enjoy all forms of music, truly. But I do tend to fall back on 70s era jams. From disco to rock and roll, I played it loud and often, anything to attempt to drown out the seemingly invisible misery attacking me.

 Month five begun with a skull cracking mouth pain. I awoke in the middle of the night screaming. My lower and upper jaw bones were throbbing, my gums bleeding. Never in my life had I endured a pain such as this. I would have rather gone through childbirth again, without drugs, than what was happening. If it didn't stop soon, I'd have no choice but to see a dentist or doctor or fucking witchdoctor. This pain surpassed the intestine liquefying grossness of the months past. When your jaw hurts, your head hurts. They go together. I took the max dose of my nerve pain medication plus Ambien, nighttime cold medicine, and Melatonin, for nine days in a row. Knocked myself out as best I could to get through whatever the fuck was happening. I was either going to survive it or overdose.

One morning I lurched upright in bed due to suddenly choking on two teeth that had fallen out. Coughing them up into my hand I stared at the bloody pool in my palm with the two teeth. I hurried to the mirror to find all my canines, upper and lower, had gone or were dangling loose. The premolars and molars on both sides were all loose as well. Spitting up blood and crying became a new normal. Every now and then I'd laugh while crying because it was such a mindblowing disaster. I was in hell. I obviously deserved it for some reason. This just could not get any worse and why hadn't I gone to a doctor? Screw what the card said. I should be in a hospital. Then, *BOOM!* Out of nowhere, like I had been smacked in the head with a lead pipe. My body crumpled and dropped to the bathroom floor, convulsing until I finally passed out.

Once I slowly regained consciousness, I realized I was still in the same spot. Groggy, in a haze, trying to blink and focus, I felt the new wrongness. My mouth didn't hurt as much but I was stuck to the damn floor. My left cheek was glued down by thick dried blood. I literally had to peel myself carefully off the ground to sit upright, leaving a bit of skin behind. Hair disheveled and matted; caked with blood and drool. The floor had a dark red, almost black-like powder substance everywhere. A few more of my teeth were scattered about.

Nauseated, I wanted to puke again, I was soaked in urine from my waist to my ankles and the room stank to high heaven. Trying to get my bearings, I sat still for quite some time, leaning against a wall and slowly letting the room come into focus. I knew it then, I was rotting, like a zombie.

Vader was at my feet, curled up and sleeping, bless his loyal furry soul. I felt incredibly fragile as if I were the thinnest glass vase about to shatter. Vader didn't look so hot either. Crawling to my phone across the bathroom floor, I discovered I had been unconscious for three days. My poor Vader was surely out of food and water. My joints were rigid and sore, I could barely walk. Hunched over like an old woman, I struggled to carry him to his dishes in the kitchen where I encouraged him to drink fresh water. After feeding him and giving him some love, I eventually made my way back to the bathroom to shower.

It was amazing; like I had never felt water on my skin before. Every cell soaked up the cool wetness while I braced myself upright, leaning forward with eyes closed waiting to wake from this most current nightmare. I washed my hair several times to get all the blood out and scrubbed my body vigorously. When I dried myself off, I noticed something curious. The majority of my scars and pregnancy stretch marks were faded, not gone, but noticeably less visible. My hair was thicker and longer by a couple of inches. Nothing much anyone else would notice, but I did. I got dressed and then took a long look inside my mouth. Touching the holes where my teeth used to be I felt something sharp. With a flashlight I got a closer look inside the voids. New teeth were coming in and they were pointy. *Oh, come* on, *is this a vampire thing? No! This is unacceptable!*

So much for going to a dentist or doctor to solve this. I didn't think that was a good idea. They might use me like a lab rat or Seth could show up out of the blue and kill us all. My head was spinning with all kinds of folklore and movie references. *Crap, I had better not be all sparkly in the sunlight. I'll be so pissed!* I went outside to test this worrying theory by sitting in my chair for a few minutes. Nope, no flames. I stayed longer to smoke a cigarette while carefully studying my skin. Pleasantly pleased I was not burning from the sunshine nor was I sparkly. So, that was some good news. *What was I, dammit? What was this?* I couldn't think straight anymore due sudden hunger. I mean, ravenous. Eating was a chore with the soreness of my mouth, I had to kind of suck and crush sideways with my gums. *Note to self about dentures*, but I continued to scarf down as much as I could. An unhealthy amount of ice cream was consumed over those days of toothlessness.

Later that night I relaxed in my easy chair. In a state of peace and calm for once. My mouth still ached but was tolerable. Whatever my body was doing I didn't know how to stop it. I couldn't alert anyone or get help. The question that kept jabbing me was, would Seth hurt my children if I told anyone, doctors and such? I didn't care much about my own survival but you don't mess with my kids. And there was still at least six months left before I would see Seth again. If he really did come back. If he even existed. Thoughts of how I would murder him began to occupy my mind. If anyone deserved my wrath, it was him. I was no angel before this started and the mental changes hadn't lessened my temper, only spun it tighter. Getting this under control seemed impossible. How do you control what you don't understand? I just prayed the worst of the changes were over.

During the previous months I had spoken to Josh and June a handful of times. Of course, I did not discuss with them my changes or issues. I didn't want to chance something bad happening to them if they found out. Too many movies warn against sharing secrets like mine. Unfortunately, movies and books were the only guide I had and so far, they were all incorrect.

Texting had been the preferred method of communication between the kids and me, especially now. With my skin looking a bit younger and the fact that I was missing teeth; a video call would be out of the question. They would have committed me to a mental hospital in a heartbeat if they saw me. They wouldn't have believed one word if I tried to explain.

My Joshua was always busy with his work. A nuclear powerplant inspector, of all things. It was hard for me to imagine that clumsy, goofy, little boy, now a man, in such a crazy and dangerous profession. There are not a ton of nuclear plants thankfully, however, that job kept him moving quite a bit over the west coast. June, on the other hand, had gone toward the more traditional job of landscape designer. She created beautiful backyards for families and hotels. Pools, trees, boulders, etc. That was her thing and she was really good at it. I was very proud of my children but as aformentioned, they would not waste a moment entertaining my new 'issues.' They'd have had me locked up. They were both firmly grounded in reality. This would have been too much for them.

My life had become a B rated horror movie of sorts. Supernatural did not yet feel accurate and would not have made for a good picture anyway. But if I were in the middle of a psychological breakdown, what with all the madness, nightmares, and body changes, it was definitely fitting for a *Jacob's Ladder* type of setting.

My saving grace was that blood didn't bother me. I had bled from every orifice over the months, in disturbing amounts. That would have been enough to give the average person pause or panic. Blood has never freaked me out. Not even as a small child skinning a knee or getting a cut. That made being a military war medic a good fit. Seeing blood is one thing but you must also accept the smell of it. Fresh blood has a beautiful metallic scent. Like having a penny in your mouth. And you continue to smell it long after it's been cleaned up. Old blood, however, has a decaying stench that repels most humans. It's an internal subconscious trigger warning you death is near. The point being, I was not alarmed or turned off by the continuous bloodletting. Don't mistake my quiet guarded nature as meekness or even weakness.

Anyway, as time passed, my new teeth grew into place. All the calcium-rich foods I was instructed to consume now made sense. It was to help grow those teeth. Three on each side of my upper jaw. Starting with the longer canines; gradually getting shorter as they went back. A little more wolf-like than vampiric. I say that because there were also four pointy teeth in my lower jaw as well. Two on each side beneath the canines. Ten new razor-sharp fangs in total. This may sound odd but they looked natural to me. The teeth didn't stick out over my lips. They fit in my mouth as if they had always been there. My smile was more intriguing than scary, as long as I didn't open too wide. Pearly whites that happened to have a notable sharpness—looked super-hot to me; badass really, but they came with an odd feature. One I wasn't expecting. Barbs.

I found out the hard way they were all barbed on the backside. Some snake species have barbs to help them hold onto their prey better. Well, that was concerning. Since those teeth were new and I was getting used to them I would often play with them subconsciously while watching TV. Kind of like when I got my braces off as a teenager and would roll my tongue over the front of my teeth feeling how smooth they were. Like a new toy, it was difficult those first few months to leave my teeth and barbs alone.

One night I touched one of my canines pushing up on it and before I knew it my finger was literally snagged on the tooth. The barb on the back of the tooth had dug into my skin. Carefully, I wiggled my finger free and that was the first time I witnessed how quickly I could heal. The puncture wound on my finger bled for only a second and then, before my eyes, the mark was gone. I saw it seal up, so I quickly punctured it again, watching as the action repeated. That was pretty neat! My new teeth were not very long, they were just short enough that maybe I could go to the dentist for a cleaning. Just maybe I could get away with saying I had sharpened the teeth myself as a dumb teenager or something. The barbs though, there was no way to explain that shit. So, no more dentist for me. I wasn't going to risk it.

Month six brought forth shedding, plus some eye and hearing changes. While undressing I discovered copious amounts of dead skin everywhere in my clothes. I was peeling, like a whole-body peeling. Because I was unsure how bad that next phase was going to get, I bolted from my house, driving into town. I needed to restock food and necessities.

It had been too long since my last trip from my protective cocoon. I tried walking through Walmart as if nothing was wrong with me, paranoid that everyone somehow knew. But there was a strange tension in the air. I looked at each person differently. Something was odd about them, they smelled funny, walked weird, and sounded foreign. I was confused and sped out of there as fast as possible once shopping was complete.

Each day after that, the amount and rate of peeling accelerated. Just gross as if I were a molting snake. At first, so much skin had died off that all my tattoos were much brighter and new-looking. Then, after several more days, they began disappearing, sloughing off, revealing almost perfect skin. I'm still kind of pissed about that. They were expensive and many were memories of past military triumphs and places. All gone now. I was looking noticeably younger. Not by much; maybe ten years, but the change was significant enough that others would wonder or ask questions. My initial excitement turned to worry. This could cause problems.

The morning I woke up nearly blind was probably the first time I panicked. All that pain and extreme suffering from body changes was one thing but it was the loss of my eyesight that truly terrified me the most. I lived alone. Neighbors were some distance away. If I stayed blind, I wouldn't have a choice but to call 911. Luckily that change was swift and my sight soon returned. I really didn't feel my vision was better, that became more apparent over time. But I did have immediate control over my eye color! How fucking awesome is that? I would stare in the mirror practicing. Blue, brown, red, gold, green, and then I began to master multicolor. I could think of the color and it would wash into my irises, just like that. My eyes didn't glow fluorescent or scary crazy like. They were soothing gradual colors, natural-looking.

Night vision had elevated considerably. I could not see a deer, for example, in full color during total blackness. What I could see at night was more akin to warm silhouettes. I knew what I was looking at and I could hear the deer beautifully if I focused. My new eyes and ears worked much the same as sonar at night. Not green-glowing night vision or a heat sensor type of thing but the shape of the animal would be in perfect detail using distance to key off of it.

Hearing and sense of smell greatly heightened as well. My ability to smell everything was on the extreme side of all my new changes and it got nauseating. I didn't understand what I was smelling half the time. A sense of smell so keen that the last food a person ate would be the first thing I noticed about them. So many odors just oozed off people. I enjoyed going to the grocery stores because the smells of the real food masked the odors of the people walking by me. Oh man, some people *really* need to shower more often! And I would like to report, from the youngest to the oldest are all over the pot game. I walked by an eighty-year-old who reeked of pot. It was in her bloodstream, but not on her clothing. Edibles probably. I really got a kick out of that one.

Also, I could hear the sounds of heartbeats. I mean, not just when I walked by people, but I could hear a rabbit's heartbeat damn near fifty yards away. Vader's heartbeat in the house was so loud! It took some time for me to block that out just so I could focus on a TV show. At night his tiny paws running through the house suddenly felt and sounded like an earthquake. I could hear a car driving toward my home long before I could see it. I was very impressed with the elevated hearing. It could come in handy later.

So, was that it? Was all the weirdness and change finished? I could've just stopped there and been very comfortable. "I'm good, no more," I begged the universe. "Please no more."

The universe laughed; more was coming.

Chapter 3
Pacing

Nine months of epic extraordinary and unbelievable fairytales seemingly come to life through my body. The whole time I struggled with thoughts of madness. Was any of it real? Was I changing or was it all in my head? And those thoughts alone started to send me into madness itself, ironically. But still, life was gradually settling down. I had gone three weeks with zero new 'upgrades' to my person. Three amazing weeks of feeling better than ever. I still didn't know what I was or becoming but I found myself, for the moment, not caring. I enjoyed not being in physical pain and confusion for once. But the other shoe would drop eventually. My constant visions told me that. It was not over.

I made the decision to take a trip a few states down to visit with my children. A mini weeklong reunion of sorts. I'd been optimistic that my changes had halted. That I would not endure anymore madness, for a bit anyway. After those nine months I was in dire need to be with my children and grand babies.

The first remark I received from them was how young and refreshed I looked. June accused me of having plastic surgery, a facelift, something. That concerned me greatly. I didn't see it as that big of a change. I hadn't gone from looking fifty to twenty. Barely ten years, maybe fifteen off and I didn't think she'd be so quick to notice. I was wrong. I chuckled a bit and waved my hand at her stating, "No, no. You know I wouldn't voluntarily put myself through surgery."

She made a grimacing face and rolled her eyes.

She didn't believe me at all. *Crap.* Would I continue to stay younger looking as they aged? How much longer would I be able to let them see me? This so-called gift Seth had given me was going to rob me of my grandma years with my family.

Josh kept trying to look at my teeth. He caught me in the middle of a laugh. I think he had noticed the new fangs but his brain probably convinced him he was seeing things. There was a question nagging him, I could see it, he wanted to ask but resisted.

The visit was more difficult than I imagined it would be. I'd had the luxury of time to get used to many of my upgrades, but they had not. The grandbabies were oblivious though and just enjoyed their time with me. I hugged and kissed those babies as if I'd never see them again. Mainly because I wasn't sure if I would. Overall, I was incredibly glad I took that trip. Especially now.

More changes.

I recall it was around month ten when the pacing began. It was as simple as walking into the living room with a cup of coffee. I couldn't sit down. I put the coffee down but I didn't sit. Didn't even notice for hours that I had been wandering around the house, back and forth. From the bedroom to the living room. From the living room to the bedroom. I played games on my phone, scrolled through Facebook, messaged some distant friends for the hell of it, but my mind was elsewhere as I walked. Something wicked seemed to be building and boiling up inside me. I paced and cleaned, went jogging but it didn't help. I was feverish, exhausted, and antsy all at once. That continued for six days, maybe seven, each day worse than the last. Finally, I crashed and slept soundly straight through the night.

The next morning arrived and brought with it a new level of hell. As I sat up in bed I found blood down the front of me, in the bed, and on the sheets. The smell ... it was a smell I didn't recognize. The blood wasn't human or at least I didn't think it was. There was a clean wildness to the scent. I stumbled to the bedroom door to find bloody footsteps headed in my direction. I followed them back to where they came from. Through the kitchen and out the back sliding glass door.

On my porch lay a deer and two foxes, dead, in pools of their own blood. It was the first time I realized I could distinguish the scent of blood from one animal to the next.

I freaked out.

Out loud I shouted, "I did this, I FUCKING DID THIS!" All the animals had their throats ripped out. They were drained of blood, the stuff on the floor must have been from the initial kill. Probably weighing half their normal body weight, they were crumpled together in a heap. Frantically I got dressed, ran out into the woods, and began to dig as large a hole as possible. I was in a race to remove all traces of what happened. If I just buried them then it never was. It would be gone. I spoke to myself, as I often did especially in times of stress. *My God, what if it had been a person? Would I be doing this to people next? Why couldn't I remember anything? I was in so much trouble here.*

After the animals were buried, I cleaned the porch deck, and then myself. The pacing started again soon after. Was it a stress thing or a hunger thing or was it just a part of my madness? The whole of the ten months came down hard in that moment. Everything I'd gone through and tried to convince myself would be okay, was NOT

OKAY! The mental breakdown was on and in full swing. I screamed and cried. This was not something I could heal from. No amount of time would help, no amount of distance.

I wanted so badly for it to just go away. None of it was really happening, it couldn't be. I couldn't do it. I had never felt as alone as I did right then. Jake had permanently gone from the world, Josh and June lived far away, and I had no one there to comfort me, no one I could tell. The worst part was, if I had not been so alone in my life, this would never have happened in the first place. And that topped off my revelations. My lifestyle had somehow brought me to the crippling misery I was in. It was all my own doing. I had asked for this. *Maybe that's what Seth meant when he told me I called to him?* I wasn't sure but it just felt like I had somehow put myself in this situation.

I was finally scared to death. I was afraid to go back to sleep that night. Afraid of doing something again with no memory of it. I shuffled to the porch after pulling myself off the living room floor. In the tree line I saw something staring at me. It was not an animal but a creature of some sort. Was it Seth? No, too early for him to come. Was it another monster as I was? My head ran wild with all kinds of thoughts and guesses. My patience had long since emptied and dried up. I watched the hidden thing in the cloak of trees and anger welled inside me. I had had enough!

The creature in the distance made no move. I was thoroughly creeped out. It was too much. I was a vampire, wasn't I? A vampire who could eat whatever I wanted, with a heartbeat, and could be in sunlight? Pure ridiculousness, absolute and utter ridiculousness! I wanted answers. I needed to know how and why I had been transformed. And why was that creature still looking at me!? I got up from the chair to pace the deck. The creature's eyes followed me, back and forth. If I admitted it to myself, I had known it was too good to be true a few months ago when I thought it was over. It couldn't have just stopped with cool-ass hearing and eyesight. Nope, what was the fun in that? Had to go for the full-on vampire monster experience!

I wondered if Seth had a return policy on this *gift* he'd given me? I would gladly take death if that was the price I had to pay in exchange for returning it. Yes, much of what I had gained through the process was phenomenal. The hearing and sense of smell, not to mention the absurdly fast rate of healing. Even the new teeth looked cool and I had gotten use to the barbs. But the killing of animals was a bit too much for me. It brought into focus the severity of what I was facing. Up until the slaughter, everything else had felt one-sided and possibly delusional. Now, there was a shift, this shit was real. I felt like giving up. What to do? What to do?

I paced the floors late into the night as Vader watched me in dismay. He'd seen me go through the most gross, unfathomable, sad, and cringeworthy changes. Yet he was still loyal and loving toward me because he didn't understand. Ignorance was bliss. Or was I simply his meal ticket? Whatever the reason, he was still here, and I was very grateful. That cat was my only solid constant.

At around 3 a.m. I got tired and decided to lie down but I locked Vader out of the bedroom. I didn't know what drove me to attack those animals and I didn't want Vader to meet the same fate. I couldn't think much more before sleep took pity on me. I dreamed away most of what was left of the night.

A peaceful dream. Although I'm not sure it was a dream but more of a memory. I was walking through the woods and came upon a chair. I sat down, smelling the night air. My eyes were closed as I called to a deer with my mind. A signal of longing for one of them to come be with me. I felt it, the signal, I could feel it wash out from within me. A large buck slowly and carefully walked right up to me. He lay down in front of me, putting his head against my shoulder. I petted him lovingly while humming a lullaby. At the point of complete trust I viciously ripped his throat open.

That part woke me from sleep.

To my surprise, the dream did not alarm me or raise my heart rate. Quite the opposite.

I felt content as I made myself coffee and sat down to watch the morning news. Vader immediately curled up on my lap wanting love and attention. I somehow knew the pacing was over for the time being. Calm had settled, my shoulders lowered, and the previous day faded.

Needing a change, I thought it had been long overdue to work on my property. The gorgeous fall leaves, yellow and red, had started their annual descent to the ground. It was time I got outside to take care of the grass and cut up a few fallen branches, etc. Get back to nurturing the exterior of my home. I had mostly ignored it the entire summer while dealing with my transformation.

After a couple more cups of coffee, I put on my work clothes, braided my now unusually long hair, put on an old hat, and headed outside. The cool breeze mixed with the scent of wet leaves was stimulating. I believe I must have been out there for nearly eight hours. Mowing the lawn, raking leaves, cleaning up the flower beds and readying them for winter. I even managed to wash my car and straighten up the garage. The wilderness in all its glory was magnificent indeed. Stopping to smell the last of the flowers held new meaning with my heightened senses. The beautiful bright yellow black-eyed Susans had never had a noticeable scent before now. Rotting strawberries and grass clippings was the smell I picked up and it was intoxicating. Amazing!

Neighbors drove by slowly to wave at me or well, to snoop and spy. Although they lived spread out, they were still around.

Gossip is a rarity in an area where everyone hides from one another, so it was with surprise that I saw Mr. and Mrs. Stockwell, my neighbors, slowly approaching in their overpriced and oversized blue suburban. I gave them a friendly wave in return. They then backed up, pulling into the driveway. *Oh crap*, I panicked.

They got out of their car.

Double crap! To tell you the truth, I was thinking, worrying for their safety. *Please don't kill these people. Whatever you do, don't kill them!* I was thinking.

They walked over to me and said they thought I had moved or something. No one had seen me outside in months and the condition of my property was not the perfection it normally was. We, as neighbors, didn't see each other often. Our homes were hidden by forests and hills but we did connect a few times a year at BBQs. That was more than enough for me.

The Stockwells were very nice people but still they were... people. Mrs. Stockwell smelled like home, comforting, like blueberry pie and lavender lotion. So strong the incredible myriad of scents rolled off her carried over to me by a breeze. Her husband, however, caused me to slowly retreat as we chatted. He reeked of liver and onions, whiskey and umm... pickled herring, I believe. I gagged and tried hiding it with my hand over my mouth to disguise the disgust as a yawn. With the way his heartbeat sounded, he wouldn't be long for this world. *Should I tell him? Did he already know?*

Interesting, an ethical conundrum. Assuredly, the first of many with my new abilities.

These were the first people I'd had a conversation with since the whole deer and fox-killing event. Whenever I made trips to town for resupply, I would avoid any contact with everyone. No looking anyone in the eye, kept my head down and just finished my shopping. It felt kind of nice talking to another human being. Mostly I was relieved I didn't want to kill them. Even though it was only idle chitchat about the weather and such; it was still a relief, and it was useful. To see if they could tell I had changed. Or if there were any triggers about myself I should be aware of, a.k.a. would the smell of their blood throw me into a frenzy? So far, so good. Sort of.

Although I didn't desire their blood, I still had an urge to harm them. Strange, they'd never invoked that response from me before.

Avoiding laughing too loudly or smiling too big was difficult. I didn't want them to fully notice my teeth. In no way did they give off any fear or apprehension. As a matter of fact, they seemed to be drawn to me. As I would take a step back during our conversation, they would take a couple steps forward. Which was odd. These were 'keep your distance' people, which I had always appreciated. But now, it seemed like they were intrigued by me, almost *enamored* with me. That was creepy. *Was I giving off a new scent of my own? Something appealing to them?*

They pulled themselves closer, making me uncomfortable and I found myself eventually wanting them to go. Needing them to go. The test was over. My senses had become overwhelmed. Saturated to the point of confusion, my heart raced. The building anxiousness shook my hands a bit; this was about to go very badly for all of us. I gingerly told them that I didn't want to lose the light so I could finish my chores.

Disappointment emerged on their faces, but they acted as though they understood. And with that they did finally leave. What a tremendous relief!

Back to work I went with a sudden renewed burst of zeal. Like I was trying to distract myself. I completed everything on my checklist. Revitalized after accomplishing tangible, normal, hard work for a change. The fresh air had done me good. Stretching out my muscles gave me hope in a weird way. Hope that I was still me somewhere under all these new layers.

I became stronger and stronger each day. Physically and mentally. Most of the health issues and injuries from the military that had plagued me in past years were gone. Overall, life was looking up and evening out.

One night while watching a comedy show, I had a revelation, a big one. During the movie this woman was in the middle of giving birth. She was screaming and angry and was asking her boyfriend why it had to hurt so much.

He, trying to lighten the mood, said, "Creation is violent and painful. Making people is hard. If it were easy, they wouldn't call it labor."

I remember thinking that was easy for *him* to say, but I paused the movie and ran the words through my head again and again. *Making people is hard. Making people is hard ...*

Throughout those first months I had been looking at it all wrong. Focused on literally surviving the process and thinking on all those supernatural fairytales we've been drenched in since childhood. Comparing what I was going through to our folklore. I had not once considered it could be DNA-related. I rolled over in my mind each change that happened, in what order, and for how long each process took. Going through it this time with my medical brain. Why I hadn't connected this transformation to physiology before, I don't know. Biology and chemistry. The most simplest of answers was staring me in the face.

I came to the conclusion that someone or something had created a DNA-altering disease, if you will. My body had been reborn over that year. From my organs to my hair, teeth, skin, eyesight, smell, and hearing. Systematically rebuilt. Who had the power to devise such a thing? The government? Maybe. They do a lot of shady shit we don't usually see. The government was always looking for ways to improve us for war purposes. Aliens? That could be it too. After all I had been through recently, who was I to discount aliens? Anything was possible. Maybe it was an experiment. A secret entity or cult trying to level up the human race. I really couldn't wrap my brain around why anyone or any being would want to give us humans the time of day. It would be better if they turned us to dust and just started over.

We don't belong here. Since I was young, I've felt we as humans should not be here. Nothing about us is natural. The majority of humankind, from the beginning, has had this egotistical notion that we're better than everything else on the planet. Touting that we're more intelligent and above all animals. We created speech, math, and advanced sciences. We call ourselves mammals because we too are made of blood and need oxygen. We can reproduce, giving birth to live young, but we are still evolved beyond any living organism on earth. That's what we've told ourselves for thousands upon thousands of years. I say and have always said, we are the freaks here. We're not like anything else on this planet and in the worst possible ways. Being superior to all animals and plant life was not enough for us. We had to also style ourselves above each other. Just to survive and live without harming anything else was not enough. We broke ourselves down into categories and classes. *Humanity* has killed more humans than all the illnesses combined since the world began. Country against country, people against people, and because of the most trivial concepts. Generic reasons to hate one another such as color, gender, religion, territory, etc. A continuous nightmarish bloodbath. Everyone blames everyone else, taking no responsibility for the absolute waste and destruction consuming our world. No, human beings are not the same as other organisms here but that doesn't make us automatically superior.

Have you ever wondered why we are so intrigued and overjoyed when we see a person commit a truly selfless act? It's because that is the exception, not the rule. We feel the need to promote generosity and kindness but those attributes should be the standard. They shouldn't have to be promoted. Sadly, none of the positive attributes humans are capable of are the standard.

We shouldn't live in a world where something good shocks us; that shit should be everyday life and in every country. A world where being decent is commonplace. It never has been though. Struggle, despair, violence, and greed have all consistently trumped goodness. Out of billions of people we celebrate a slim few empathetics trying to change the rest of the world, preaching and urging others to be fair, kind, and giving. Their efforts haven't worked enough to tip the scales, though. As a whole, our own nature won't allow it. Like we're allergic to just allowing others to live out happy lives.

Humans are a mistake. We're the true plague; above and beyond all others. We have decimated our own home. We, the *superior race*, have violently consumed one another and destroyed what was once an amazing planet. We don't belong here.

I'm not expecting anyone to agree or disagree with me. I'm not looking to add myself to the fight. I just don't understand why anyone would want to deal with us in any capacity. Who would choose to upgrade *us*, to what end? Can we change for the better? I don't see it.

Well, that's my rant on the human race. Pieces of it. Sorry, I just wanted to bitch and let off steam. I can also report that thankfully I'm no longer a part of the human species. At this point in my story, I hadn't fully grasped that notion yet, but I was growing excited at the prospect of not counting myself among the mindless human hordes. The year was almost up.

Would Seth show up? Would he dare? Would I get answers to all I had survived? And would I allow him to live after his explanation? *All good questions,* I thought. I hoped he had something really good to tell me; I would've hated to clean up his blood off my floor. Too much blood had been spilled in my home lately.

We would soon discover my fate and what this monster affliction meant.

Chapter 4

The Wait is Over

Climbing out of an amazing and much-needed bath, I put my robe on intending to start an ordinary day. As I passed by the front window, I heard a car door shut and I could smell something delicious. Like all of the warmest spices on earth rolled together. A gorgeous well-groomed man walked up my front porch steps as the car he arrived in drove off.

It was Seth.

Winter had come again and the one-year wait was over. I had never been a hundred percent sure I would see him again but there he was. He used the front door in daylight, like a normal person. I opened the door before he could knock. I was breathing heavy, seething.

"I hope you've picked out your last words because I've been planning your murder for months now!" I snapped at him.

He chuckled a bit at me, completely unfazed. "You always seem to be in a bathrobe. Do you own regular clothes?"

"Do you want to die on my porch or in the living room?" I asked him. I invited him in telling him to wait while I put on *regular* clothes. I went to the bedroom, locking the door behind me and set my 9mm handgun on the bed. As I dressed, I could clearly hear him fixing himself a cup of coffee in the kitchen. The audacity! Oh, I was definitely going to put a bullet in his brainpan.

I came out and took a seat in my easy chair across from him, 9mm in my lap at the ready. He pretended not to notice it or perhaps he just didn't care. I noticed that his heart rate never elevated. That set me back a bit. If he had no fear of the weapon I was holding then it might be because he knew it couldn't harm him. *Dammit*. It was worth a try though, but whatever kind of being he was, was already proving to be above the threat of violence.

Seth's eyes brightened as I sat down. "There she is. Looking all lit up inside; feels like light itself. And dressed like a normal person too," he said in an almost condescending tone.

He really was such a beautiful man. It was difficult for me to be my usual sarcastic self, though, not impossible. I turned my head sideways confused because he had said '*feels* like light.' That was weird.

He sipped his coffee and casually gazed at the pictures around my living room with a slight grin on his face. There was an air about him so serene it was like watching jellyfish undulating. We sat silently for what seemed forever to me. I had so many questions but couldn't seem to voice them.

Eventually, most likely feeling my anxiousness, he spoke, "Ask me everything that is forefront in your mind in this moment."

I tried to speak calmly at first but my questions got faster and faster, like a spray of bullets. I wasn't waiting for him to answer between. I couldn't. This was a year in the making and I needed to get it all out. What am I? Are you the same as me? Are you Death? What or who created this ability for me to change? How long will it last? Will I live forever? Why did you pick me for this curse or gift? Who dropped you off and are they coming back? How many of those like me are there in the world? Why are you so cute? Where did you come from? What the fuck is that creature in the woods that's been following me everywhere? Is this real? WHAT HAPPENED?! WHY?! I mean, WHAT. THE. FUCK. MAN!

With each question my temper grew, throwing my hands in the air and all around. Like an Italian telling a grand story; my hands would not be still. I could feel that pull or need to pace the floors starting but I forcibly kept my butt firmly in the chair.

Seth held up one of his hands in the stop signal to make me pause. With a smile on his face, he softly asked me to take a break and settle down.

My emotions and senses were insanely heightened. Tears began to well and I shook; my body trembled with worry. It was too much and for whatever reason I was finding it difficult to control myself.

He sweetly put his finger to his lips. "Shh shh shh, it's going to be okay. You are going to be okay." He sat back against the couch, getting comfortable and crossing his legs as he began.

The irises of his eyes fluctuated brown and then into blue and gold and I immediately commented on how neat that was.

"You saw that? And it didn't do anything to calm your mood?" Seth asked puzzled.

"Of course not," I replied. "Should it have?"

"Interesting," was all he muttered in an intrigued tone. He then attempted to answer most of my questions. "I am not Death. But if I had not given you the gift you would have died within about six weeks," he explained.

As it turned out, I supposedly had a heart condition I was unaware of, and in the grand scheme of life, had been scheduled to pass away in my sleep. Seth told me that I was a similar being to him and a few others around the globe with this gift. They nicknamed themselves Evols thousands of years ago, short for Evolved Humans who possessed this new DNA.

I stopped him to make him clarify the name. "Evols? You guys have lived thousands of years and that's the best nickname you could come up with? Come on, man. That shit sounds fake." I then continued embarrassing myself further. "You do realize Evol sounds a lot like the word evil, don't you?"

That got him perturbed a bit but he remained calm. "No, it's not a fancy nickname. Honestly, Evols generally have little interest in labels. And you do realize that you are making fun of your new people?" he asked.

I laughed out loud. "I have been making fun of humans since my birth; fifty damn years. That includes laughing at myself. I'm not about to change anytime soon."

He smiled and continued. He explained that no one had any clear answers as to where the Evols came from nor how they started. There were a few that had spent their extra time searching for the answer to that riddle but so far had only created more questions. Some Evols, not many though, argued about our origins all the time. A handful felt it was biblical and some just thought it was truly a natural evolution. While others thought it had to do with aliens. The fights about it could get quite contentious. Our kind still had divisions over what we were or the rules we lived by. The extremists even tossed around the idea of killing Evols that didn't meet their expectations.

Angrily, I interrupted him by mumbling under my breath, "Evolved, my ass. Kill me now."

"Yes," Seth remarked. "We are unfortunately in some ways still small-minded beings. But overall, Evols are nowhere near as bad as regular humans. Over the centuries most cease to be human altogether. Our anatomy internally is not human, but it takes time to shake the human instincts," he insisted.

He wanted me to trust him. I could feel how hard he was trying to keep his patience with me. That was concerning. I nodded in response. I was still all ears and willing to absorb his words. My brain felt like it was ready to explode but I needed him to continue. He tried to lay out the basics for me of this new life I'd entered: All Evols heal rapidly and do not succumb to illness or disease. That makes our lives much longer than regular humans, however, we are not immortal. We're still an organic being made of flesh and blood. We can and do die eventually. Also, we heal faster and become physically stronger over time. Right now, as a newborn Evol, I was still vulnerable and would be for the next century. Seth told me there were extreme ways I could be killed in my current young state, like explosions or beheadings ... of course.

Seth had transformed four hundred forty-eight years ago in the fifty-fourth year of his human life. *Damn, he looked amazing*, I thought. For being fifty-four or well, actually five hundred two years old in total, he was gorgeous. Unbelievable and nuts but I tried to focus back on his voice instead of his face. After a pause in the moment, I apologized, "Sorry. I'm listening, continue."

He rolled his eyes and took another deep breath, preparing to get the rest of the information out. Our hearing and sense of smell rivals the most evolved animals on earth. There are even some Evols with such keen senses they know where you were born just by your scent. Such as, if you were born by an ocean or desert, they can smell that deeply beneath your skin. And just like regular humans, each of us are also unique with slightly different attributes after the transformation.

My teeth, for example, were not like his but he said we'd get to that later. I wanted to get to it immediately but clearly, I wasn't running the show.

He continued to inform me that as I met more and more Evols I would notice the vast majority looked like young forty-year-olds. Perhaps by trial and error it was found that our gift could not be passed to the young. He explained it was too powerful for a younger body to control. Evol emotions were easily elevated and could be destructive. The young would expose us in the most devastating ways through impulsive anger issues. Plus, for obvious reasons, choosing someone closer to middle age reduced the chances they would reproduce a child. And the elderly didn't receive the gift simply because they would not survive the transformation. Often, the chosen were people that keep to themselves completely. They were not in the eye of society anymore nor did they want to be. They were content being on their own and it was less likely they would share this secret with anyone.

I was on board with that and it was the first believable thing he said that made sense to me. However, it felt like the ultimate oxymoron as well. Gifting those who have next to no life, some don't even want to be alive, and giving them an everlasting extension of life? Sounded fucktarded to me. Sort of a waste maybe to give this to those of us who no longer participate in life. "How old is the oldest Evol living?" I asked him.

"Nine hundred sixty-three years old. His name is Tamson Gluster. You may get to meet him one day," Seth answered. "Furthermore, on average, after the eight hundred year mark, Evols do start to show aging. If you come across an Evol who appears more elderly or weathered, there is an excellent possibility they are well up into their nine hundreds or more," he said.

With that knowledge my theory of the government being responsible for this gift was shattered. The government hides a lot from us but not even they knew what DNA was a thousand years ago, let alone how to manipulate it. I began to lean back toward the aliens theory; they were just fucking with us for fun. Seth also said Tamson was not the first of our kind although he was currently the oldest. So, that meant I could live a thousand years. *Gross.* I wasn't sure I wanted to be here for a thousand damn years. Jesus, I couldn't stand people now, how would I tolerate them for a thousand years? Without killing them all?

My head was spinning again by that point. I needed a break and Seth knew it too. He offered me a breather and jokingly said I could bring my gun if that made me feel better. We strolled our way outside so I could have a smoke. I felt weak as I made my way to the back porch. My knees and even my back buckled a little.

"Lucas and Sara, that's who dropped me off earlier," he said. "They are expected back in about two hours, with food. We will all need it by then. They are Evols too and excited to meet you. Well, Sara is. She and Lucas are about the same age, around four hundred, give or take. But she acts much younger. She is also one of only a handful of women Evols," he explained.

I gave Seth a disapproving look, projecting again my feelings that Evols were not really evolved.

He giggled. "No no, it's not like that. If our push forward in this world still requires us to remain hidden; then we can only gift the hidden people. Women, as a whole, are usually more outgoing creatures than men. There have been few good candidates for this new life in the female realm as it were. It has to do with finding asocial people, not sexism," he assured me.

Okay, I'd let that one slide but I was not convinced. I started rambling on about how incredibly painful the transformation had been and how they really should warn people.

In the middle of my whining Seth busted out a question, "Why does it smell like a mass grave back here? It didn't last year. I know something very gory happened right where I'm sitting but I can't see anything. What in the blue blazes happened?" he exclaimed.

"What in the holy hell makes you think for a second that I could answer that question?" I asked, letting out a snarky noise. Letting loose, I ranted about the animals I had slaughtered with very scant memories of the massacre. I demanded he discuss my teeth with me. I wanted to know why he didn't have them and why I had sharp-ass barbs that I kept catching my tongue on.

The reaction was not comforting. His mouth hung open, his eyes widened, as he ran both his hands through his hair. He urgently snapped at me to grab a small mirror so he could take a closer look at my teeth. We both got up to go inside. I put my weapon away as I retrieved the mirror. By that time, I felt a gun would be useless. I could sense that if I took a shot at him, I'd be dead before the bullet even hit him. We were too far in the weeds for me to still be concerned for my safety now.

I brought him a dental-style mirror and sat myself down on a kitchen chair.

As he examined my teeth, particularly the backside, he further concerned me with his words. "Emma, I told you Evols are all slightly different. Curiously though, in all the Evols I've encountered thus far, none have had teeth like yours. These barbs and you feeding on animals are nothing I've heard of before," he said, taking the mirror out of my mouth.

I put my two thumbs up. "Super, I'm a freak even in this new life."

"My, my, you are a sarcastic creature, aren't you?" he told me in an almost scolding tone as he took another look at the barbs.

Before I could answer with another sarcastic remark, he uttered, "They're hollow, the barbs are hollow," he said before almost frantically asking me for a potato and a knife.

I just got up to retrieve them. I wasn't in the mood to ask why anymore. He cut the potato longways in half and had me bite down on one of the halves. I carefully took my teeth out after biting down. He sliced the potato in half again along the path of the teeth marks. Inside was a pale silvery-blue shiny substance. It was gooey like a lotion or jelly.

I got him a Ziplock bag and he scraped off the substance, putting it inside the bag and then stashed it in his coat pocket. I asked him if it was a venom or a paralytic. And how would I find more information.

He stayed quiet as he slowly walked toward me. With his clasped hands over my hands, he sighed. As he focused on my eyes, he ordered me not to tell any Evol about my barbs. Not yet anyway. He was going to ask an older friend of his, Dr. Maximillian Harris, who worked in the Evol archives located in Jerusalem. He said he trusted him with his life and also trusted he would keep the information to himself.

Seth didn't know what my barbs were or what the weird goo was leaking from them. Because it was unknown, he wanted me to stay quiet about it. He explained that Evols were cautious and fearful of being discovered. Some could take my uniqueness as a threat.

I pushed away from him; stepping back a few feet. Raising my hands up at him. "Wait, wait, wait! Are you telling me that I'm actually a freak among the freaks? Are you fucking kidding me? Does this mean you also don't know if or when I will open another animal like a juice box?!" I was panicked and angry. Back to frantic, like earlier.

He shook his head no, meaning he did not know if it was going to happen again.

I backed up further as a deep growl came from a place inside me. A surprise for both of us. Three hundred sixty-five days this horrid nightmare had been building and by God, someone was going to give me real fucking answers to my misery. My emotions were pushed to their limits. A small piece of me was still convinced I was in a fever dream. I backed away a few more steps, rage building.

Seth stealthily stepped forward, paused only for a second watching me carefully and then leaped. He desperately attempted to grab and soothe me. He tried to wrap his arms around me as I fought and struggled. Seth was insanely strong. His skin was not hard like stone, however I felt like I was trying to push against steel. I took a couple swings at him which he caught. I wiggled and protested, even had this immense drive to bite him although I didn't.

After successfully subduing me, he began to cradle me in his arms. Swaying from side to side, urging me to take deep breaths. Doing the one thing I had truly needed for that whole year.

Finally, I relented. I couldn't keep it up, I was all out of fight.

He squeezed me, tight. Our heartrates slowed together and began to beat as one. An act of a real evolved human being. Not an attraction type of caressing but one of empathy. That gave me hope it would somehow work out; that I would be okay. This was not a soap opera from a fantasy romance novel, he was not seducing me. He was genuinely looking out for my wellbeing. We shifted down to the floor where he just held me.

Chapter 5
Too Many People in My House!

Today you are You, that is truer than true.
There is no one alive who is Youer than You.
—Dr. Seuss

There was a knock at the door. Seth and I got up off the floor. I had calmed myself and let much of his information sink in. For the time being I was optimistic but that feeling would come and go, dramatically. On the other side of the front door window, I saw a petite, redheaded, golden skinned woman waving excitedly at us. *Oh no, nope. None of this welcome party crap in my house.*

Seth opened the door and the short bubbly woman bolted toward me, hugging me as if we were old friends who hadn't seen each other in years. It was a one-sided hug as my arms were pinned down. I had no interest in hugging a stranger. My personal space had been invaded all too quickly.

A gruff stocky man with a scowl on his face showed himself to the dining room table, carrying bags of Chinese take-out. Seth pulled the woman off me just as I began to softly growl. She backed up a bit, stunned by the warning sound and squinty eyes I had given her. Seth then officially introduced me to them both, Sara and Lucas. Sara smiled and waved at me again. *Gross, weird little teenage girl*, I thought. Lucas, on the other hand, barely made a nodding head gesture. That was more my speed. Sara walked back to the dining room to help him lay out the food but kept her eyes on me as she left. So focused on me that she nearly ran into a wall; that would have been awesome.

I attempted to keep my composure, reminding myself that I had zero idea what any of them were capable of. I didn't know what I was capable of so I couldn't defend myself against them. My mind kept darting from one wild abstract thought to the next. This was not what I envisioned as a child. If you were to ask a kid what a typical day in the life of a super being would be; this would not be their answer. About to sit around a table to eat dinner. No, that was not what any of us imagined. That made the situation more suspicious. It was too normal. Too mundane. *Madness,* I thought. I had gone crazy and this is what it looks like. Trapped with three strangers all up in my space being intrusive. In my younger days they'd have been fucked by then. Make no mistake, we'd have been brawling.

The obnoxiously adorable redhead was too eager.

"I was hoping Emma would be gracious enough to give me a tour of her home before we eat. Would that be okay, Emma?" Sara asked as she seemed to be jumping from her skin.

I would have rather drank from an anal gland but instead smiled and replied, "I guess that would be okay. Not a problem."

"Wow! What's with your teeth? I didn't realize Evols were creating vampires now, are we? Or dogs? That's crazy. Have you seen this, Seth?" Sara commented.

"Dog? Is that what you just fucking said? Would you like to be the first to get mauled?" I asked while moving in particularly close so I could look down at her a bit. It did feel good to be taller than someone for once.

*Cue brawl music.

Sara leaned away, nervously putting her hands up to brace herself. "Oh no. I'm sorry. I didn't mean it how it sounded," she insisted.

Seth scolded her, "Sara, are you that naive? There are all kinds of unique Evol transformations. It's not a big deal."

*Cut brawl music ... *dammit.*

He was clearly trying to make my fang issue appear benign. Even though it was not how he had acted about them earlier. I sensed Sara's body tense. She was giving off an odor of fear and apprehension. *Afraid of me? She was afraid of my teeth? That might work to my advantage,* I thought. I hoped that meant she didn't want me to show her around anymore. No such luck.

"Still want that tour?" I asked her.

She nodded. "Yeah, that'd be great. Let's go. You wanna come with us, Lucas?"

"Nope, that's okay. I'll be here watching the food get cold," Lucas replied.

My home was not large. The tour wouldn't take but a couple of minutes. Within those minutes she hit me with a barrage of questions. Enthusiastic and bubbly. My brain was screaming as we made our way from room to room. If I could sense fear in her, could she sense anger in me? Hmm, that would kind of take the surprise out of life if we could all sense one another's mental states. I tried to keep the introductions to each room brief but not so brief she would think I was being rude. Again, I didn't know what she was capable of. If I said the wrong thing she might flip the house upside down, literally. I had no clue.

Then the tour was over and we headed back to the dining room where the boys were chatting. Seth got up to help me gather plates and silverware out of the cabinets. Sara and Lucas opened the take-out containers.

Seth leaned in close whispering in my ear, "Try not to be sarcastic with Lucas. He's a medium-aged Evol but has an ancient, grouchy personality."

Swiftly, a deep voice from the other room bellowed, "I heard that!" Lucas barked.

We all sat at the table. Sara made a point of positioning herself across from me, leaving the boys to sit across from each other. She stared at me in an almost fangirl way. Lucas dug right into the food, seemingly oblivious to all else. He was well-built with amazing caramel-colored skin. Difficult to see under an enormous amount of arm hair and medium length beard. I imagined in his human life he was one of those guys who appeared to be wearing a sweater with their shirt off. People we would nickname 'bear' or 'the wolfman,' due to an abundance of hair all over. He could be described as burly, I guess. Very dark auburn brown head hair sprinkled with salt and pepper highlights, and kind green eyes. He didn't look all shiny and new as Sara did with her childlike glow. Interesting they were both in the four hundreds. However, Lucas looked more like Seth, age-wise.

While I was eating, I noticed Vader down by Lucas's boots. He was rubbing against his legs. That was highly unusual. In fact, it had never happened before. Vader was a very sweet cat but he hid from everyone except me. Well, the extreme few people who have ever stepped foot in my home, which I could probably count on one hand. "So, do any of you have noticeable talents as Evols? Like superhero stuff? Are we still even human? Or is that rude of me to ask such questions?" I blurted out.

Sara answered quickly, like she was about to burst, "Oh, between the three of us, only Seth has anything truly extra. We can all do much of the same things, but Seth is special. He's a Gifter and that also comes with perks. He's your Gifter as a matter of fact," she explained.

I looked at Seth and guessed that meant he was one of the few able to infect humans with this DNA-altering crap. As he had doomed me with a year earlier.

He started to answer but Sara jumped in to answer for him, "Every two hundred or so Evols born there will be one that just knows they are allowed to pass on their evolution to others. And no, we're not considered human any longer." Jokingly and without thinking it seemed, she continued, "Seth is my only freakish friend, that is, until you. Vampire teeth and all." She looked up at me smiling. But before I could get angry questions out of my mouth, she continued with more, "Gifters also have the ability to ignore gravity for a moment which makes them appear to fly in a sense. It's how they make it around without being caught. Or escape in case a human flips out and tries to hurt them. Not that a human *could* hurt them." She laughed.

The tension lessened as I grinned, turning to Seth. "Well, that explains a lot about my first two encounters with you," I remarked.

Lucas rolled his eyes at Seth. "Playing flying parlor tricks on humans again Seth?" he said.

I wondered why Seth had told me not to be sarcastic with Lucas when he was obviously quite sarcastic himself.

Seth ignored the comment. "If all Evols were able to make other Evols, it would be mass chaos. Only a few have the responsibility of being a Gifter," he said.

We went back to eating as another awkward silence followed. Then Sara began asking me a bunch of questions again. The urge to bark at her or throw my food ran across my mind several times. If this was to be my life now, non-human, oddity with fangs, then why not do whatever the hell I wanted? At least I'd amuse myself while these 'people' were invading my home.

Back to Sara, something was off about her. Supposedly, Evols were mostly shy loners and Sara in no way fit that description. Not only did she not look to be a young forty-something; she really looked to be in her twenties. Acted like it too. She talked non-stop, barely taking a breath. I felt as though I was watching a bad reality TV show. That was the annoying level of high-pitched nonsense noise she was spewing. As Sara continued to ramble, my mind wandered further and further. I was getting irritated and my heartrate sped up. I felt the need to pace growing stronger. It was her and that hundred mile an hour mouth of hers. Waves of heat began to radiate off me. Anxiousness caused my nervous knee to shake under the table. Laser-focused as I was on her, I didn't realize the boys were trying to get my attention. Suddenly, Lucas kicked my leg under the table, hard. It shocked me and a, "What the fuck?!" slipped from my mouth.

Our eyes locked.

"Cool it," Lucas calmly told me.

"Can you read minds or something? What did I miss here?" I asked.

"No, we cannot read minds. We can, however, feel tension, heartbeats, breathing, and emotions. Just like you can. And your emotions are too much in the red zone right now. You should calm yourself. We're not here to hurt you," Lucas explained.

I chuckled once and sarcastically snapped back at him. "So, you kicked me to prove you're not here to hurt me?! That was your plan?"

Sheepishly he lowered his eyes back to his plate with a grin. "Fair point. I guess I didn't think that one all the way through," he replied.

That's it. I'd had enough. If this was real, then let the chips fall 'cause I was done with this shit show. These people were in my home, uninvited. After the year I'd been through, I wasn't really inclined to take crap from any one of them.

Seth suddenly blurted at me, disrupting my inner rant, "Holy shit, Em! Your eye color! It's purple—"

"What?" I began.

"—with fiery gold rings!" He was getting quite excitable.

A deep rolling growl emanated from my gut. The table shook fast, vibrating the plates and glasses. Everyone sat up straighter; alarmed by what I was doing. Lucas immediately looked at Seth; wanting him to control me or do something.

Seth was just as surprised as the rest of them, but he quickly reached over to put his hand on mine. "Emma, maybe we should all just take a moment to remember that it's been a big day for you."

I took a deep slow breath and felt the speed of my heartrate lessen.

Seth smiled, patted my hand, and said, "There, see, all better now."

We moved our plates back to their normal positions in front of ourselves. Sara quietly apologized for referring to me as a freak and then finished her dinner. As an Evol, she didn't seem to sense anyone else's inner struggles, unlike Lucas who fucking kicked me. I just hoped the day would be over soon. Three people in my home was three too many people. There was a reason I didn't have company over often. People in general suck. These weren't people in a sense, but the same irritation came along with meeting and getting to know them. I wasn't going to be shy anymore. I asked what I wanted to regardless, "Alright, let's go down the rabbit hole for a moment. What's up with all the nightmares, hallucinations, and madness I've been enduring this last year?" I placed my hands on the table and stared at them all.

Lucas took another crack at speaking to me, this time gentler, "Unfortunately, that seems to be a standard side effect of the gift. As your body rebuilds, your mind also undergoes a rewiring of sorts. An explosion of neurons, we believe, triggers mental instability and nightmares. That portion of the transformation should be over soon," he explained.

"How many newly gifted commit suicide before you return?" I asked. "Because I have to tell you, I was damn close on several occasions. I thought I was petting Vader one night but he wasn't there and I bawled for an hour. UNTIL, he then just waltzed by me as if it didn't happen. Cause IT DIDN'T!" I angrily told them.

"Madness is the biggest hurdle and something we all went through," Seth answered. "I'm glad you survived. The butterfly is only beautiful because the caterpillar was brave enough to transform." He tried an optimistic grin.

Lucas rolled his eyes. "Jesus, I'm going to be sick."

I agreed with Lucas and pressed Seth harder, "You didn't answer the question, Seth. How many commit suicide before their transformation is complete?"

"Many, Emma. Many, I'm sorry to say," Seth replied.

I was too angry to continue so I dropped it. Once we finished dinner, Sara elected to clean up the dishes and take-out containers. She insisted and basically pushed me right out of my own kitchen. I gave in and escaped outside for a break, a cigarette, of course. The night air during falling snow always made me feel better; it was relaxing, calming.

Lucas came outside too and sat next to me. "You know, you'll stop smoking soon," he said.

"Oh yeah? Not in the mood," I barked back.

"Not because it's some Evol rule or anything but because your new DNA won't allow it for much longer. Right now, everything is still changing and settling in your body but eventually, you will simply just stop. How amazing is that?"

"Huh, that's good. I bet millions of humans would like it to be that easy. To just be able to quit an addiction," I commented. His words had a calming effect.

He nodded in agreement and then closed his eyes, seemingly letting the day's tension go.

I would say the silence felt nice if it wasn't for being able to hear Sara in my kitchen talking Seth's ears off. Still, I was getting more comfortable with Lucas and I already liked Seth. Two out of three was pretty good odds. It wasn't just because Sara talked too much that I was having an adverse reaction, there was a bad vibe overall about her.

At the time, I set it aside as just me being me. I mean really, I had only met three Evols. I knew zip about this new life or who they were. Time would tell, I couldn't judge them all over one dinner, or one night. My brain was still trying to think and act like a human, which very much added to what my perceptions were at the time. That would change as well.

"Hey Emma, I know you couldn't see what your eyes did in there but between that and the shaking of the table, you'll have to work extra hard to control your emotions. One wrong move from a rude stranger at Walmart and you'll take the place down," Lucas remarked.

"Did they really change that much?" I asked, confused.

"They went all gold and fiery like Seth told you. He wasn't making that up," he said.

"Is that something you've seen in other new Evols?" I asked.

"Nope."

"So, others have control over their emotions sooner than I obviously have?" I asked, still trying to get information out of him.

Lucas gave me a side eye and let out a sigh. "I've never seen anyone do what you did. You have an electricity within you. We can all sense it. I don't feel it's a bad thing. But you should be aware of it so you can practice controlling it. It's important you get a grip on your abilities. Your physical strength will grow significantly over decades but this voltage you carry is turned up already. Be careful," he explained.

I switched gears then, suddenly tired. I didn't want to talk about me anymore or all my unusual features. "I saw my cat, Vader, loving up on you. He never does that. Do you have cats or maybe something on your pants that drew him to you?" I asked.

"Oh, that. After I was reborn, Evol animals started coming at me from all directions. Seth thinks it's one of my natural powers, so to speak. I don't know. Watch this," Lucas replied. He stuck his arm out into the air and almost instantly, a robin landed on him.

That was pretty cool. Not what you think of as superhero maybe, but cool nonetheless.

"It can get annoying when I'm trying to get work done outside. Critters just show up to bug me."

I could tell he was holding quite a bit back. Something about himself he was hiding. Maybe something about me he was reluctant to say. I tried not to pry too hard this time. We continued to chat about nothing in particular, and before long, Seth drew our attention when he clapped his hands from inside the house.

"Okay gang, it's time to go! Let's get ourselves together and leave Emma to rest."

Oh man, was I relieved to hear that. I needed sleep not just rest. Sara and Lucas put their jackets on at the front door. Sara gave me a strong hug again and told me she'd email me soon to chat. *Please, no.*

Then Lucas shoved a blue folder into my hands and in an emotionless, flat tone said, "Welcome to the Evols."

Yeah, his grumpiness was growing on me, big time. They went down to the car to warm it up while Seth said his goodbyes to me.

"Go through the paperwork in the folder carefully," he said, hugging me. Then laughed, stating, "Back when I turned Evol there were no such things as welcome packets. It was a, *figure-this-shit-out-as-you-go,* mentality." He left me with one last thought, "For the first fifty years, give or take, your emotions will easily be triggered. Try to avoid anything too upsetting or sad. I'm very serious about this. There's a huge difference between human rage and Evol rage. Same with heartbreak. It's often life changing," he paused. "Also, my contact info is in that paperwork. I'll be writing you in a matter of days to answer more questions. Take care Emma." And with that, he walked outside giving me a wave and a smile.

It had been an incredibly stressful, long-ass day. All I wanted in that moment was to find Vader and unconsciousness in my bed. The words kept spinning in my head, *I'm not human anymore? I am not human anymore. Fact, I am not human.*

It's a difficult concept to wrap your brain around. I locked up the house tight, turned off all the lights, and crawled into bed. I didn't even crack open the folder. I was satisfied with the answers I had gotten thus far. There were most certainly a thousand more questions but what had transpired gave me enough to ease my mind. I would dive into all the paperwork, rules, or instructions, later. Instead, I separated myself from everything that had occurred, compartmentalizing the day. Knocked out cold, I slept like a rock, and continued to sleep for the next day and a half.

Chapter 6
Sinking In

I looked at the welcome packet while watching the morning news. There was a rule sheet which really only had one rule reading 'Do not allow humans to discover you're different.' Well, that was straightforward. The penalty was a Gifter would be forced to eliminate me along with the humans who had found out. *Nice.*

'Gifters are the only ones of us who possess the ability to create Evols and destroy them,' continued the sheet. I thought that was interesting. Seth could have killed me if I had flipped out during the transformation and told someone. If I had gone to the hospital, the doctors would've found unusual blood test results, even organ displacements, or impossible iris color changes, not to mention my fangs. He would've been forced to erase me and the hospital staff. It was a pretty good failsafe when you thought about it. Glad I didn't try to shoot him. My intuition had been correct about his ability to kill me.

The paperwork continued on to explain that my Gifter had no tracking device on me. He or she wouldn't know if I was in trouble or danger. We were not linked in any supernatural way, so to speak. Except in one important aspect. The only connection my Gifter had to my blood is they could feel the moment I died. That is, if I were to die one day. In a case such as that, he, in this case, Seth, would be responsible for ensuring my body was properly disposed of. It was to keep a medical examiner or anyone else from discovering anything unnatural or out of the ordinary.

If I had questions or needed my Gifter, then it was up to me to contact them. They were not babysitters. A relationship between the gifted and their Gifter was solely up to those individuals. Seth did explain when he was at my home that, centuries ago, many Gifters did stay close to their progeny to help them through the difficult year, but that nowadays, humans had cell phones and technology at their fingertips, and tended to freak out or panic easily. It had been found that leaving the newbie alone for a while actually caused less stress and weeded out the weak from the strong. *Uh huh.*

There was also a brief explanation that stated Evols didn't have presidents or rulers or any type of organized government. There was no official registry so to speak, with the exception of the Gifters and they were responsible for knowing who their progeny were. I liked that a lot. My decisions were up to me and I could live where I wanted to. It did, however, mention a committee of sorts that oversaw severe infractions. People who, in extreme cases, ensured the safety and stability of the Evol nation. *There's a hit squad,* is what my mind said. A committee meant someone, somewhere was calling the shots and it didn't sound like I'd want to meet them. So, I couldn't run wild *exactly*. Interesting. So it wasn't a free-for-all, and a panel of Evol killers were watching from somewhere to keep the peace, to keep their—no, *our* secrets.

Another sheet of paper detailed funds that would be sent to me bi-annually over the next ten years. It was suggested I invest in properties of my choosing as well as trading stocks from around the world. Due to the long life in front of me I would need to provide for myself in the future. Rotating the buying and selling of multiple homes and land ensured a steady income. It would also afford me places I could stay at and or hide in, at a moment's notice. I thought that was pretty damn rad.

They were giving me money to get me started in this new life. Trying to set up the new Evols for success was a sign of a long-standing responsible company or in this case, culture. I wondered if there had ever been a newborn Evol who took the money and just pissed it away. Gambled excessively or bought fancy cars and such. If they had, I bet their Gifter made a visit to them. Or maybe they just let that person wallow in the poverty they created for themselves. More questions for Seth. I started to get the impression that I had signed up for a timeshare scam or cult. A secret squirrel club.

The folder contained an invitation to a reunion. It was called a Gathering. Every fifty years the Evols would meet up at one of the estates owned by an elder. The Gatherings lasted around three days and was a chance for us to connect and share our experiences. The next Gathering was scheduled to be held in seven years and the host was none other than Tamson Gluster at his home in Spain. *Well, lucky me,* I snickered. Transformed just in time to go to a party at the oldest living Evol's humble abode. A whole bunch of outcasts and loners turned into longer living outcasts and loners, then forced to socialize. To tell you the truth, even as I read, I still believed I had just gone mad. Trapped in an elaborate cabin fever dream. It didn't matter that I'd had three people in my house all day recently or that this folder was in front of me. A piece of me was in denial.

I took a break and went outside to stare at the trees and snow, mulling over what Lucas had told me about the electricity in my body. At the same time I was thinking about his words, my hands began to light up with heat. When I broke my concentration to inspect them, they cooled down. I continued thinking about what Lucas had said and my hands became warm again. It occurred to me that I was causing it to happen by focusing on the electricity conversation. Sometimes all you need is another person telling you what's inside you to bring it forth.

I closed my eyes a moment and focused on my hands, imagining the electricity inside. Urging it to surge through me toward my hands. Suddenly my palms began to glow. Heat upon heat. And just like that, a ball of purple light appeared. *As if by magic*, I thought. A ball hovered just above my hands. It was an orb. *Neat!* I laughed out loud, marveling at how awesome it was. I didn't know what it did, but it was cool as hell. I could do something superhuman, otherworldly, and it felt exhilarating. If it wasn't for my new family's visit, who knows how long it would've taken me to find this gift.

A sudden knock on my door caused the purple orb to instantly dissipate. *Dammit!*

I saw through the window that it was Mrs. Stockwell. She came right in with neighborly familiarity and maple syrup in tow. She and her husband made maple syrup to sell and sometimes she gave away excess bottles to her neighbors. It was wintertime so she wanted to get rid of their overflow stock before they made more in the spring.

As I was putting the bottles in the cabinet, she got nosy. I had left the folder on the table with the paperwork all spread out. My heart began to beat fast as I thought if she saw what was on them, she'd wonder what was going on. So, of course, she started picking up the papers.

Shit! I panicked. Not a year old in my new skin and about to be destroyed by some mysterious committee because I let a neighbor into my home.

"Oh, how fun! What are these?" she asked.

I quickly took the papers from her, stacking them together nervously. I put them back in the folder and tried to get around the issue. "Oh nothing. Just research on a project you know. Something to pass the winter days," I explained, hyperventilating a little.

"Research on Egypt or some country? All those symbols look like hieroglyphics. What kind of project?" she asked, pressing further.

Huh? They looked like English words to me. I opened the folder a second to look again. How was she seeing symbols and not words? Taking yet another look at the papers, I still didn't see whatever it was she was seeing. *Am I the one who was nuts?* I wasn't sure what to do next, so I shrugged my shoulders and played along with her. "Yup, that's what it's for. Just an ancient Egyptian language. I have no clue what it means. I thought it would be fun to translate it. You know, learn something new. Never hurts to delve into different things," I told her.

She smiled and then made a disapproving comment. Something to the effect of, people up here don't do weird things like that.

Well, if I wasn't already the flighty odd hermit of the mountain I would be after she got done telling others of this. We changed gears and chatted for a few more minutes about regular things. Local gossip and such. Like who the new town selectman would be and the scandal of how he attained the title—by sleeping with the widow of the last selectman. There was damn near no one in this one-horse town and yet there were still plenty of tabloid tales.

As soon as she was out the door, I took a hard look at the

paperwork. It *was* all in English. *What the hell?* I should've been used to things not making sense by then, but this was truly strange. I mean, how was it possible to perceive two languages in the same paper? Another question for Seth. Speaking of, later that day I exchanged my first emails with him.

He informed me that his friend, Dr. Harris, wanted to meet me over a video call soon to discuss my teeth. I wrote him back to confirm I would be available anytime and asked again about the creature in the woods because he hadn't answered me when he was at my house. I asked why I slept so much and if that would level out over time, and then about Sara. I wanted to know why he had brought her along and why she looked so young. I thought the young were not to be gifted. I only asked three questions to start with. I wasn't in much of a panicked rush as I was when he visited. I would try to break up my questions little by little now that the initial shock was past.

When he returned my email, he said he didn't know what the creature in the woods was and in fact, hadn't seen anything. Not to say I was seeing things but it could be something just attracted to me as my new self. He explained there were other beings in this world that we didn't know much about or understand. *But ... he saw nothing in the woods?* How was I seeing it and no one else? Was it a ghost? Another made-up vision created by my brain misfiring and changing?

Seth suggested that if the creature had not approached me nor harmed me then it probably wasn't worth worrying about. *Who says that?* So, it hasn't hurt me which means we just pretend the damn thing isn't staring at me all the time? I don't know, sounded reckless.

The sleep issue would take time, he informed me. My new body was forever fixing itself, so it burned a lot of energy, even if I was just sitting still. Over time, an Evol, on average, will sleep about fourteen hours a day. If for any reason I found myself awake for a prolonged period, then in turn I would also sleep for an extended time to catch up. By the same token, the reason why he instructed me to eat copious proteins and calcium was due to how fast my body was going to change. The number of calories burned during the process was astronomical.

It was at that point while reading his email we realized we were both online and started instant messaging.

"So, I can assume you didn't mean for that calcium to help me grow these new teeth?" I asked.

"No, that wasn't a part of the plan or regular process. I'm hoping Dr. Harris will have some answers for us," he replied before continuing. "Honestly Emma, I don't know how you survived that part of the transformation. After I came home and thought about what kind of agonizing pain you must have gone through; I just don't think any of us would have made it through that. I really don't."

"It wasn't pretty," I said. "I almost lost my cat because he was alone and hungry while I was passed out on the bathroom floor for three days; convulsing and bleeding profusely," I replied in an almost angry tone.

He gasped. "Oh my God Emma. I wish the rules had been different because if ever I was needed to be with a newborn, this would've been it. It really was that horrible, wasn't it?"

"Yeah, it was," I simply stated.

Seth changed the subject and started explaining Sara to me. He assured me Sara was in her forties when she was gifted but her skin repaired much better and faster than most. Some people just got really lucky in the body repair department. As far as why she had come to the house, that had been Tamson Gluster's idea. He was an elder so he, at times, tried to push Evols out of their comfort zones and felt she needed the experience. Also, since I was a woman, it was thought to be better to have a woman with Seth and Lucas to make me feel more comfortable. I understood that. It made sense. Shortly thereafter, we wrapped up our conversation for the time being.

The very next day I received a video call and answered to see Seth sitting next to an older-looking gentleman. Much like a movie professor complete with the cliché bowtie. He had a sweet soft face and graying hair around his temples. An average-looking white man with brown eyes. I could imagine him in a spy movie for some reason. There was a beautiful warming glow about him but also, I suspected a devilish side as well. Dr. Harris.

"Nice to meet you, Dr. Harris. I appreciate you taking the time to speak with me," I said.

He brightly smiled and replied in a slight Russian accent, "Please, call me Max and I could not wait to meet you either. Before we get started, could you please indulge an old man and show me your teeth?"

I nodded, "No problem." I smiled big and opened my mouth a bit. Moving my face around so he could see them at all angles.

"Outstanding!" he said, appearing suitably impressed. "Here is what I found in the archives. The last record of teeth such as yours was around 1,200 years ago. There isn't much information about them, but they appear to be nothing more than a rare occurrence. Like when humans give birth to triplets without fertility assistance," he explained.

"Do they have a name?" I asked.

"Angel teeth. They're called angel teeth for a couple of reasons. First, the enamel has a feathery shape, curved to look like angel's wings. And second, not to scare you, but they are also called angel teeth because they make the owner appear to be the Angel of Death." He laughed and shook his head back and forth. "I wouldn't worry about it sweetie," he assured me.

The 'sweetie' would've normally irritated me. You know that condescending tone that often comes with it? However, I viewed his as more grandpa-like. He was, afterall, a thousand years old. It was to be expected that political correctness wouldn't exactly be followed by Evols all the time. And Max in no way appeared to be an arrogant man.

"So, the word angel doesn't refer to anything biblical, right?" I asked.

"Oh no Emma. Not at all. Just a nickname for the shape of the teeth. From a distance they look like, well, like vampire teeth to me, or maybe you'd prefer the word *fangs*," he insisted.

"Okay, to be crystal clear, I'm not an angel. For sure, right? Is it also true I'm not human anymore either?" I asked.

"Correct. We call ourselves Evolved Humans simply because we used to be human. However, our new DNA is too far-off to be considered human. What exactly we are is still a mystery, so we just stick with the term Evol for now," Max explained.

"What about the pale blue shiny goo that Seth extracted from the barbs of my sharp teeth? And what about the animals I killed?" I asked, more concerned.

He took a breath in and shrugged his shoulders. "Well, we haven't been able to identify that substance. It's not a venom or neurotoxin, that we know of. Not one the world has come across yet anyway," he said.

"And the feeding on blood?" I was getting worried again.

"That seems to go along with the teeth obviously but in all our records, the feedings only consisted of animals. You, my dear, are why there are legends of vampires. Though, no records of an Evol feeding on humans exists. That's not to say it hasn't happened," Max tried to say in a calming voice.

Seth popped his head back into view of the phone and gave me a big smile. "See, you're fine and everything will be okay."

I tried to sidestep his overconfident cheery comment. Sorry but drinking animals dry was a big deal to me. I refocused and brought up what happened with my neighbor. "I have one more question. My neighbor came over to my house unexpectedly. She saw the paperwork from the folder I was given. I didn't show her. I panicked when she started looking at it. Anyway, she said it looked like hieroglyphics. I was confused because it looked like English to me!" I exclaimed.

Seth and Max giggled. "That's a cool trick huh?" Seth said. "We developed that many years ago. You didn't know you could now read other languages, that's why you saw what you thought were English words. To protect our information, the welcome packets are in a language that no one else can read except Evols."

"Wait, I can read *any* language?" I asked.

Max answered and had a question for me, "Yes, ma'am. You can read and speak any language now," he said with a smile. "Have you found it difficult to eat regular food, I mean with the fangs? Do they get in the way?"

Out of all the questions flying back and forth, this one sounded the most normal to me for some reason. "I was surprised how little they affect me when eating. Almost like they've always been there. I have on occasion bitten my lip by mistake, but my eating habits haven't slowed down because of the teeth. I'm not having difficulties if that's what you're asking," I replied.

"Excellent news. Thank you, Emma," he said. He grinned and

instructed me to call him anytime I had questions or concerns, especially if there was something Seth didn't have answers to.

Seth chimed in to tell me he'd call again soon so we could talk more. He also mentioned that he had given Sara and Lucas my email address so I could get more opinions and experiences from different Evols. Getting used to this new life was to be a healthy mix of wanting to learn everything and allowing some things to just chill and be okay as was. Max and he both encouraged me to try living for a couple months in peace. Relax and let it all sink in before making any large decisions. We hung up the phone and instantly I felt like a ton of bricks had been lifted off my chest.

I'd been so paranoid about my teeth. Our human horror culture put me in such a fearful state of what I could be turning into. People fantasize about becoming vampires, werewolves, or fanged beasts of some kind, it's alluring for sure but when it happens to you, everything you were taught was impossible shatters like the largest mirror, splinters of yourself no longer recognized as your reflection. I was a predator now. A real one, an unknown, unseen miracle who may have evolved beyond the whispers of legend.

I was thrown far from you, human, my thoughts seemed to say.

After the video call my heartbeat slowed as all my muscles untangled. I was finally beginning to wrap my brain around everything. The words, *crazy* and *mad* weren't ringing in my head as loudly as before. It was a great feeling. There was to be a future for me, a new beginning, a path that I was in control of to cut as I pleased. Sitting still in the easy chair with my eyes closed, I let go of a year's worth of strife and pain.

A short time later, I heard my email notification *ding*.

And then another and another and another.

I reluctantly got up and opened my inbox to find messages from Sara. Many messages. *How did I go from being a grumpy hermit loner to a cheerleader's best friend?* Fuck.

Chapter 7
Ripped Open

Heartbreak is like having broken ribs.
On the outside you look fine, but with every breath, it hurts.
—Greg Behrendt

Two years had passed by in a flash. Although my body was significantly different, my day-to-day life stayed much the same. I did invest in some real estate here and there around the world. A villa in Italy and one in Scotland to start with but I mostly stayed on my remote mountain. I purchased the properties without even seeing them in person. It was hard for me to branch out. It's just not in my nature. Dropping what I was, and that normalcy of human routines and ticks, felt downright impossible. And it had been difficult to reconcile that I was going to potentially live for hundreds of years. I was semi-excited about the possibilities but I also didn't know where to begin. Breaking the shell of my cocoon was an ongoing chore.

My creature was still stalking me. Now I even noticed it during the daytime. It appeared as a shapeless clear silhouette, but I could feel it was there. Like the remainder of gum under your shoe; there's always a bit of a tug with each step, reminding me the creature was ever present. At night, of course, those two beady eyes in the darkness would watch me. I kept thinking one day I would find out its identity but until then, I mostly ignored it. One of the many mysteries yet to unfold. To me, my creature felt like a secondary mystery. One that could wait; I obviously had plenty of time on my hands to figure it out.

Trying to expand my new abilities I did practice the ball of light thing often. My purple orb. One time, I even thought maybe it could be a weapon, so I attempted to throw it but the orb stayed within my hand. I stood in my backyard vigorously trying to shake it off my hand, looking like a moron flailing my arm around. I had no idea what its purpose really was, yet it did come in handy as a flashlight. My nighttime walks through the forest became more fun as I could illuminate the pathway. Even though I wasn't in need of light to see, it was just nice to see the world in color rather than sonar.

I discovered a new power of floating or hovering just a few inches above the ground. Not in the way Seth could do it but it was still pretty awesome. I hadn't shared with Seth or anyone about my purple orb. I wasn't sure if it was another oddity I should keep to myself or not but I did ask him about the recent hovering. I wanted to know if it was a sign I could be a Gifter. He told me that was not how he found out he was a Gifter. It was a feeling or pull to draw yourself closer to loner humans, and it didn't start happening to him until he was in his fiftieth year as an Evol. There was a development stage for Gifters; their power takes time to mature. So, I guessed I would just have to add hovering to the growing list of weird shit I could do.

I did eventually respond to Sara's emails. She started to grow on me overtime. We actually went on a short vacation together to Fiji if you can believe it. Crazy, right? 'A girl's trip' she called it. I learned how to block out much of her chatter and she knew it although she didn't seem to mind. I admired that about her. She was who she was and rarely muzzled herself to please others. Sara didn't share many details about her human life. I found it curious how often she would change the subject as soon as I asked anything about her time before the gift but we were at least getting along. I had very few friends before becoming an Evol so I didn't want to make enemies of the slim few new ones I had recently acquired.

Sara exuded innocence. I could get around some of her outward annoyances because I felt her genuine spirit and kindness. My feelings that something was off about her still lingered faintly in the back of my mind however, what she was showing in the foreground was winning me over.

Seth kept great tabs on me. He checked in often and we had some amazing heart-to-heart conversations. We talked about Evols and our pasts as regular humans. I considered myself lucky that I was not only given this gift but also that my Gifter was a solid person. Oddly, even after two years, I still had many questions, and he was always there to help me out. His patience was endless, a perfect temperament for a Gifter. Eventually, Seth brought his husband to my home, Eric. His hubby was sweet but also mischievous, super funny; I would laugh to tears every time I spoke to him.

Seth and Eric had been together for two hundred years. It wasn't until meeting Eric that the idea occurred to me; Evols would have to partner up with other Evols. Having such long lives, we couldn't realistically pair up with a regular human. They'd know something was wrong with us once they grew old and we did not. Nevertheless, I was not looking for a soul mate. Another trick of Evol DNA was that ordinary sexual hormones were stalled for quite some time until one's emotions became more controlled. Regardless of the secluded life I led, I used to have quite the sexual appetite, which vanished after the transformation. The usual turn-ons changed. My new appetites were triggered by a whole new set of senses that I had yet to master. Shit, up until that point, I was still having trouble distinguishing hunger from thirst let alone anything more complicated.

Lucas and I grew much closer as well during those first two years. He wouldn't travel with me to other countries, but he did come visit me on the mountain. The strong silent type for sure. However, once he got comfortable a whole lot started rolling out. One day he and I were taking a walk in my woods and we sat down, just chatting about nothing in particular. A rabbit slowly hopped over to him and sat by his foot. I'd never seen anything like it but Lucas wouldn't pet it. Instead, he tried to pretend the rabbit wasn't there. Within no time at all, two rabbits were by his feet, a fox behind him, and omg, the squirrels were ganging up on him. I teased him, calling him Snow White. It was bizarre how drawn to him the animals were. Lucas just ignored them all, telling me that if we were to spend time together, I would have to get used to it too.

He'd had a rough start as an Evol. His Gifter didn't show up for nearly three years after giving Lucas the gift. I felt so bad for him hearing that. One year was too long in my mind to wait for answers. Especially after going through that most painful and confusing experience. He was without answers for three years. When his Gifter finally had showed he really didn't explain a whole hell of a lot. By that time, Lucas was convinced he had gone crazy. Seth had heard about Lucas through one of the other Gifters and decided to pay a visit. Thus, began a long-lasting friendship between them. As far as Lucas was concerned, Seth was his true Gifter because Seth had taken the time to care. His physical Gifter was a piece of garbage. More proof that Evols, mentally, could be the same as regular humans. They may have evolved their DNA but that didn't change their compassion or intelligence. Either you're willing to change and grow or you're not; it's that simple.

Lucas and I had a magnetism between us. It's hard to put into words but there was an unmistakable pull. We never acted on it in any way. Not even so much as holding hands. I'm not sure as to why we never let ourselves fully commit to what we were both feeling. Eric would throw out suggestive comments, teasing us at times. He saw what was so clearly there and tried to encourage it but we'd brush off the comments and ignore him. Both of us were still very content with being on our own. Having our separate lives. Living in our own little loner worlds. Whatever attraction was there would have to wait until we were ready, if ever.

There was an incident with a couple of nasty hunters I should mention. Compared to the horrid events that will unfold later in this story, my encounter with the hunters was mild. At the time though it felt serious to me. I owned some forty-two acres that surrounded my home. It was mostly all forestry land and perfect for my new need to feed on animals. Even when it was not my feeding time, I'd often take long walks in the woods late at night. Being basically impervious to serious injury or illness made my trips into the forest more enjoyable. No diseases from ticks or mosquitos and animals most certainly didn't try to attack me. It had become my own little secret world right in my backyard. Evol vision was extraordinary to behold.

Anyway, while hanging out in the middle of the woods one night, listening to the owls hoot, I caught the scent of something that didn't belong: Wild Turkey whiskey. Yup, I could distinguish between types of liquors and food from the smell of a person's blood, and from quite a distance. Jealous yet? Don't be. This smell was emanating from two humans somewhere close to me. My land had *No Hunting* signs all over it but that didn't deter everyone. I started walking toward the smell and then heard whispering. They were high up in a makeshift deer stand. Suddenly, a shot rang out and a sharp pain hit me in the shoulder. Like a red-hot fire poker shoved through my flesh. They shot me! My eyes lit up, I doubled over in pain and let loose a deafening screech.

"Holy shit Jim! You shot a person! What do we do?" one of the hunters shouted.

"We have to kill them. It's the only way to hide this shit. Take the shot man! Take the shot!" Jim exclaimed.

It was at that point the trees and ground began to vibrate; a small, localized earthquake beneath us. The men tried to hang onto the tree but were unable to steady their rifles to take another shot at me. They were drunk as skunks and had just attempted to murder me for walking on my own property! *Yeah, bad move fellas.* Both of them finally fell from the deer stand onto the ground. I heard their bones break as they landed. One shattered his femur and the other broke his clavicle. *Outstanding!* I thought to myself and smiled brightly.

As they tried to get their bearings, a deep growl rolled out of me. I'd of course become accustomed to that when I was angry, but it was not what they expected. I walked up on them quickly, removing their rifles and slung them over my shoulder. The very shoulder they had shot me in. It was almost healed already. The bullet had passed through so the healing was damn near instant. The men looked up at me and I suppose they saw my golden eyes illuminating my face. I couldn't see my own eyes, but I could see the light radiating from them.

Upon giving them a sharp toothed grin, they started yelling, screaming uncontrollably. I believe I heard the word witch a few times. And demon. I crouched down close to them.

"Never hunt here again. I know the owner of this property. They wouldn't appreciate your presence, even less knowing that you tried to murder someone. If I find you here again, you will not survive our next meeting. I suggest you hobble out of here, now!" I told them.

I didn't have to say it twice. They helped each other up; trying their hardest to leave. I emptied their weapons of ammo and then broke them into pieces. Tossing the pieces around the forest as I made my way home. Never had an issue with hunters again.

Also, a few months later while chatting with a neighbor, they told me their hot gossip about some local boys getting admitted to the Xavier Mental and Wellness Hospital. Apparently, they had gotten drunk one night in the woods somewhere and chased by an animal. That's what the doctors assumed but the boys kept saying there was a witch in the woods. Eventually, that kind of talk put them in a nut house.

I would say I felt bad, but I so did not. They were poachers, drunk, shot a person (me) by accident, and then tried to cover it up by murdering said person. Nope, I didn't feel bad in the least. I was proud of myself. I had controlled my temper. That was a rare occurrence when I was human and as an Evol it had been particularly difficult. A few broken bones were the minimum of what I could've done to them. Spending some time in a rubber room might be good for them. I thought of it as a public service.

Often, I wondered what Seth had been thinking making me a part of his outlander nation. I self-secluded, not to protect myself from anyone else but to protect others from me. Taking a firm hold of these new gifts and urges was a most tedious ongoing struggle, indeed. My children, Josh and June, had slowed down their communications with me. I wasn't sure if that was on my end to fix or possibly just a lull for the time being. They were both busy with work and kids of their own. I was torn in between pushing harder to see them or cutting ties now because either way, they wouldn't be able to see me over video chat much longer without blowing the whistle on how I was not aging. To be honest, I avoided making the decision. I wasn't ready to deal with losing them this soon.

Well, time moved on again as it does. In my fourth Evol year, my sweet baby boy Vader passed away. That was a heartbreak for me. With my insanely elevated senses I felt there was something wrong with his breathing and heart rhythm. He was sixteen years old and, with the exception of my Evol-ution period of change, I spoiled him every day possible, so I believed he lived a good life. I considered my gift as a blessing for the first time because I knew Vader's time was coming to an end and I was able to be with him. Instead of me finding him one day dead behind the couch, I was able to hold him, pet him, and shower him with extra love until it was over.

After his passing, I decided it was time I checked out one of my new properties. I needed a change. My mountain home no longer felt the same without Vader running around. So, I packed up the house to get ready for my new adventure. I choose Scotland as my first stop. It had been a dream of mine for years to go there, and I felt a positive vibe and glow about my next steps in life. As I made my way through the house, putting items in boxes, I realized I hadn't touched the stuff in the basement.

On a shelf sat a large plastic tub labeled, *Jake*. It gave me pause. That was where I kept my deceased son's belongings. He passed away at nineteen from a car accident. I hadn't opened it in many years, especially after Seth's warning about how high Evol emotions could run. My brain vehemently told me not to even touch it. My heart, on the other hand, needed to look inside one more time.

I broke the seal on the plastic tub and removed the lid. Immediately, I breathed in deep. I could smell my child so clearly. I gingerly picked up his jacket that lay on top of the rest of his things, brought it up to my face and took in another deep breath. Suddenly, I was frozen. I could smell amniotic fluid. His amniotic fluid. It felt like heaven and pure light. Oh, could this be real? How amazing was this? Another deep inhale. I couldn't get enough. I closed my eyes as the image of his birth appeared. Me, holding my sweet newborn Jakey. Studying his tiny hands and peering into his beautiful eyes. Then the image changed to when he was two years old and I was playing a chasing game with him; running around the living room. I could hear his incredible little giggle so plainly that I couldn't help but smile. The image changed again to when he was five. Then again and he was older still. *An unbelievable gift*, I thought, until they got faster.

His life was speeding by me. I felt it all, smelled it all, heard it all; it was completely real and tangible. Then a sense of panic began to course through me. I knew where those images were headed. I tried to make them stop but I was in a locked-down mental state of terror. I could not move. I could not put his jacket down. The memories moved on, older and older he got. My heart was pounding inside my chest. I needed it to stop. It had to stop; his death was approaching fast. Finally, I saw myself standing on a street corner at night. I knew where I was. It was the corner where Jake had died.

I was not present when the accident occurred years before, but somehow, I recognized where I was standing. I saw Jake's car coming down the road and I tried, franticly, to wave my arms for him to stop.

He wouldn't look at me. I technically wasn't there. In the other direction came the Mac truck, barreling out of control. A clash of thunder as devastatingly loud as an explosion as the two vehicles collided in slow motion in front of my eyes. I saw my son's body fly forward into the windshield. I heard the cracking sound his skull made. Echoing out in my head was his death. On repeat, looped, until …

I dropped his jacket as my mouth hung open in anguish. Air moved from my lungs but made no sound. No sound until finally the outburst of an earth-shattering, wretched scream came forth from a place in my soul that only mothers know exists. The basement walls shook, the ground shifted beneath my feet, and glass jars exploded, hitting the floor like little grenades. As that devastating cry of pain rang out from inside of me, I fell to my knees.

Then, just as suddenly as that horrid event started, it came to a screeching halt. My body collapsed hard onto the broken concrete floor. I shook momentarily, akin to experiencing an epileptic fit. My heart stopped beating and the basement fell silent.

***

Seth, six states away, was watching a movie with Eric. They had just gotten comfortable on the couch after eating dinner, having planned a cozy date night in for themselves. Abruptly and intensely, he received an unsettling feeling in his gut. He jumped to his feet with lightning-sharp shooting pains hitting his head as his heart raced erratically. A picture of my face popped up in front of his eyes and he bent over, throwing up violently on his living room floor.

That was his Gifter sense telling him I was dead, but it had never been that visceral of a reaction before.

"No! Emma!" he screamed.

Chapter 8
How Big of a Freak am I?

Seth grabbed Eric's hand and promptly used his Gifter's ability to escape gravity. They hopped in and out of the stratosphere from state to state, arriving at my home within thirty minutes.

Silence of the greatest volume, only the shuffle sounds of their footsteps approaching my home. The door was unlocked. They cautiously walked in and relief washed over them as they heard a heartbeat. The trickling noise of running water was also confusingly heard. They didn't know where it was coming from or if it was even my heartbeat thumping slow.

Seth and Eric scoured the house room to room but found only some moving boxes scattered about. Then Eric opened the basement door; he could smell me. He motioned to Seth that I was down there.

As they descended the stairs, they couldn't see me yet but could definitely feel me. My breathing was faint, but more troubling was my heart only beat four times per minute. I may not have been dead, but it would only be a matter of time at the rate my vital signs were degrading. When they found me, I was lying on the floor in a large puddle of a gooey substance mixed with streaks of blood, covered in a silvery-blue sheen, as if I had sweat that goo out through my pores.

Unconscious and shivering with cold.

Eric spotted a burst pipe along the wall. The basement was filling with water, he quickly turned the well pump off. They picked me up to carry me upstairs, but had a difficult time of it holding onto me. That stuff I was covered in was a slippery, gross slime. They got me upstairs to the living room where they discussed what to do. Not wanting to set me down on a bed in my slime-covered condition, Seth decided a bath would be best and it would help to raise my body temperature. They gently lowered me into the bathtub.

Eric hoped there was enough water in the hot water tank to fill the tub. Seth stripped off my clothes, letting the warm water wash over me. Eric snickered and Seth looked up at him, wondering what could be funny in that moment.

Eric put his hands up. "Dude, when she realizes we saw her naked she's going to be all kinds of pissed off," he said.

"This is not the time for jokes Eric!" Seth snapped. "We've got to get this weird slimy stuff off her. She's ice cold and maybe that's because of this goop. Emma usually radiates heat; it just pours out of her. I don't understand why she's this cold."

Seth and Eric dried me off, dressing me in sweatpants and a T-shirt. They laid me in bed and thought about what to do next. Seth started dialing Max's number and told Eric to call Lucas but absolutely no one else. They stood in the bedroom staring at me while talking to the others.

My heartbeat was still weak and thready. Max never heard of anything like what they found but he was going to start digging through the archives. He was also told of the goop I was covered in and how it resembled the substance that was extracted from my fangs. Lucas bolted from his house the moment Eric told him. It was going to take him some time to reach us since he didn't have Gifter powers. He would have to arrive the old fashion way, by car.

Eric then called a local plumber to fix the pipe in the basement. He didn't know how long I would be unconscious or how long he and Seth would be at my house. The water needed to be turned back on if they were to stay awhile. When he spoke to a willing plumber, they confirmed they could be out in the morning.

Seth and Eric switched off, lying down on the bed next to me, their Evol body heat keeping me warm. They slept but wanted to ensure they were close in case I woke up.

The next morning the boys were watching the local news. A small earthquake had taken place in my area the day before. That explained the burst water pipe in the basement along with the broken glass and mess down there.

Seth called Max. "Listen, I don't know if this is anything important, but we were just watching the news and there was an earthquake here at Emma's house yesterday. It happened the same time I felt her die Max," he relayed.

"Hmmm, I don't know if that means anything. It might have been just coincidence. I'll investigate that too," Max said.

Shortly after their conversation, the plumber arrived with a cleaning crew. Eric led them to the basement through the outside bulkhead. He didn't want them in the house with what would've looked like a suspicious situation. A woman in bed unconscious and two strange men wandering the home. The plumber told Eric that he'd been their third call in the local area. He thought it was odd the earthquake had been centered just around my home. Two other houses close by had also reported burst pipes and cracked foundations. While the men fixed the pipe and vacuumed out the water; Eric drove to a hardware store to buy concrete patch. He wanted to kill time, he said; make himself useful by patching the cracks in the basement.

Lucas pulled into my driveway twelve hours later. Seth and Eric had no news for him because I was still in a coma-like state. He went to my bedside and sat quietly. He was listening for any changes that might occur such as heartbeat or electrical surges. When he touched my arm, he was taken back by how cold I was. The boys explained they didn't know what that was about, and Lucas piled another blanket on me and sat back down. Nothing about the situation appeared normal, not even for a person in a coma. I was still slightly sweating that gooey substance from the pores on my forehead. Lucas would wipe it away with a washcloth throughout the day.

Seth and Max spoke to each other often to go over the details of how they had found me. Max was beside himself, not having any answers. Lucas was worried, racking his brain for anything that might turn the situation around.

While he was standing out back watching the sunrise over the trees on the third morning, a mouse found its way to him. It hopped onto the top of his boot and just sat there looking up at him. And that's apparently when an idea hit him. He later said, they all felt they had tried everything else already.

He swiftly went inside to speak to Seth. "Hey, does Emma still drain animals? I mean, has she done it since the first time she told you about it?" he asked Seth.

Seth was puzzled but answered him, "Yes, she has a couple of times since then. Why?"

Lucas walked back out to the porch yelling that he had an idea. He sat down in my chair to wait. With his natural ability to attract animals he was hoping he could lure something big to the house. Thirty minutes went by and a bunch of squirrels with a raccoon showed up. He kept shooing them away. Forty-five minutes more past and then he heard it. The crunching of leaves made by hooves in the distance. Finally, a lumbering good-sized bull moose came into view. It sauntered down the pathway directly to Lucas, lying down in the grass beside the deck. Lucas got up to gently pet the beast.

Eric and Seth watched through the window in awe.

Lucas turned to Seth and mouthed the words, "Go. Get. Her."

Seth ran to the bedroom and picked me up. My heart rate had dropped down to a mere two beats per minute. He carefully carried me outside and Lucas told him to place me by the moose. Seth's eyes widened, fearful the animal would hurt me, he shook his head no. Lucas rolled his eyes with impatience. He took me from Seth's arms and laid me on my right side leaning up against the moose with my head resting on its massive neck.

"How do we get her to drink? She's in a coma for Christ's sake!" Eric whispered so as to not spook the moose.

With a smile on his face, Lucas held up a big hunting knife. The boys knew he was about to slice that moose's throat. As he walked toward it, my left hand twitched. Lucas paused and stepped back. The three of them watched as I began to show signs of life.

With my eyes still closed, I lifted my left arm, wrapping it around the moose's neck. I was seemingly hugging or caressing it softly. Then, in a flash, I ripped out a huge chunk of tough hide with my hand, exposing the carotid artery. The moose did not move a muscle, hypnotized by the power of my touch.

Seth and Eric, however, stepped further back up against the glass door, grimacing.

My eyes opened, I turned my head to its throat, and sank my teeth in. Blood came spurting out of the animal, spraying outwards from the sides of my face and flowed down the front of me. A moose is such a large animal that I didn't have to work for the blood. Its own heart pumping did the job. Each beat forcefully shot blood everywhere, warm and wonderful, it tasted amazing.

Eric began violently heaving and then ran inside to puke. Seth gagged repeatedly but bravely tried to stick it out until Lucas told him to just go inside, which he promptly did. Lucas sat down in my chair to keep watch. He could hear my heartrate pick up little by little.

After I'd had more than my fill, I sat up, leaning against that most generous moose. I was groggy and didn't seem to know what was going on. Looking up at Lucas, I smiled big, covered in blood, and spoke. "Lucas? Hey, why are you here?" I asked.

He smiled lovingly and replied, "Hi beautiful. Oh, I was just in the neighborhood."

I positioned myself upright, sitting a little straighter. My brain was taking in the carnage I was covered in. The realization hit me that the obvious dead moose I was leaning on had been killed by me. A wave of embarrassment and horror rolled across my face as tears welled up in my eyes. I was confused and on the verge of panic. Questions raced through my head. *Had I killed the moose in front of Lucas? Why was he really there? Why could I hear Seth and Eric in my house? What the hell was going on?*

Lucas seemed to feel my panic. "Hey, hey, hey, it's okay. You're okay. We are all okay. No one judges you. We're just happy you're back with us and alive. We can talk about it in a little while. It's okay sweetie, I promise." He tried to calm me down and reassure me, helping me to my feet and heading to the bathroom so I could clean myself up.

We passed Seth and Eric sitting at the dining room table. They were both very green-looking and silent. Eric was attempting to concentrate on not puking again. Lucas told me to just keep walking and not worry about them; they'd be fine.

While I showered I tried to figure out what the hell had happened. Maybe I had gone mad again? Crazy like before when I was transforming. *My mind snapped,* I thought. It could have been due to the stress of moving to Scotland. That had to be it. Just a small slip backward.

When I walked out of the bathroom, Seth immediately grabbed me tight, hugging me. He asked how I was feeling. I answered that I felt fine and wanted to know where Eric and Lucas were. Seth said he had sent them out for some food and I made a weird face at him. I wasn't super hungry since I had just drained a moose. The thought of food in that moment made me want to gag.

He laughed as he ushered me to sit down at the kitchen table. On my open laptop he called Max for a video call.

Max answered and his mouth dropped. "Emma! Oh, thank God! You're alright? How do you feel?" he asked.

"I feel good Max. What's going on?" I replied worriedly.

"Emma, something happened to you in the basement. As far as Seth could tell, you were going through a box of your son's clothes? He and Eric found you on the floor next to that box. He thought you had died. You've been out cold for three days. What do you remember?" Max said with bated breath.

I was taken aback by everything he explained but tried my best to recall. I recounted walking down to the basement to pack some boxes. I had opened Jake's plastic tub and my mind went into overload. And then I was with my children. All of them when they were really little.

It was like a dream but completely intact and realistic. As if I was there, back in time in that very moment. I was a spectator. At one point while I was with them, I heard someone call to me. I went to the window and as soon as I looked through, I woke up outside my house.

"Interesting," Max mused. "That is odd but we're going to figure this out. Until we do, I instructed Seth to take care of your son's box. He has stashed it away in a safe place. Later, when your emotions calm enough, you can have it back, ok?" Max said, watching my reaction. "As soon as I get all my research materials together I will send you what I find," he added.

I was shocked and still confused but I continued to nod. "Okay, sounds good Max."

As we hung up, the boys returned with food. Everyone ate, even me a little bit and we kept to small talk. Something lighter than what they had been going through over those three days. I had many questions but the atmosphere in the room didn't feel like it was the right time to get into it.

The subject of the broken water pipe came up. Eric ensured all of us that it had been fixed and cleaned up. He said the basement foundation should be okay, but it would be a good idea to have a professional inspect it, which I wanted to get done, especially since I was planning on moving away for a while.

After dinner Seth and Eric announced they needed to get back home. We could talk more about everything that occurred later over the phone. Lucas agreed with them that he too had to get back to check on his pets. I didn't want them to leave but understood they must have left their homes so quickly they needed to get back to take care of things. How fortunate I was to have this new family, truly. I don't believe anyone from my human world would've come to my rescue so willingly.

While saying my goodbyes to Lucas at the door, I overheard Eric whispering to Seth.

"Thank God she didn't realize we saw her naked. We might get out of here alive," he said.

Obviously, he'd forgotten about my elevated Evol hearing. I whipped my head around and barked, "WHAT?!"

"Nothing, we have to run. Love you. Take care. Call you later," Seth said, panicking as he grabbed Eric to pull him out the door.

Eric smiled and waved goodbye as they left.

Chapter 9
The Lost Ones

Comfortable in my new cozy home on the West Coast of Scotland. Four months had passed since the incident on the mountain. Moving to Scotland had been the first long distance public travel I had completed in years. Having to deal with so many people during the process sucked, I mean really sucked. Loud and smelly. I was unprepared for how overwhelming an airport would be with my senses. Speaking of that travel across the Atlantic, I had another scrape with the humans. And with some horrid former humans. It happened at the Boston Logan International Airport.

I was standing in the security TSA line and noticed a couple of Evols far at the front. It shocked me because I hadn't seen any of our kind out and about in public before. I felt proud and a little naughty that we had a secret others around us didn't know. The two of them spotted me as well. One of them gave me a small welcoming smile and we went back to waiting in line like nothing was amiss. Then they went through the metal detectors.

When it was my turn to get into that MRI-type metal detector, shit went wrong. As soon as the scan began, the machine went haywire. The monitors blacked out and the metal detector made loud blaring noises. An agent asked me to step forward so she could manually inspect me. She used her magic wand and all was good but, due to the confusion of the machine, she was suspicious. She aggressively began to pat me down. And that set me off.

That stupid damn growling started. I didn't know how to control it. It hadn't happened in a couple of years, not since the hunters. I closed my eyes, thinking, *fuck me*. All hell was about to break loose. There were two bomb sniffing dogs off to the side who went ballistic. Barking and pulling their handlers in my direction. If TSA wasn't already looking at me, they were by that point. One of the two Evols I'd seen earlier was putting his shoes on and saw the commotion.

He came over toward us as more agents showed up. He went over to the conveyor belt where the passenger carry-on stuff was. Meanwhile, I had an agent in my face asking me questions and on instinct I flashed the golden rings in my eyes. She backed up, confused, she didn't know what to do. I could tell she wasn't sure she had seen what she saw. Her brain was probably trying to shield her mentally.

Suddenly, another agent was pulling the guy in line behind me to the side and made an announcement. Before I knew it, my agent said I was free to go but that other guy was getting the third degree. I grabbed my things and went to the bench area to put my shoes on. Holy shit was that close.

One of the Evols came over and told me not to sweat it; he had taken care of it. I asked him how and he said he had dropped a bag of edibles in Third Degree's stuff on the conveyor belt. TSA had their hands full with him now. I looked up at him after tying my shoe; laughing and thanked him. Unfortunately, it was then that he noticed my sharp-ass fangs. He excused himself quickly and left.

When I walked by them both on the way to my gate they gave me the dirtiest looks; noses turned up and shaking their heads. *Well, fuck. So much for making new friends! Assholes.*

Thankfully, once on the airplane the ungodly distractions and noise of people completely cleared my mind of those dickheads. And by the time I landed in Scotland, all that mess had faded. Such an amazingly beautiful country; the drive to my new home was breathtaking. The cottage sat atop a knoll overlooking the ocean, close to the village of Arduaine. That's quite a bit west of Glasgow. I had hoped to be closer to Edinburgh, however, when you fall in love with a home, that's it. Edinburgh and its famous castle had been on my bucket list. I did make a few overnight trips to see it on several occasions.

My creature followed me to Scotland somehow. I'd been curious to see if it would, if it could. It most certainly did. Shocking to see it this time on the airplane, I continued to ignore it though. If it wasn't bothering me then I wouldn't bother it. Just another weird fact of being who I was. The creature would watch me in the yard practicing and cultivating my abilities. I often wished it could speak to me, tell me how I was doing, etc. The levitation trick had grown significantly. I was up to three feet off the ground. Seth still didn't understand what that was about. He didn't know anyone else who could float, so to speak, apart from Gifters. I was discovering more and more unique attributes on an almost monthly basis.

The purple orb remained a mystery, absolutely zero clue. On the plus side, I was getting physically stronger. Disappointingly not as strong as I had hoped, not yet anyway. When people keep assuming you're a vampire you start believing it too. Human depictions of vampires were beings of immense instant strength and speed. I could open a jar of pickles by myself but not lift a boulder over my head. Meh, compared to how strong I was before the gift I would say I was making leaps and bounds in that department. Slowly but surely, I was finding that moving furniture or chopping wood had become non-strenuous activities. That was another helpful gain for me in the pursuit of independence. I did, every now and then, randomly try to pick up that boulder though. I knew one day I'd do it!

My kiddos, Josh and June, were taken aback when I broke the news that I was moving to Scotland. Since Jake's death we hadn't been close anymore. None of us talked like we used to and what little we did was spread out by months at a time. We had drifted significantly over the years, dealing with the loss and I really drifted once being gifted. I think June took it better than Josh. She sounded resigned but I still detected anger in Josh's voice. I remember he cut the call pretty short after I'd spilled the beans.

My appearance and their age were getting eerily similar. It wouldn't be long before they looked older than me. I didn't have a great excuse for moving halfway across the globe, but it was a good way for me to begin the physical process of cutting my ties with them, I figured they'd been well-prepared. It had to be done at some point.

I could not get enough of my new surroundings. Sincerely, couldn't have been happier if I tried. Close to perfection and by that, I mean it was stone cold quiet out where I lived. The loner life still fit me like a glove. My Scottish cottage atop that pristinely vibrant green hill overlooking the sea was heaven. Not a neighbor in sight! However, I did travel into town occasionally. The people there were atypically kind. A very happy bunch that took everyday life in stride. Loud though, they spoke and laughed in full volume and with complete joy. A little nosy and curious, of course, as pretty much all folks are in small towns. They were also full of superstitious folklore and fairytale stories. They loved spinning yarns to each other and with me. I was the foreigner and the new kid on the block. They sought me out when I was in town so they could gab my ears off with talk about banshees and changelings, kelpies and fairies. The Loch Ness Monster. If ever I were to fit in among mystical weirdos; that was the place to be. Or at least fit into their lore; if not with them exactly. But it was close enough, I thought.

An elderly man at the post office was particularly cautious of me. I had laughed too hard at one of his jokes, revealing my unusual vampiric dentalwork. I covered my mouth to finish my laughter, but I think it was too late. He looked at me differently after that day. He knew something was up with me.

From then on, he would act rushed around me like he was too busy to chat. If he had been seriously concerned about me, he didn't alarm anyone else to it. Good thing too. I would've hated to leave and been unhappy to have to eliminate him or those he told.

The food in Scotland was okay. I wouldn't describe it as the best cuisine I had been exposed to however, I wasn't averse to it either. The delicacy haggis. Many people find it disgusting but I found it intriguing. Traditionally, it's a mixture of ground up animals and oats with spices, all stuffed into a sheep's stomach. And I could literally smell it more than a mile away. Haggis, to me, is a good stink if that makes sense. The taste is not really my thing but for whatever reason, I *do* enjoy the smell of it. I can pick out each individual animal that went into carefully creating the haggis with my super senses. It's quite fun, like a culinary detective game.

Fun fact, it *does* snow in Scotland. Did you know that? Particularly in the northern regions but also where I was on the west coast. I didn't mind. I preferred it colder as you may have guessed by my snowy mountain home. Even more so, now it was important for me to be in cooler weather. My Evol body ran like a steam engine. Constantly radiating heat. That saved money on electrical bills, another bonus. Yeah, I fell in love with everything about my cottage, including the small villages surrounding it. And most definitely the weather! Everything I needed and wanted was right there. A patch of forest with animals for feeding, seclusion and privacy, cool breezes, the ocean, and incredible views.

Not long after I moved into the cottage, a package was dropped off at my door from a Dr. Maximillian Harris. Seth had undoubtedly given him my address. I was confused for a moment until it occurred to me what could be in the box. Inside, there was a small book with a note attached:

Emma,
I hope all is well with you. I thought you might find this useful or at least interesting.
Read the chapter on The Lost Ones. *You can return it to me at the Gathering if we don't see each other before then.*
Take the best of care,
Max.

The book appeared very old and delicate. It was titled *Volume 6: Evolved Fairytales*. That piqued my curiosity. Was it his answer to what happened to me? Or was it just something about us as Evols he thought I would enjoy? Anything was possible when it came to Max. He had so much historical information in his head and his favorite pastime was sharing the evolution of 'us.'

I made myself comfortable in the little reading nook by the bay window facing the ocean. Carefully, I opened the fragile book to the chapter he had suggested and began to read.

The Lost Ones

Eons before humankind there were beings of no name who inhabited the Earth, composed of the deepest joy and love. They stood tall but walked soft with very long, beautiful hair streaked with gold. Their skin glowed with a remarkable natural sheen and they gave off a warm light from inside that lit up even the darkest of nights. They lived much longer than what we would consider normal; their average life span was eight hundred human years.

Many of these beings had long, sharp teeth, similar to those of a tiger's so as to feed on wild animals but in no way were they feared. They were gentle creatures, singing or humming to their prey, giving thanks for what they were about to receive. It was said, the reason they took such care with the animals was because as these beings aged, they did not die but instead transformed themselves into an animal. Effectively recycling back into the food chain. This ability sustained and replenished the Earth's bounty perpetually.

The world was much different from what we know today. The sky and atmosphere was pristinely clean. You could see the moon and stars at all times even during the day with the naked eye. Fertile ground was an understatement. Theirs was the richest soil that has never been seen since their time. They grew and farmed plants and foods of the likes humans could only dream of, working together in harmony and peace to ensure every being had what was needed to not only survive but to thrive.

They never knew war, strife, famine, or even hostility between tribes. The reason for this was not only emotional superiority but also their ability to time travel. Within their bodies was a substance called Shimmer, *which could be exuded through their skin. This incredible fluid's name derived from its glistening appearance. Shimmer triggered the time traveling process and helped to lubricate the being's transition between the fabrics of space. On rare occasions, if an issue arose that could disrupt their utopia-like lives, one of them would Shimmer back in time to find the source of the problem. They could correct the issue before it had a chance to develop into a war or struggle.*

Although they were as close to perfect a being as there was, there were a slim few who tried to disrupt that perfection. Shimmer was used to assist in changing that person's perception before anything permanently destructive ruined the seamless flow of their world. When a natural weather event threatened crops and food supply, it could be corrected with the use of Shimmer. Transporting themselves back far enough to ensure the proper preparations were made to protect the crops during the future weather disaster. Shimmer was an invaluable resource that kept their world rotating smoothly in a perfect circle of love and safety.

One day, over the course of a single a day, their existence was wiped off the face of the Earth. There was a great resurfacing of the planet. Fire and rock swept over the globe, killing the beings and changing the structure of their world. The changes forced all elements to change; oxygen and carbon levels, oceans and land masses, and even sky coloration. Earth appeared as new. A reset of the planet itself.

Some of us believe the resurfacing happened due to an error during a Shimmer event. Possibly something went wrong while jumping through the fabric of space, triggering a planetary shift from its orbit and causing a catastrophic remodeling. Others believe it was an act of God. Whatever the truth of the resurfacing, it did not kill all of the beings. A small handful, we believe, escaped the rapture. They hid within the folds of time out of reach of instant annihilation of their kind.

These few came back to find their home, as they knew it, gone. We call them the Lost Ones. Their Earth not only looked radically different but there were also new creatures: humans. The Lost Ones kept themselves hidden as best they could. Over the centuries, many of them died off by changing into animals, which when mistakenly observed, gave rise to our related human fables and myths. When a Lost One found themselves trapped in a city with no animals to feed on, they would attack a human in desperation. The witness of such events would bring about tales of vampires. When at full strength and in bright sunlight they had the appearance of magnificent angels. That was their allure. Don't be fooled. We do not know much about them or even what their true name was, however, a Lost One's power would be too great for our world.

It is not known if any still exist today or how many could be left. But if any of these ancient beings were among us, our world would be in danger. The existence of Lost Ones could mean another planetary rapture.

I put the book down, shaken. What kind of fairytale was this? If you really wanted to scare children, then tell them this. Watch out for the Lost Ones, kids; they'll destroy the planet after turning themselves into animals. No wonder the Evols aren't allowed to have kids. For this reason, right here! Who even wrote this? Crazy.

I called Max a few weeks later to ask him to meet up with me. I needed to know his thoughts on what he found and why this fairytale was so important. He suggested we meet in London, insisting it was in the middle of a crowded place. He reminded me that Evols didn't like crowds, so they tended to stay away from big cities. They put our senses into an uncomfortable overdrive. Although Max and I would not like it either, he felt it was imperative no Evols saw us or heard our conversation. I agreed and we set a place and date to meet.

I tried to hide how ridiculous I had felt the story was; wanting to hear his explanation before laughing at him. The longer I was an Evol, the more I believed I had died. I must have passed on from a heart attack and now I was in a weird, fucked-up Dr. Seuss movie. Two thumbs up from this girl. If this was how I was to spend my death then so be it, there were worse ways to live a dying existence. If I was truly alive then, so be it. I couldn't wait to hear Max's theory. Who knew? Maybe it would make sense somehow, or I maybe I'd walk right out in the middle of the conversation. We would see.

I needed to conduct my annual feeding first. I had learned to plan ahead to avoid that horrid pacing when I denied myself. The Scottish countryside offered an abundance of large deer roaming. This new need of mine to devour animals had given me even more reason to live a solitary lifestyle. It wasn't something I would want a human catching me perpetrating.

I sat outside and patiently waited. A stellar looking stag approached.

How grand he was. Proudly, his magnificent rack hung prominently over my fireplace after that night. With my appetite sated, I packed the following week for my trip to London.

Chapter 10
The Hidden Outrage

People run in packs because they don't feel safe alone.
I run alone because I don't feel safe in packs.
—Muhammad Ali

I was meeting up with Max in a London diner in the middle of what seemed like chaos to me. It was just another busy day for the folks of London but for me, the crowds felt like a battlefield. The noise level of all those humans was absolutely deafening. I was in physical pain navigating my way through the congested streets. By the time I arrived at his table, I was exhausted.

Max stood to give me a big hug. It was great to see him in person, finally. Time was still a concept I gauged life by, so the mere five years I had been talking to him made our meeting a long time in the making. To Max however, he had dropped the concept of time centuries ago, so maybe he didn't feel the length of our friendship the way I did.

The first thing he did was teach me to block out everyone else around us. He said it was a talent honed over the centuries, but he was going to give me a crash course. If he hadn't tried to train me in that then, I wouldn't have been able to sit there or pay attention. He could feel how incredibly uncomfortable I was. The trick, he told me, was to concentrate on the person you were talking to and only that one person. Concentrate on their heartbeat and breathing. Make a solid effort to focus on their scent and slight body movements. Keep your eyes locked with theirs as much as possible. If you can get your heart rhythm on the same page as theirs, you will be able to block out the humans in the room.

We sat quiet and motionless for some time while I focused on him alone. It started to work, and I increasingly felt better. Earnestly and carefully, I narrowed my senses until everything centered on him. He had my full attention in no time at all. An excellent trick indeed. I could see all the people around us but not really hear them or even smell them. I remember wishing Seth had shared this secret with me earlier. It could've come in handy during my move to Scotland.

Airports are a hotbed of grossness and noise. If humans could sense what I could; no one would ever go to an airport again. People stress at airports over late or canceled flights. Stress causes stench. Arguments with the people they're traveling with, fights during phone conversations, overheated tempers all over the place. Feeling the need to shower after traveling is an understatement for an Evol. Anyway, I digress …

Max and I ordered our food and drinks. I had become much more relaxed and relieved. When the time felt right, I reached into my backpack and gingerly removed the near decayed storybook. Sliding it across the table and into his hands, he placed the book in his briefcase and then looked at me pensively. He told me the first thing I needed to absolutely grasp was this …

"There is a hidden faction of Evols who consider themselves guardians of our evolution. They believe we should be always in an evolutionary upward trajectory. Meaning, any Evol born with something out of the ordinary could threaten our progression," he warned.

I stopped him there. "What you're describing sounds very much like the white supremacist movement but the Evols I've encountered are all different colors and backgrounds. Hell, even Seth, Lucas, and I, distinctively look like all parts of the world," I commented.

"It has to do with our abilities and DNA structures, not with color. But yes, they are very much a supremacy type of faction," he replied.

I nodded with anger and disappointment. I understood what he was saying. I didn't like it, but I understood and listened carefully as he continued. Trying to keep an open mind, trying to keep my composure.

"Emma, you can never tell anyone what I'm going to share with you. Not yet anyway. I haven't even told Tamson. Not Seth. No one. Tamson and I are each nearly a millennium in age. We have been friends for most of that, but I will not share this with him either," Max said.

That made me sit up a little straighter wondering what could be such a big deal. What had I gotten myself into? I leaned forward, ensuring I was completely focused on him and his words.

Max took a breath and began, "I have a theory, Emma. You might be linked to a Lost One or possibly even *be* a Lost One. That pale silvery-blue substance that came from your teeth we tested? That was the same stuff you were covered in during your coma event last year. I believe that to be Shimmer," he explained.

"Hold up, I was covered in it? When Seth and Eric found me in my basement passed out because of Jake's keepsakes? No one told me that. I wasn't covered in that substance when I woke up outside. Why do you think it was Shimmer?" I asked.

Max explained his theory to me. He believed that when I was going through my son's memorabilia box my Evol senses took over so completely that I was truly about to die. He didn't know what I saw but it was strong enough to stop my heart. In that instance I bled Shimmer, allowing myself to shift back in time to a place and moment I was most happy. He said it would have been lightning fast; a millisecond. My body physically left the house mid-fall and then reappeared on the basement floor. He thought I had most probably saved my own life.

I sat back in my seat letting his words absorb. None of it made sense to me. Not a few years back I was a human, living a life of seclusion with scant special abilities. A stellar medic in my heyday, a novice painter, and a more than okay cook but a time traveler? No, that wasn't on the docket, I chuckled to myself.

So I challenged his theory. "Okay, you believe that when I thought I was dreaming of being with Jake, I was really with him? Back in time? And you think that was possible because I am a Lost One? But that wouldn't be possible, I was born human, Max. One hundred percent human. No abilities or unusual behaviors. Just plain old human," I insisted.

He nodded in agreement. "That is true. I'm still trying to make that fit into my theory. But do I believe the foreign shiny substance inside you is Shimmer? Yes, I do. There really is no other explanation. Are you an actual Lost One? I don't know for sure."

I looked down at my plate and began eating. He could see I wasn't buying what he was selling. There were too many holes in his theory, and I had grown impatient or rather, frustrated. Max tried to further state his case. He said all he knew for certain was that a human had been reborn Evol with teeth similar to mine about a thousand years ago and then he vanished. Gone and erased from our records. Max didn't want the hidden faction to think I was different in a bad way. If or when they found out about my teeth, we would want them to see them for what they were—an evolutionary leap forward, not backward. He touched my hand as if to console me.

I took a few deep breaths, trying to stave off tears. I was despairing. In human life I had been different and now as an Evol I was still different. I successfully stopped myself from crying but the pain of my thoughts lingered. Besides the cool tricks I'd learned and the neat colors in my eyes; I wasn't seeing the benefit of being an Evol right then. The bare bones of it sounded too human. Nasty vicious creatures, bent on controlling others to how they felt life should be. Could any being or creature outrun the ridiculous ideology of, 'I'm better than you, so you must die?' I was feeling like maybe I should ask Seth to end me. Truly, why would I want to live a thousand years dealing with the same crap I saw humans do to each other? Instead, I tried a new tack. "Hey, I have a question about that thing called the 'resurfacing' in the story. What's that all about?" I asked.

Max's eyes lit up; he loved talking about those types of things. "You know the big bang theory? Of course, the time when humans thought the world began. Well, we believe Earth was already here. It was here and then a cataclysmic event took place, completely changing it. The resurfacing," he explained.

"Okay so there wasn't a big bang, ever?" I asked.

"Oh, there was but it had been long before the humans' so-called *big bang*," he insisted.

"Interesting. Not sure about that either. Ya'll are weird. Do you know that? I guess I fit in where that's concerned. Your fairytales are fucked-up though," I said while chuckling.

Max laughed out loud. I think my belligerent nature amused him. Once we had finished our meal, I took that opportunity to ask him how he became an Evol.

He gladly told me his story. He was born and raised in a harsh isolated village on the outskirts of Konakovo, Russia. Food was scarce and the government hostile. *Much like now*, I was thinking. Of course, that could've been my ignorance showing. He and his wife had one child who died when she was just three years old. Now he knew what had killed her, Smallpox, but back then they had no name for it. How he and his wife did not contract it he didn't know. Many years went by, living in terrible conditions in his war-torn starving village. They decided not to have any more children. They didn't want to bring another child into that frozen hell.

Then, one day, as he was out hunting far from the village, he heard a commotion in the distance coming from the direction of his village. He saw what looked like glowing fire and smoke in the sky, and panicked and ran back to his home. When he arrived, out of breath and weak from running in the snow, it was to a demolished town. Outside his tiny shack of a home was his wife. She had been raped and her throat slit. The government had swept through their town killing everyone in sight. Burning homes and taking any food they found.

He wept over his wife's body but he was alone. The intruders had gone. No food, no home, and no wife. He couldn't even bury her. If one of the soldiers returned and saw a grave, they would know someone had survived. Taking his one rifle and nothing more than the clothes on his back, he left and walked into the forest where he stayed for five more years, alone. That's where his Gifter had found him. Forty-three years old, no wife or child, no home, and no desire to be around people again. He too had mistaken the visitor as Death but he was unafraid. He welcomed it.

Thinking on Max's story, I began to wonder how many of us Evols were tragic misfits. The orphans of the world. Beaten down by tragedy and loss. Betrayals, violence, and heartbreak is what brought many to solitude. It was not unlike my own story. Those of us that had given up on life and humanity have been given a second chance. But to what end? We couldn't be seen or heard, so what was the meaning of it? It just seemed to be another way to punish us by forcing more years on us upon this hell hole we call Earth.

After finishing his story, we left the restaurant. It was both a relief to move around and stretch our legs but also an irritation due to the noise outside. Strolling the streets of London, we spoke about other, more regular Evol topics. There were still a lot of tricks I had to learn. Max talked to me about how not be recognized by another Evol. Contact lenses would be my friend, he said. There were many subtle ways Evols noticed one another, like the way we moved —strangely. It had to do with our heightened senses going haywire around humans. We sway, almost as if we're floating, very intentional and slow. But it was our eyes that truly gave us away. Our ability to fluctuate the colors in our irises was unmatched by any other.

The brilliant flowing dance of rainbows was something humans didn't readily notice and if they did, they didn't understand it. Our colorful eyes were the first thing an Evol keyed in on. Particularly since we also have unbelievable eyesight. Max said wearing contact lenses could mask the color change so that a random Evol on the street would not notice me. And, since our bodies stay continually healthy, our hair grows at an alarming rate. It was a good idea to cut it often and in the current fashions so that I fit in.

I highly enjoyed the strolling part of our visit. I'm always down for learning new things and broadening my education in any capacity, and Max was a most welcomed teacher. He was patient, kind, and had a song in his voice. Soothing.

We parted ways with a tight hug. He traveled back to America and I to Scotland. You might think Max's theory haunted me, that I had sleepless nights running it through my head over and over, but that was not the case. To tell you the truth, I gave it little thought beyond that evening. Don't get me wrong, I immensely respected and appreciated Max. I had, to that point, never encountered such a highly-educated, sensible, and yet astutely blunt man before. Nevertheless, I didn't give much credence to any of it. I might have been in denial or maybe I just tucked it away to protect my sanity. But at the time, I was too contented with my new life and where I was living to be consumed by fairytales. I also didn't tell anyone a single damn word about what we spoke about. I may have been in denial, but I wasn't looking to get lynched either. To say I was shocked to find out there was a bigamist faction within the Evols would have been a lie. I was still too human to be surprised that brutally tragic morons existed in any form or creature. It was disappointing but unfortunately, not surprising.

Better adventures were on the horizon.

Scotland considered me a foreigner and as such by law, I had to leave about every six months for a couple of weeks before I could return to the country. It's an immigration thing. I was on the fifth month of one of those and I couldn't decide where I wanted to escape to—Italy, France, back to the United States or maybe I'd just hop over to Ireland. While discussing it with Lucas, he blurted out that I should stay with him at his home in America.

Lucas, like most of us Evols minus Sara, was the stay-the hell-away and get-off-my-lawn sort. I accepted his invitation, of course, even though I was a little surprised. I did miss him and the safe comfortability I felt around him. The effect and hold he had over my emotions intrigued me, drew me in closer. Was it a power of his? There was definitely a sense of security when I was next to him I couldn't ignore, so yes, I wanted to visit him. He also lived next to a thick forest, so that was a bonus for my habits. I purchased plane tickets and bought a few Scottish souvenirs for Lucas. He wouldn't wear the T-shirts, but I figured he would appreciate the gesture.

So, what does a retired ex-human do all day, you ask? Whatever I wanted to I guess would be an appropriate answer. More than half the day's hours were taken up by sleep and the continuous evolution of my DNA. The rest of the time I often used for castle hunting. My new hobby that also helped me learn the land and its people much faster than if I stuck to the house. I was the lone mysterious woman seen sitting outside old ruins and castles, sketching for hours. Then once back home I'd paint what I'd drawn. It was a way to keep me grounded and not focused so much on the hocus pocus Evol gifts I was becoming too comfortable with.

In the weeks preceding my trip to America, I began to have unusual dreams. Each seemed to be a piece of a whole puzzle that I was, so far, unable to put together. A new world perhaps, I couldn't tell you. There was always a lavender sky in the dreams, streaked with weird colors. I didn't recognize any of the plant life, so close to our own trees and shrubs but just not quite the same. Something akin to pine trees but adorned with large red spiky fruits I didn't recognize. Low growing vines you'd see in a pumpkin patch but there were no pumpkins. It was nearly jarring this peculiar sprawling vegetation. And in each dream a wolf would appear. Once, the wolf led me to a large meeting hall. On a different night, it led me to a village. But the village was empty, it looked as though the people had vanished in the middle of dinner. The kitchens were deserted but food was cooking over a fire and personal items were strewn about. A ghost town.

In these dreams the wolf was oversized with an outstanding raven-black pelt. Something I'd seen on a nature show or in a movie most likely. During one dream, I was standing next to a great golden lake that gleamed with silver and ruby jewels just under the surface, and in another I was on a brilliantly-green hill overlooking the vacant village. In another still, I was standing in the middle of scorched earth with emptiness all around.

Sometimes in the dreams I was the person experiencing everything and sometimes I was seeing myself wander around. Whenever I saw myself, my eyes were lit with what looked like black opalescent rings. Black and shiny and they glittered in the light. The dreams became consistent enough that it felt like a message. But what message I had no clue. Foreboding maybe or memories, possibly. One thing was clear: this new world I had created in my mind was felt in every cell of my blood.

I attempted to put the dreams aside. There was still so much about being an Evol I didn't understand. Most of the odd things that happened to me I would brush off as probably being a side effect of my new life. Dreams come and go; they don't always have to mean something prophetic. They could've been the product of *The Lost Ones* fairytale Max had encouraged me read. I was trying to rationalize. Brains are good like that. Inventing crazy stuff in your mind after reading a book or watching a movie. Hard to shake the nearly orgasmic feeling that came over me when embroiled in those dreams though, and a familiar sense of belonging prevented me from fully dismissing them.

Well, once again I was going to stay in denial and focus on my upcoming trip to see Lucas. I was very excited about it. A little normalcy would be good for me. Back to being next to Lucas was even better.

Chapter 11
Stop Asking Questions!

My flight arrived late but I made it without killing anybody on the airplane with me. I figured out that noise-canceling headphones were the way to go. At least one of my overacting senses could be quieted. All the people scents were another problem. Let's just say I held my breath often. It's a sad state of affairs when the teeny plane bathroom smells better than the person you're sitting next to. On the plus side, there hadn't been the same debacle at the metal detector as before.

Lucas was waiting for me out by baggage claim. He gave me the usual side hug. In case you were wondering, he and I had not gotten any closer physically over the years. I would say the apprehension between us was just a him-and-me issue but many Evols stayed uncoupled. The reasons why most don't marry is unclear and frankly, I wasn't interested in asking. I was, at the time, just elated to see him again. He felt like home to me. Our genetic makeup is far removed from a human's where relationships are concerned. The same appetites don't exist in the same way or space. Meaning, what once triggered my attraction was off now, different. The recognition of pheromones with Evol super senses threw all I knew about attraction out the damn window. Imagine not knowing the smell of bread. So, how would you know the smell of toast cooking? Pheromones are the same in a sense. As a human I couldn't tell you what they smelled like so then, as an Evol, I was picking up these new scents and was just thoroughly confused as to what they actually were. It was difficult to explain back then and honestly, I'm not entirely sure I understand it any better today. When I figure it out, I'll share.

We stayed fairly quiet for most of the drive. He knew what crowded flights and airports were like and he let me unwind peacefully. He did warn me that both of his Great Dane puppies would be all over me. And they were, they were an excitable pair. I was thrilled to spend some time with pets again, dogs or cats. I still missed my Vader and one day I planned to adopt another kitty. *This was going to be a great trip*, I thought. Watching the East Coast of America pass by me as we drove was amazing; familiar and comforting. There was a chilled vibe in the air. Total relaxation was to be the tone of the trip. So, I thought.

Lucas unlocked the front door to his home. He let me walk in first and ... *surprise!* Many people were there. They jumped out to greet me. I threw him a *what the fuck?* look and he apologized, promising he had nothing to do with it. Sara was the first to come running up and hug me. She had the energy of an atomic bomb and despite myself, I had missed her too. Yeah, *shocker*. Seth and Eric were there, and Max was sitting in the corner of the living room waving at me with a big smile. As I was saying my hellos to everyone, new people joined us. I wasn't a fan of new people especially in a surprise situation but what was I going to do?

Eric quickly made the introductions, "Emma, this is Tamson and his two colleagues, Greg and Myra," he said all fancy and official-like.

I told them all it was nice to meet them and then I pointed at

Tamson. "Tamson? Mr. Tamson Gluster? The gentleman hosting next year's Gathering?" I asked.

"Yes, the one and only," he said. "What terrible stories has Max been filling your head with about me?"

I laughed and told him none. Tamson stood not much taller than me, maybe five feet, six-seven inches. He most definitely had some age showing. A few wrinkles and laugh lines, gray hair kept short and tidy. There was the mere hint of Malay about him and I noticed right off that his smile and laughter were incredibly infectious. He was buff though, really built, far beyond what you'd expect from someone of his age. I mean, even for an Evol he oozed strength and assertion more than others I had met thus far. Not in a scary way, neither too aggressive nor stand offish. He was a close talker. One of those people who feel the need to get right up on you super-close to your face. I'm not comfortable with that. I didn't like it as a human; I most certainly didn't like it as an Evol.

Nonetheless, we got comfortable in the living room and Lucas took my bags to the guest room. I had been so focused on meeting Tamson I didn't notice until we sat down that his two friends were human. I suddenly became paranoid that I had laughed or smiled possibly too loudly when I arrived. They might have seen my teeth. *Crap, crap, crap,* I thought. I looked over at Max with worry and he patted the top of my hand softly, letting me know everything was okay.

Tamson asked how I was getting along in Scotland. It appeared to be code because of his human friends in the room. He was really asking how I was adapting to being an Evol. I just nodded, said it was fine and looked down at my feet for a moment. I had become accustomed to nodding in front of humans to hide my fangs. Turned into a bad habit that was hard to break when in the company of Evols.

Lucas came back to ask if anyone needed drinks and said he was going to get the grill fired up. I excused myself and bolted up to help him; needing to remove myself from the spotlight. Max snuck into the kitchen while I was chopping bell peppers, poured himself another glass of wine, and asked if I was okay. I told him yeah, great, and I really was. Starving was an understatement though. The best way to accomplish eating sooner was to help with the prep so cooking went faster. He took his wine to the living room and rejoined the others. People truly did seem to be enjoying themselves in there. Sara and Eric were by far the loudest and most giggly. It felt good to hear them all but I was happier in the kitchen.

Lucas and I took a break from cooking so he could give me a tour of his home. He showed me where my room was and the all-important puppy room. His dogs had their own ginormous room with dog beds and toys everywhere. Interactive balls with treats in them. They were locked in there for the moment, due to the company, but they didn't seem to mind.

Seth passed us in the hallway and apologized about the humans, "Tamson thought it would be good for you to get used to being around humans in a relaxed setting."

I flashed him a dirty look.

"I know, I know, but he just suggested it would be good for you," Seth tried to play it down.

"He does realize I flew here on an airplane full of humans, right? Nobody died and I have been around many over the years." I was feeling annoyed. It was presumptuous of him to do this and I found that I didn't appreciate it. "Is this about my stupid teeth again?" I snapped at Seth as quietly as I was able.

"I truly do not think this is about your teeth, Emma. Tamson is just an overly cautious kind of guy, many Evols are," Seth replied.

"Yeah. Sorry, I just need to get food in my stomach," I said, backing down a bit.

Seth shrugged and Lucas gave me another side hug and suggested we got back to making dinner. My stomach could not disagree. As we walked back outside to the grill, Tamson's two human friends were saying their goodbyes to Seth and Sara. They, Greg and Myra, had to get back home to relieve their babysitter. I couldn't shake the feeling Tamson had heard me talking to Seth in the hallway. It was difficult to have private conversations in a house full of people who can literally hear a flea fart.

Seth returned to the backyard and asked to see how high I could elevate but I felt embarrassed doing that with the others watching and refused. He suggested we take a short walk in the woods while dinner finished cooking. Out among the trees, away from all the unexpected people, I could breathe. We found ourselves in a clearing where I demonstrated some of my new skills and abilities. Sort of like his own magic show. He beamed with pride. Since he was my Gifter and my good friend he took my progression to heart. But I couldn't ignore my stomach growling any longer, so we returned to the house, finally, food.

Dinner was wonderful and, thank God, not a minute too soon. Either I was going to eat real food, or I would've eaten one of the forest animals and in no way cared who watched. I can honestly say it felt like a real family throughout the whole meal. Comfortable and playful. Max told jokes that kept us in stitches. Tamson and Max had many amusing tales about each other that had Lucas and Eric rolling with laughter. Those two had gotten into the hard liquor earlier so they were laughing at just about anything anyway. Tamson treated me exactly the same as any of the others. He didn't stare at my teeth or ask me too many questions. He was very friendly and accommodating. The night was a huge success.

Sara, Eric, and Lucas started clearing up from dinner, and Max and Tamson took their drinks outside to sit under the stars for after-dinner cigars. Music was blaring in the living room, puppies running through the house—someone had opened their door—and everyone was feeling good vibes. I felt that was a good time to get Seth alone. My guest room was on the other side of the house and with the music playing, it was unlikely the others would hear us. I lured Seth to my room under the guise that I wanted to show him the gifts I got for Lucas. I sat down on the bed while he was mocking the T-shirts, teasing me that there was no way Lucas would ever wear them. That's when I asked him the question that had been bothering me for some years. Since the very night I had met him.

"Seth, what did you mean the first night we met? The night you were on my back deck. What did you mean when you said I called *to* you?" I asked.

Seth put the T-shirts down, walking over to a chair beside the bed. He sat and stared at me for a moment and then he shook his head, no. "I don't want to share this, Emma. I'm not sure it would be good for you. Knowing some things can cause more issues than not," he explained.

"Please Seth, I need to know. It's been long enough, how did I call to you?" I pleaded.

"Okay," he began. "Many years ago, when you were in the military and on a deployment in Iraq, I was there too. I had been helping a new Evol of mine at his home. In the middle of the night, I was awoken suddenly by your image and name. You asked me to help you," he said.

"I don't understand how that would be possible, I was still human,"

I replied, confused. *Iraq?* "Which time in Iraq? I've been there like three times."

"You were covered in blood. I felt your pull strong enough that I got out of bed, put my clothes on, and walked six blocks to an area I'd never been before. It was there I saw you being helped into a military vehicle by your unit. You were covered in blood and brain matter, head to toe. I could smell it wasn't your blood and I don't know what happened, but at some point during that event, you called to me," he explained calmly.

I sat stunned for a minute. I remembered. Of course I did. I could never really ever forget, just bury. Over and over again. I didn't want to share the whole story of what had occurred that night. Seth was right, some things should be left unknown. Knowing can make things worse, but I'd opened this can of worms ... I had locked that night away and thrown the key out. I was a hard bitch to kill long before Seth had gifted me this new life.

Regret quickly set in, knowing then I shouldn't have asked him anything. I also knew I wouldn't be telling him or anyone that story either. I gave him the CliffsNotes version of what had gone down instead. "That was the night two enemy insurgents snatched me from the convoy and dragged me away. Let's just say they didn't complete their mission of whatever hell they had in store for me. I came very close to dying and truly thought at one point I *had* died. But I still don't know how I called to you during that," I explained.

Seth had no answers for me. "I don't know either Emma. It's never happened before, not to me or any Gifter. Max and Tamson had no knowledge of such a thing ever occurring. But it did happen to you and me that very night. An anomaly maybe," he said.

"What happened between that night in Iraq and when you finally came to me? When you found me on my mountain years later?" I asked.

"I watched from afar and checked in on you from time to time. You still had a full family life. You were working and fairly social. It wasn't until you moved to that mountain some eighteen years later that I decided to take a closer look. You had proven above and beyond that seclusion was a great fit for you. So, that's how we met," he ended with a smile.

"I see. Thank you, Seth. I appreciate you telling me. One more piece of the puzzle put to rest," I said, smiling back. It was not at rest though. I just wanted to make him feel better about telling me and trusting me with the information. In my mind I knew what he had told me meant something was wrong with me. Not just as a freak Evol with pointy teeth but as a human too. There had been a defect I didn't know about. Max's theory on the time traveling substance he called Shimmer did not give me pause; it was just a theory. But what Seth had just told me sent me into an internal panic. *Damn me and my fool-ass questions!*

To add insult to agony, Seth unloaded one more thing. "Since you brought up the first time we met, I need to tell you something else. Do you recall that deep growl that spooked the deer?" he asked.

"Of course I do. That was crazy. I haven't heard you do that since," I remarked.

"You haven't heard it from me since because it didn't come from me. It came from you. Even though you were still human, something in you or around you made that noise. A warning signal maybe, possibly sensing my presence even before I landed on your deck," he explained, pausing. "You also made that noise in your dining room when I brought Lucas and Sara over to the house. Evols don't normally growl when they get angry. You do," he said.

I just nodded my usual, go along with it, nod.

Seth went back to looking at the T-shirts. *Awesome*, I thought sarcastically to myself. *I'm not only a freak with vampire teeth, I'm also an animal.* All that time, I truly thought Seth had made that growling noise. So, when I began doing it too after my transformation it hadn't seemed like a big deal. I assumed everyone could do that. Boy, was I sorry I had pulled him aside to ask questions. *Arggggggghhhhhhhh! Stop asking shit! It never goes well!*

Chapter 12
Not So Fast

We made our way back to join the others in the kitchen and asked if we could help. Sara made a snarky comment about how great our timing was because they had just finished. She then switched gears in a flash, reinvigorating her mission of ensuring we attended the Gathering. Even though it was still almost a year out she could not stop talking about it. It had been Tamson's bright idea to put her in charge of the invitations and decor. Being ancient, as he obviously was, didn't make him automatically smart. Sara was driving everyone up the wall with all the Gathering promotional speeches and hoopla. However, I felt relief was in sight as she wasn't spending the night at Lucas's.

As the day's festivities drew to a close, I became thoroughly exhausted. I excused myself to go upstairs. I had trouble falling asleep at first, due to what Seth had told me but before too long, I was knocked out, nearly paralyzed by the weight of the day.

Dreams engulfed my sleep. That incredible place with the lavender skies was my destination once more. Walking alongside my wolf companion, I was a spectator again. Stalking myself, it seemed or someone who looked like me. My eyes were black opalescent rings to match the color of my wolf. We were in a forest near a cave. It was an entrance to an underground cavern of some kind. An old woman emerged from the cave and petted my wolf. She escorted us to a pond on the other side of the cave. When I looked at my reflection in the water I saw only the wolf. I couldn't see myself.

Suddenly, ripples in the water pulled me from sleep.

I rose around 11 a.m. stretching and yawning to find a note on the floor next to the bedroom door. It was from Lucas telling me good morning, take my time, and that coffee was in the kitchen, and he would be outside completing a few chores. I got dressed and braided my hair, feeling refreshed but still in much need of coffee. Upon opening the bedroom door, I was assaulted with love by two excited puppies. The house was dead quiet and calm apart from their happy gaggle. A complete turnaround from all the ruckus of the previous night.

I poured myself a cup of coffee and looked out the window to see Lucas running from a bear. Promptly, I spat the coffee into the sink and began to bolt outside to help him until I saw him suddenly stop and change direction. And then change direction again.

He wasn't being chased for the purpose of being attacked. He and the bear were *playing together*. I settled back down as I watched them through the window, relaxing again as I poured more coffee. I wasn't a person who panicked much as a human, a good trait for a medic. Seeing this at first was admittedly alarming but just as I had done many times in the past, I was able to calm quickly—my Evol DNA greatly helped with that too. "Well, this isn't something you see every day," I said to the puppies. "You see Daddy outside playing with that bear? That's why you're inside the house with me."

On the kitchen counter was paper folded in half with my name on it. I opened it to find there were four more sheets of paper inside with a handwritten note on each one. From Sara. The content was about the Gathering, *again*. She desperately wanted me there. Not all Evols went to every single Gathering. It was an open invitation to all but on average, only a handful would show up. Many spaced out their attendances to every few hundred years. In the letter, Sara told me that I would be one of the lucky ones to stay at the mansion. Most stayed at the surrounding villas or hotels. As per tradition, I, a newcomer, was invited to stay in the mansion with the other new Evols. She continued to ramble on about the events during the three-day celebration. What clothes I should bring and what to expect. I put the letter down. I had heard more than enough about the big party. It was a year away still and not high on my agenda.

Turning my attention outside instead, Lucas waved me over to join him. I stepped out, still holding my coffee, careful not to accidently release his puppies. He encouraged me to meet his friend, the bear. I shook my head no and smiled. I mean, it was a friggin' bear!

"Oh, come on, she won't hurt you. Tova is an amazingly sweet bear," he assured me.

Tova was massive. A grizzly bear. We're talking about a one ton, eight foot tall when standing, grizzly bear! And at that moment she was lying down in the grass letting Lucas feed her blackberries.

The pull toward the beast was strong. She was incredible, there was no question. I loved all animals and knew my DNA would heal my body instantly if she attacked me but I wasn't stupid. Sweet or not, she was still a monster-sized bear. It appeared these Evols had forgotten their human fears or maybe it was just Lucas who'd outgrown mortal worries. After all, fear itself is a mortal gesture of something believed to be higher than oneself. In turn, immortals forgo such, believing themselves higher than high. At that point in my journey, I still clung to some semblance of normalcy, immortal or not.

I sat my coffee cup down next to his and cautiously approached them. "Tova, huh? That's a pretty name. It's Viking. Where did you come up with that?" I asked.

By then I had reached them and Lucas took my hand to put it on her back. Helping to ease my fear, we pet her together. She lay all the way down and seemed as happy as a clam munching on her blackberries.

"I don't know how I came up with Tova. Some years ago, I saw her when I was taking down a tree in the backwoods. She wandered over to me and the name just popped into my head," he began. "I said the name, Tova, out loud and she leaned into me. So it stuck." He shrugged, like bear-naming was a regular thing *in these parts.*

"Well, this takes your Snow White talents to the next level," I said. "I better change your nickname to Grizzly Adams! Have animals always been this attracted to you? I mean, before you turned Evol?" I asked.

He seemed to consider as he scratched Tova's belly. "I did have a natural caring side for animals, and some did seem to be very comfortable around me. I guess it just magnified after the transformation." He chuckled.

We spent a few more minutes with Tova until she got up, retreating into the woods. After she had gone, Lucas let the puppies out of the house. They ran around and tussled as we simply sat, soaking up the summer sun. Lucas mentioned there had been an earthquake in the night. A small one but it was all over the news that morning. He asked if I had felt anything. *Nope.* I was passed out, asleep and dreaming. I remember he shot me a weird look as if I should've known about the tremor. Possibly he was confused because if it had woken him then it should've also shaken me awake too. But he dropped the subject after that and we moved on.

I was excited to show him something anyway. Before my flight I had made up my mind to show him my purple orb. So then, standing right there in his backyard, I produced it in the palm of my hand.

His eyes sparkled with intrigue and awe. "What is that? When did you figure out you could do it? So cool! Why is it purple?" he asked.

"I figured out I could conjure it not long after the first time we met. And I have zero idea what it does! No clue man," I replied, chuckling. Lucas reached his hand forward to touch the purple wonder as I tried to quickly yank it away. "Don't Lucas! I don't know what this thing does yet!" I snapped.

But it was too late. His finger grazed the top of the orb before I could remove it. A scene of sorts flashed in my mind within the split second his skin made contact. "Whoa. That was freaky. I just got an image of you when you were much younger. A teenager maybe. You were on a cobblestone street, kicking a ball around with other children," I told him.

"No way! When I was little, I played outside in the street with the town kids all the time."

"Neat. Maybe the purple orb shows me the past or something. Memories and such," I said.

Lucas reached forward again with his whole hand attempting to grasp the orb fully. I turned away and forced it to dissipate.

"Nope. Not happening Lucas. Not yet. I have to be sure this thing won't hurt you. Just because that one experience was harmless doesn't mean the next will be," I explained.

He relented, laughed and appeared to be okay with that for the moment. I didn't believe at his age, coupled with his natural attitude, that much scared him. But he let it go for my benefit.

We sat down on the porch and sipped our coffee. He then asked me what I wanted to do for the day and I replied by raising my cup, showing him that I was already doing it. He looked relieved. Perhaps I'd given him peace of mind knowing he wasn't going to have to entertain me while I was there. Sightseeing or being on the go wasn't something either of us were into much. I craved and required only the peace his isolated home afforded.

It was a kickback couple of weeks. We both had a love of music and played his records near non-stop. Music was surely one of the few reasons I survived the agonizing transformation. His collection of vinyl records had me wishing I'd kept up with my collecting as well. Every genre you could imagine. Some incredibly old, some foreign, and some a bit newer from the 1970s and 1980s. I would pick a new genre each day and we'd listen to everything in it. We watched movies and took long walks in the woods, played with his dogs and talked about our lives as young children. As easy going as two people could be with each other.

I shared with Lucas the story of the hunters who I had found on my property and he laughed so hard I thought he was going to wet himself. He had a not dissimilar experience after moving into his home some hundred years ago. The hunters were not so stupid or drunk to shoot at him though. He had picked up a boulder and thrown it at them, roaring that *all* the woods belonged to him. They ran and never came back. There were stories about Lucas's woods ever since. Tales of a wolfman or Sasquatch that roamed around, threatening to kill any hunter he came across. The image made me smile fondly.

It was an outstanding carefree vacation. Full of laughter and light-heartedness. Even though I missed my remote home in Scotland, I never regretted a single moment in Lucas's company. We had brief encounters of catching one another's lingering glances. Maybe purposefully walking a bit too close so as to brush our arms together. An odd affectionate dance of two souls committed and yet not ready to embrace.

As all good things do, my time with him finally came to an end. He drove me to the airport and for the first time, gave me a full hug. Not a side hug but a whole-body, real hug. It felt nice. Alarming and unusual but nice. That made me want to stay even more. Nevertheless, I boarded my plane after saying our goodbyes.

Arriving in Scotland, I could barely contain my excitement of seeing the cottage. I stood on the bank of my front yard, gazing out at the ocean. Not realizing just how much I missed it until I was standing there in the moment. I unlocked the front door and put my bags down in the bedroom. Several messages were blinking on the answering machine. They were almost all from Sara. All about the Gathering, of course. Every message was from her except for two. One from Seth, checking in to make sure I made it home okay. And one from Lucas, telling me his puppies missed me and that he hoped my flight had been tolerable.

I unpacked my bags and wiped the dust off the tables and countertops. I opened the windows throughout the house to let the amazing ocean air float in and removing the stale smell of a house that had been locked up and empty for weeks. Man, I loved my modest two-bedroom cottage. Open quaint kitchen, window seat nook, and the previous owners had built a spectacular bathroom. Most cottages such as this have bathrooms you can barely turn around in. Mine was gorgeous, updated fixtures, large tub, and heated floor. The home was complete with creeping ivy framing every archway. What more could a woman ask for?

I drew a hot bath, sliding in with pure happiness; resetting my mind after all the travel and loud humans I'd had to deal with over the last twenty-four hours. Visiting Lucas had been incredibly eye-opening, informative, and amazing but, as always, traveling there and back was stressful.

As I soaked in the tub, I let the stress go and hoped there would come a day when I could spend time with him again. While lying there in the tub, I found myself getting excited about the upcoming Gathering. It would be my first and I'd get to meet more Evols. Sara's constant chipping away at me about it was working. I wasn't going to tell her that though. If I did, she would try to get me involved in the planning and party planner was in no way on my list of things I wanted to accomplish. However, I was now most definitely on board with going. Seth and Eric would be there. Lucas would be a wild card. Apparently, he had only been to one Gathering since he was turned some 400 years ago. I'd dropped subtle hints, giving him positive encouragement to attend during my visit but … it was anyone's guess if he'd come.

The months sped by and I was still living a basic wonderful life. I had begun to worry that I hadn't heard from Sara in weeks. You would think that would've been a relief, but it concerned me. It wasn't like her. I had tried contacting her a couple of times, which was not in *my* character, but she had been short with me. She made up excuses to get off the phone, my emails to her were left unanswered. I spoke to Seth, asking if he knew what was going on. He was very surprised and taken aback and had no idea what her issue was. Eventually, we just agreed that maybe she was too busy with the Gathering party planning. It was coming up soon and she was most likely buried in last minute preparations. I also questioned Seth about how many Evols normally attended and what the atmosphere would be like, etc.

"Well let's see," Seth began. "When I was first gifted, the Gatherings reached a capacity of about 300 to 400 people. Recently, however, the last two reunions have dwindled in size significantly. Around one hundred guests, maybe, attended the last time. I'm not sure why the number has dropped so drastically."

"That's too bad. Not that I was looking forward to being among a crowded mob of people," I chuckled, "but I was hoping to meet as many Evols as I can in one shot. Just to get a feel for our kind."

"Even if the numbers are small this time, you will still get a good mix of personalities and backgrounds," Seth stated.

"Awesome," I replied. And I meant it.

A few weeks later I received a video call from Sara. Normally, I would've tried to ignore those types of calls. She could talk for hours and hours, but that time I answered, hoping she was her old self again, happy and giddy, chattering a mile a minute. It wasn't the case. Not by a long shot. She was solemn and a little stone-faced.

"Hi Emma, I know you weren't excited at first about going to the Gathering and I think ... maybe you shouldn't come this time," she blurted out.

I was speechless to tell you the truth, it was a true curve ball. But I had to say something, "I had my misgivings in the past but I've been sort of geared up about it recently. Why shouldn't I come?" I asked.

"Well, you're new, like *really* new and young as an Evol. I'm just thinking you would be more comfortable after some time passes. The next one is only fifty years from now and I'm sure you'll be more settled and ready for it then," she nervously explained.

"I don't understand, Sara. You have been on me for the last *two years* about attending this thing. Why the sudden change? What's going on?" I demanded.

Sara looked away from the phone as if she was checking to ensure no one was around. She appeared to be scared and panicky. She turned back to me shaking her head, almost watery-eyed, like she was on the verge of crying. *What was going on? Did it have to do with me? Was it her? What the hell?*

She got in close to the screen and angrily whispered, "Just don't come Emma, don't come!"

And with that, she ended the video call.

Chapter 13
The New Toy

*We're all a little broken. But last time I checked,
broken crayons still color the same.*
—Trent Shelton

I had no clue as to what just happened or why. Did Sara really just tell me not to show up to the Gathering? Did I offend or hurt her? Immediately, I called Seth and ran through the conversation with him. He wasn't sure what to make of it either and explained that he was also getting mixed signals from Sara. We felt something bad must have occurred or was about to. My video call with her only solidified the gut feeling Seth had that Sara was in trouble. He and Eric had already booked their villa for the Gathering; they were going regardless.

Seth was significantly pained and worried by Sara's sudden attitude change. In all the years he'd known her she had never displayed such distressing antics. Whatever the reason she was trying to prevent me from attending, her efforts only made me that much more determined to go. One way or another, I was going to find out what was going on. If I had to go to the Gathering just to corner her face to face, then that's what I was going to do. No one stays the same for 400 years and then flips out overnight for no damn reason.

When the big event finally arrived, I flew over to Spain and got into a cab headed to the Tamson Gluster Mansion. The cab driver pulled into the driveway, and it was as if I had stepped into a Spanish romance novel. Absolutely not a house or even a regular mansion. The magnificence of his home rivaled the Alhambra Palace. I asked the driver to double check the address. He assured me we were at the right location. I stood, speechless, as the driver retrieved my bags from the trunk. Tamson, with welcoming open arms, walked out through the humongous entryway doors. He instructed a staff member to take my bags to a guest room as he invited me in, leading the way.

I stopped, it seemed, every couple of feet to look around. Incredible high cathedral ceilings, walls made from large blocks of stone, floors of marble, and priceless works of art and sculptures adorned each new corner. Many of the ceilings had breathtaking murals. The only other place I'd been with pieces of ancient art displayed everywhere like this was the Vatican in Rome. It was a true castle in my eyes. One that overlooked an ocean to boot. The one thing that stood out as not time period appropriate were all the security cameras.

Tamson ushered me down a long hall to my guest room and me to make myself comfortable and even take a rest if I needed it. He announced that dinner wouldn't be until 7 p.m. and I should just relax until then.

My room was exquisite. A king-sized bed draped in the softest silk duvet I had ever touched. Opulence dripped with silver, gold, and royal red decor. Tapestries, oil paintings, and even an antique porcelain tea set! Uncomfortable was the first word that popped into my mind. That extent of glamour was not my taste.

Nonetheless, I unpacked the dresses I had brought to get them hung up so they wouldn't wrinkle further but found, upon opening the closet, that there were three dresses already hanging. A small tag with *Emma*, hung from each gown. Those dresses far surpassed the beauty of the ones I had for the occasion. Maybe they knew going to fancy parties wasn't something I'd had to dress for in the past. I wasn't offended in the least. The dresses in the closet were stunning. If some rich dude was handing out free gowns, then why not?

Double french doors led out onto a wondrous balcony. As I opened them a warm sultry breeze rushed over me. The stone terrace spanned the whole of the backside of the mansion. As I leaned against the thick strong railing, I lost myself in the view of the Balearic Sea. Almost too unbelievably beautiful to exist. The extreme grandiosity of the mansion did not suit me but that view most certainly did. Tamson had definitely saved all his pennies to gain such a perfect property. Of course, he'd had a thousand years to build his fortune. *Was this something I could strive for in the future?*

After a short nap, I got up to shower off the airport grime I felt I must be covered in. Graciously, I donned one of those incredible gowns and nervously strolled down the hallway trying to find the main dining room. Following the sound of commotion and laughter, it wasn't a difficult task to accomplish. Oh, when I tell you the dining room was breathtaking, it was an understatement. There were two large chandeliers lit up with candles. Round tables draped in blue satin and adorned with flowers, gold rimmed plates and silverware, place cards, and more candles. Huge museum-worthy oil paintings hung on all the walls and even more candles atop pedestals lining the perimeter of the room. Apparently, Tamson was partial to the old ways of illumination—using candles—because I did not see an electric light switch anywhere.

At first glance, as I looked around, I felt like I was witnessing the fanciest junior high school prom. People were talking to one another and giggling here and there but they were spread out in odd numbers. Everyone had on tuxedos and gowns, appearing regal on the outside, but also giving off an awkward vibe, like pre-teens at a school dance. *Nervousness?* I wondered. I didn't mind. I realized my apprehension about going to the Gathering was unfounded. It should have occurred to me that it wouldn't be a free-for-all frat kegger. Our kind of people are mostly shy pacifists.

Seth had not exaggerated the lopsided presence of women to men within the Evol population. There were maybe seventy to eighty people in the banquet hall and I believe I spotted fifteen women at best.

Max saw me before I saw him and joyfully shouted over to me, waving his arm in the air and beckoning me to him. "How wonderful and elegant you look, Emma," he said, beaming. "Dinner is going to be served soon and I made sure you were sitting next to me, along with Seth and Eric too, of course."

His words put me more at ease, knowing I would not have to sit with a bunch of strangers. I scanned the room and saw Sara off in the distance. She was trying not to look back at me; like she was hiding. *What had I done?* I wondered. I must have done something to offend her, but my mind boggled. The moment she noticed I was headed toward her, she bolted! My progression halted, I causally swayed my way back to Max.

"Have you seen Lucas? He wasn't one hundred percent sure if he was coming," I asked.

"No, I haven't seen him yet, my dear but he still may show. We'll be here for two more days. You never know with Lucas. He hasn't been to the last three Gatherings so your guess is as good as mine," he said.

A soft muffled bell begun to chime, indicating dinner was about to be served. We made our way to the tables and seated ourselves. Tamson raised his glass of champagne and gave a short but rousing speech, welcoming us all to his home. While we were eating, I again saw Sara. She was sitting at Tamson's table, looking distracted and irritated, and still refusing to make eye contact with me. Seth leaned to the side toward me and whispered that something was definitely wrong. She hadn't so far been the social butterfly of the party this year. She wasn't annoying anyone with her painful consummate chatter. He was going to investigate while at the mansion. I nodded, agreeing that he should go on a snooping mission.

At one point into that delicious dinner, I felt many eyes on me. The hairs on the back of my neck stood up. People from other tables kept staring at me and whispering to each other as they peered in my direction.

A little later, Max came over, placing a calming hand on my shoulder. He told me not to worry. I was just simply the *new toy* of the group. It happened with all new Evols and it would wear off quickly, he assured me. I didn't like the term and I tried to put it out of my mind while I enjoyed a gorgeous dessert set in front of me. I ought to mention that whatever thoughts may currently reside in my head are apt to temporarily disappear whenever chocolate enters the picture. So I sat in my happy place, ignoring the unwanted attention, and instead, delighted in every bite of that chocolate crème brûlée.

Following the completion of our meal, people stood and regrouped into small cliques, talking about this or that. Tamson called everyone over to a table in an effect to show off his latest invention. Sara tried to stop him it seemed to me. I couldn't tell what was said but she looked upset again and was pulling on his arm insistent about something. I saw Tamson shake his head *no* and her face as he snapped at her. Sara hurried off in a huff, ostensibly to check when the drinks service would be brought out.

I had just started to head in her direction when Eric abruptly grabbed my hand. "Where do you think you're going, Emma? Surely not to bed already?" he asked.

"No, I'm not going to bed. I was going to see if Sara was okay. We haven't spoken since I arrived. I wanted to catch up with her. You know, girl talk," I told him.

Eric pulled me close. "Sara is fine, I'm sure. Just more of her over-exaggerated emotional crap. You need to stay here and check out Tamson's new gadget. He's always coming up with craziness. Come on, come stand with us and watch," he demanded.

I relented and stood next to Eric and Seth. We were in the back of the group that had gathered around the table. Although the recent exchange of words had seemed contentious between Sara and Tamson; they hadn't appeared to faze him in the slightest. He gleefully waved us all over to him and we viewed a little machine that looked like a handheld electronic temperature monitor. You know, the ones in doctor offices that a nurse puts to your forehead? To me, that was all it looked like. I was also brand new to the Evol world and had to mentally kick myself often to not be so cynical. That was a continual hurdle for me.

Tamson picked up the device and proudly announced that it could tell you what your Evol age was. On the underside was a tiny needle that punctured your skin. It then calculated your Evol DNA from the small drop of blood it collected. A lot of 'Whoas' and 'Awes' arose from the crowd. He clarified happily that it only told you your Evol age, starting from the day you were gifted. Not your total age of being on this earth. Tamson then invited a gentleman in the group to be the first test subject of his amazing contraption.

"Okay, tell everyone how old you are in just Evol years, Rick," Tamson requested.

Rick replied dutifully, "Four hundred twenty-eight."

Tamson activated the device and pressed it over one of Rick's fingers. He then held it up, waiting for it to work its magic. In a matter of seconds, a digital number popped up, 428.

Many people in the crowd got a kick out of that. *A pretty neat parlor trick*, I thought to myself. Not exactly a technological marvel by any stretch of the imagination, just something fun to occupy everyone for a few moments. Another person volunteered and again the device gave their age.

Eric pushed me forward past the others in the crowd although I was in no mood to be the center of attention. "Get in there, Emma, try it out. Don't be shy," he said, in an almost bullish tone.

Reluctantly, I stepped through the sea of faces ogling me. I imagined the whole room erupting into flames. Or a bomb going off. Anything to make that moment stop. I was rethinking my decision to attend. I felt like a dressed up ugly duckling forced to do tricks for the locals. Eric would surely pay for doing this to me. I would make sure of it somehow. Regardless, I played along and held out my index finger in front of Tamson.

Tamson grinned excitedly. "Okay, tell these good folks how old you are," he instructed.

"Eight years," I stated bashfully.

Some of them snickered and giggled and Tamson motioned his hand down. "All right, all right. We were all brand new once. And for some of us, it was so long ago we can't even remember the day it happened." He pointed at Max. "Isn't that right, my friend?" he asked.

Max laughed and nodded. "Right you are, old friend."

Tamson turned back to the giggling crowd and continued, "You're all just jealous. And you know it!"

Everyone shrugged their shoulders and laughed in agreement. He put the device over my finger and a sharp prick jabbed me. A second later it displayed four blinking zeros. I looked up at Tamson, worried something had gone wrong.

"It just needs to be reset," he laughed. "Glitches happen with any new technology, more especially with the machines I create." He waved at the room in easy dismissal.

His guests got a good chuckle out of that one as well. He reset the machine and tested it on himself. The digital numbers popped up, 970. "Okay, there it is, reset and ready. Let's try again on you," he said.

Once again, the four blinking zeros appeared.

There was a ripple of disquiet in the gathered crowd and I could almost feel their stares refocusing, recalibrating. As if I wasn't self-conscience enough, this was not helping. Tamson played it off with another joke. A bell started chiming to let us know drinks were being served on the balcony. *Saved by the bell*, was what went through my mind.

The guests slowly dispersed to the balcony and Max took my arm to escort me as we walked. He was such an old fashioned gentleman. I did enjoy his company if nothing else.

"Don't you think on it, Emma. It's just another broken toy in a long line of garbage he's invented over a millennium," Max insisted.

I nodded and smiled, reassuring him that I was fine. But it was me who felt like the broken toy. Two more days of sensing judgment and being stared at was not sitting well with me. *This was a mistake,* I thought. I wasn't good in social situations, why had I thought this would be different? Awkward and brash is how I'd handled crowds or large events in the past. I had tried to keep quiet; stand in the background not wanting to be noticed. Eric had shoved me to the center of attention, essentially paralyzing me. That had taken away my ability to snap back sarcastically or even reason sensibly in the moment.

I couldn't shake the feeling something bad was coming. That Evol age machine would just be the first in many uncomfortable exchanges in the following days. Oh, how I wished Lucas had been there. Or that I was back in my cottage safe from all those curious peering eyes. How were these Evols mingling among one another so freely? Weren't we all misfits and recluses? Was I the only one there having an anxiety meltdown? I guessed so because the rest of them seemed to be doing just fine. Again, I was a freak among the freaks. Not even when surrounded by people like me did I feel settled or relaxed.

I would focus my attention to other matters. Sara. I'd never been a person who took a snub to heart. If someone didn't like me or want to be around me then I was good to go with that. Not a whole lot bothered me when it came to other people and their issues, but for some reason Sara's sudden reversal had me agitated. Call it a sixth sense if you want, but whatever was going on with her was more than a small glitch. I would have to find her first to confront her about it.

Sara was missing from the balcony cocktail event. I didn't see her for the rest of the night but I found that I was too stressed and tired to keep looking for her. Seth and Eric began to argue. A lover's quarrel, possibly due to Eric's over drinking, and Lucas wasn't there. Feelings of regret overshadowed the good experiences I'd had since arriving and I began to debate if I should change my flight and leave in the morning or not.

Excusing myself, I bid Max a goodnight and pleaded exhaustion to the host. I planned to sleep on it and would make the decision in the morning. For now, I just needed to remove myself from the crowd as quickly as I could.

Chapter 14
Collation

I was rudely awoken the next morning by a pounding knock at the door. Refusing to shake myself from a most excellent dream and not wanting it to disappear, I was ensconced in my made-up lavender-skied planet. A place that was beginning to feel like home more and more. That dream had started to become my escape from the stressors of the everyday world. People are vicious beasts, but my purple paradise was gentle and kind. Floating on the vacuum of silence and taking in the warmth of the sun was all I required to reset and refresh.

KNOCK! KNOCK! The pounding on the door persisted, growing louder. Who the hell would dare wake me at this hour? In a raspy irritated voice, I shouted. "Yeah, what is it?"

"Room Service, Madam," came the reply.

Clearly, it was not. I could tell it was a man trying to disguise himself with a woman's voice. Clumsily, I rolled out of bed and shuffled to the door, opening it with attitude and my hair in a tangled nest. "Lucas! You weirdo. What are you doing?" I said, relieved to see him.

He pushed a cart through the doorway that had a pot of coffee and blueberry scones upon it. I smiled as I followed him over to the french doors where he set up his little breakfast buffet. He looked good. His beard had grown longer but recently manicured, nice Lucas-type attire a.k.a., blue jeans and an ironed flannel shirt with the sleeves rolled a bit. Although we were in Spain, I could still smell the forest on him. Even the scent of his puppies lingered. That made me wish we were at his home instead of Tamson's lavish midlife crisis mansion.

"I wasn't sure I'd see you at this extravagant gala," I remarked.

Lucas laughed. "Neither did I to tell you the truth. I just decided at the last minute and hopped on a plane. I crashed at Seth and Eric's villa last night," he continued. "What happened? Seth and Eric are fighting. Eric didn't even stay at the villa last night."

"I don't know exactly. Sara is acting weird and standoffish and Eric was actually a tiny bit mean last night. He was arrogant and unusually pushy. But then again, he was also drinking like a fish. Who knows?" I told him.

He nodded. "Seth noticed that too. I believe that's what their fight was about. Eric's attitude."

We sat a while and ate our scones. Sipped coffee with the balcony doors open. That was what I needed to get my mind right again. Lucas, scones, coffee, and an ocean breeze. Life always felt better around Lucas. He was easy going and funny. What more could a girl ask for?

"So, what's on the docket for the second day of this shindig?" I asked.

"Well, it's been a while since I've been to one of these things." He smiled. "I think today is just more of a meet and greet like last night probably was. It's a beautiful day so you should expect most of the festivities to be held outside. Seth and I are on a mission though. You enjoy the party. Ha ha ha," he teased me.

"What mission and why can't I come too?" I sharply demanded.

"It would look too suspicious if all three of us were running around like the Scooby gang. You're the newcomer so you have to be seen. Seth and I are going to check out the mansion. Oh, and try to find out what the hell is wrong with Sara," he explained.

That made sense and I relaxed. "Ooooooh. Well, you boys have fun playing your mystery games without me. I'll be snacking on every chocolate dessert Tamson lays out on those banquette tables down there," I said, smiling as I pointed at the grand immaculate lawn below us that looked to be getting set up for another day of cajoling.

He finished his coffee, telling me to stop being so lazy and get dressed. He'd see me later and we'd get to talk more then. After giving me one of his infamous side hugs he left me to it. I readied myself and then took another moment to stand out on the balcony. I inhaled the ocean air with my face turned upward, basking in the sun. When I looked back down, I noticed a couple dozen Evols had arrived. It was then I truly saw the difference between the way humans and Evols physically moved. We did sway and almost float. It was like watching flamingos in groups perform a dance—hypnotic and often disorientating.

Do you remember being ten years old thinking anyone who was thirty was really old, and your grandparents were relics? How about the way older adults acted or how they spoke? All weird to a child, wasn't it? Most kids live in worlds of strange proportions. Now, imagine being an adult of half a century surrounded by 'older' people of many centuries. You'd want to hear some wild conversations. Once Evols lose their human habits a whole new train of thought begins. They're nuts! Super fucking nuts with colorful dazzling eyes and swaying bodies. I dig it. I could watch them all day long. Then I saw Sara and getting down there became my only thought.

Quickly, I made my way to the back lawn area, still racking my brain over what I could have done to cause her to behave the way she was. *Was she finally fed up with the way I often dodged her calls?* I'll admit I was not the coziest of friends to her all the time.

I casually strolled over to Max and he introduced me to a few of his colleagues. One of whom was bold enough to ask to see my teeth. Max winked at me to say it was okay. I flashed a big smile so they could see this fiend's dangerous vampiric razors. After which I excused myself, stating that I was in need of more coffee. On the walk to the drinks table, I saw Sara coming toward me. She instantly veered off, trying to avoid me again. Purposely, I swayed my body into her path. "Sara! How are you? We haven't had the time to catch up since I got here," I said.

She looked around with a forced friendly grin on her face. Through her grin she tried to make it appear as though she really wasn't talking to me. "Emma, I don't think you should be here." She waved at a guest in the distance still pretending she wasn't addressing me. "I'm begging you, please leave. Now. Go now, Emma!" she almost pleaded.

And with that, she moved around me, jogging over to a group of guests. Loudly greeting them and laughing as if the moment had never happened. I didn't understand. Was there a problem with me or was there someone who was going to be a problem for me? Just then, another guest asked to see my teeth. My face finally fell flat and I turned away. I didn't want to be their sideshow entertainment. Seth and Lucas were off on some fact-finding mission and I was alone in a sea of people intrigued by my fucking pointy dentition.

A diversion was what I needed. The closest direction I could use to make my escape would be to walk down to the shoreline. I located the long arduous-looking steps that led to a private beach. The strength of the waves coupled with the wind made it possible for me to think, which was a welcome break. All the sounds and smells of the people above on the lawn vanished before the raging water. I stayed there alone for hours. Lost but feeling better.

On my way back up the stairs Seth and Lucas were heading down the steps to me. "Hey there, Shaggy and Fred," I greeted them.

Seth giggled. "Lucas told me we were the Scooby gang. Listen Emma, everyone will be getting ready for another stupid fancy dinner soon. During dinner, Lucas and I are going to slip out while everyone else is concentrated in one spot," Seth said.

"Is this about Sara? Has she spoken to either of you?" I asked.

"She's avoiding us as well. Eric is trying to get back in Seth's good graces though and he appears to be his old self again. Lighthearted and joking in his normal style. That's one of the two acting right at least but Sara is still a concern," Lucas replied.

"Sara told me to leave, guys. I cornered her on the lawn a few hours ago and she told me to leave, she sounded pretty frantic!" I explained in a worried voice.

They looked at each other. "Umm, she might be right, Emma. While Lucas and I were skulking around we heard some... distressing things. We won't get into it now but just be aware of your surroundings," Seth warned.

Whatever that *meant*, I wondered.

Later that night, during dinner in the grand dining room, I was studying one of the magnificent paintings on the wall. It was of a mother and her two children, bathing. It had to be at least a thousand years old. The intricate details I was able to detect with my Evol eyes opened the painting into an astonishing world of its own.

Max came up beside me and remarked how a painting like that had the power to trap your gaze indefinitely. He then told me dessert was waiting. That instantly broke my attention.

***

Seth and Lucas roamed the castle-like mansion. They separated down different halls, going from room to room. Seth almost passed by what appeared to be a hidden room with a pink door. He stopped, backtracking when the pink color caught his eye. It most definitely did not match the rest of the decor and the door was ajar, so he nudged it open further.

There was nobody in the room. He was standing in what looked like a teenager's room with frilly bed linens, posters on the walls, colorful jewelry on a glass surface, and makeup strewn about over a night table. But all of it was covered in a thick layer of dust.

A bookshelf in the far corner was lined floor to ceiling with old books that had numbers on their spines. Sequential numbers starting with 1616. Seth climbed up the library-style bookshelf ladder to the top and pulled out the top-most book. When he cracked it open, he quickly realized it was a diary. By the looks of the handwriting, it belonged to a young child, maybe eight or nine years of age. The text was accompanied by rude scribblings and drawings of hearts and unicorns. He was baffled. Were those books from the previous property owners, the first owners of the mansion? He skipped ahead to the book labeled 1630. For a while, he skimmed through a few passages, reading bits and pieces, when it hit him that the numbers on the spine were years. Each book number was a year not a title.

As Evol we know no language barriers because our brains constantly correct for us anything written, and so Seth translated the diary entries into a more modern-day English prose. Then he came across something interesting:

Dear Diary,
   Dad told me that today was the day my life would be forever changed. Today is the day I will receive the gift. I have waited so long for this! Dad has total faith in me and knows that I will be perfect in every way. This is the start of my new adventure.

Seth almost dropped the book. Those diaries had been written by someone's daughter. An Evol's daughter and in that passage, she couldn't have been more than twenty or twenty-two years old. Seth's mind spun with thoughts. Who the hell would do such a thing to their own child? Was Tamson the father of that child? It was his house. His thoughts were interrupted by Lucas, as he stepped into the pink room. "Come here, help me look through these books!" Seth whispered excitedly. "Go through the later years. I think these books belong to a child of Tamson's!"

Without a thought, Lucas began pulling books off the shelf, scanning the contents, throwing them on the floor as they pulled another book and another. The boys didn't care much about how they handled the delicate books. They were guys on a mission, not international secret spies. Plus, Lucas was definitely a 'bull in a china shop' kind of guy. He just went for it.

Lucas began reading through a diary labeled 2023. "Listen to this," he urged Seth. "'Dear Diary, Dad is having me go on a home visit. A new Evol I'm to help with Seth and Lucas. He's trusting me to branch out and take on more responsibility finally. I'm especially excited because the new Evol is a female, like me.'"

"Sara!" Seth and Lucas exclaimed in unison.

"She's talking about our first meeting with Emma!" Lucas said.

"Emma was right about Sara, this whole time. She saw Sara was different, why didn't we sense anything?" Seth asked Lucas.

"Sara is Tamson's daughter, and he turned her Evol when she was way too young. There's not an actual rule against it, yet there is," Lucas whispered.

"The young are a dangerous gamble, plus you deprive women of having babies when they're gifted too early. It's unconscionable. There's no excuse for Tamson's actions. Turning his own daughter is—" Seth hurried his words.

"—the greatest betrayal," Lucas finished for him.

In that moment, panic and indecision momentarily froze them, but something forced them to continue. They frantically sped through the rest of the diaries, finding more and more passages of Sara spying on me for her father, Tamson. In her defense, some entries stated she didn't want to spy on me anymore, but that Tamson wouldn't allow her to stop. They found entries about my teeth—that she had feared me at first but then found she truly liked me and didn't care about my teeth anymore, another passage detailed an argument with Tamson where he beat her near to death for attempting to stop her observations. Finally, they both found the very last entry in the very last book labeled 2030:

Dear Diary,
I say this to you and you alone. There's something very wrong with my dad. He's changed and seems to have grown angry at and disgusted by Emma. I'm afraid for her. I think

he's going to do something to her at the Gathering.
I must secretly try to stop her from coming. He can't know.
He would surely beat me again but I must try.

That was enough for Team Shaggy. Lucas and Seth sprinted from the bedroom and outside to the lawn party in progress, calling out for me.

"Emma! Emma!" Seth grabbed Max by both shoulders; demanding to know where I was or if he'd seen me.

Max was bewildered. "I think she's still in the main dining room," he said.

Seth told Max that I was in trouble and together they, and a few of the guests, headed back to the mansion, running up the stairs to the dining room.

***

I was still standing in front of one of those magnificent paintings.

Tamson's voice behind me startled my peace, "Enchanting, isn't it? Pay close attention to the vase the mother is using to pour water over her children."

I focused my attention on the vase. The deep colors of it mesmerized me into an almost hypnotic state. The room was silent. I was lost. My ears picked up the sound of something metal scraping across the marble floor. Then came a scream that saved my life:

"Emma!"

As I turned, I saw Tamson intently holding a large, double-sided axe over his head; about to bring it down on me. Lucas, running at full speed, pushed me out of the way as the axe came down and Tamson buried the medieval blade deep within the back of Lucas's skull. A thick mist of blood sprayed my face and the front of my gown. Seth knocked Tamson to the ground as Max, with the other guests, began filing into the dining room. Eric pulled Seth off Tamson. Yelling and chaos between everyone ensued.

I balled my hands into fists, bellowing at the top of my lungs a drawn-out, "Enough!"

The whole mansion began to shake violently, the chandeliers swung from side to side, the stone and plaster walls erupted in a network of spider lines, and the marble floor cracked down the middle as it shifted. When the shaking stopped and the dust settled, I was on the floor trying to yank the axe from Lucas's head. I got it free, then flung it across the room. Cradling his head gently in my lap; I begged him to heal. He was unconscious and his heartbeat faint. A disturbingly large amount of blood pooled beneath his head. I covered the gash in his head with my hand and kept repeating to him that he'd be all right. He had to hold on; he had to heal, I whispered it in his ear.

The growling animal inside me was seething. Roaring out angrily.

With a gleeful smile, Tamson slow clapped four times. "There it is ladies and gentlemen. Do you see? She doesn't belong with us! We are evolved. She's a mistake. It happens but we shouldn't suffer because of mistakes like her," he insisted.

Shocked faces stood still, not knowing what to make of it all. What had happened or why.

Max spoke up suddenly, "You're the Nazi leader of that garbage faction, aren't you Tamson?" he asked.

"Nazi? Nazi!" Tamson barked back. "Look at me! I'm the furthest from a Nazi. I was born in a village near Chukai for Christ's sake! This has nothing to do with color, status, or even religion. I am simply ensuring our kind continually makes strides forward! She's an animal, Max!" Tamson snapped.

"But that is the very definition of Nazi, Tamson! You're systematically trying to eliminate those you feel are not *perfect* in your eyes," Max replied.

Tamson continued to rant about how I was nothing more than a beast, a creature. He reminded everyone that I didn't even register on the Evol age device. I wasn't supposed to exist.

It was all nonsense and I didn't care.

It was then I slowly tilted my head, revealing my intense eyes of flaming gold bands. Burning like the sun; they lit up the dining room as if it were daylight. Mercury appeared to be streaming down my face; silvery-blue tears that glistened. I could see Max standing behind Tamson who was facing in my direction.

Max silently mouthed me one word, "Shimmer."

He was telling me leave; vanish if I could.

Tamson pointed his finger at me. "Look at her. Look at what she did to this place. She is the epitome of abomination!" he cried.

I closed my eyes while still holding on tight to Lucas. With the sound of a thunder crack and a flash of lightning, we were both gone. Seemingly vaporized.

Seth told me later that the onlookers backed up, searching for us. Even Max put on a show of pretending he didn't know what had just happened. Tamson looked relieved; he probably wouldn't have wanted to kill us both in front of everyone and it was then that Seth seized his chance. He dramatically doubled over in pain, pushed his hands against his head and fell to his knees screaming, "I think she's dead. I felt her leave!"

Eric bent down to Seth. "Are you sure? This isn't like the last time?" he asked.

Seth nodded with tears in his eyes. "I believe so. I mean, I think so. It felt different! Very different! She's gone man," he claimed.

Chapter 15
Sins of the Father

*If you think tough men are dangerous,
wait until you see what weak men are capable of.*
—Jordan B Peterson

Seth had missed his calling; he should've been an actor. He knew there was an excellent shot I wasn't dead because his internal senses felt the same as when I had fallen in the basement, but his performance was convincing enough that the guests looked solemn or remorseful.

Tamson gave off a glow of vindication and pride. Seth had no clue, however, if Lucas was alive or not. He wasn't Lucas's Gifter so he had no internal feelings about his status. We were safe somewhere was his hope. Seth's relief was that we'd gotten out of there before Tamson tried to kill me again.

"Good riddance," Tamson announced to the room. He then addressed Seth, "I told you not to gift her, Seth. I told you that when you came to me asking if I had ever heard of a human calling out to a Gifter. I told you to leave her be. This is on you. This is *all* on you! She was never supposed to be one of us, never!" Tamson scolded.

Sara was furious. "Seriously? This whole time you've been a bigot!

All these years I trusted you and looked up to you and here you are, a Nazi bigot asshole!" she yelled at Tamson. "Emma couldn't even pass on her teeth. She had a hysterectomy when she was still human. What is your deal?!" Sara asked, her anger rising.

"I'm not a bigot! I'm protecting us! Eric witnessed her tearing into a moose! She behaved like the animal she is! And what if she were to become a Gifter? What if she passed on her teeth in that manner? We don't know!" Tamson replied.

"You told him? What the hell?" Seth questioned Eric, shocked and pissed.

"Emma was weird, Seth! Maybe Tamson is right. She just disappeared, just now. Who does that? Who *can* do that? It's not right," Eric replied first to Seth, then to everyone.

The handful of guests still in the dining room gave Tamson disapproving, disgusted glares. They wanted no part of his opinions or actions and one by one, began to leave. Left standing with Tamson were Max, Sara, Eric, and Seth. Max demanded to know why Tamson tried to kill me. Seth announced that the whole thing was despicable and moronic. Sara too demanded Tamson explain himself. She wanted to know how he had become the monster he was. Shouting and accusations galore.

Tamson then vehemently defended his position; why he felt his way was best for everybody. He told them the story of how he had found the light: "My Gifter, long before he turned me, was visiting an elderly Evol in the Americas. This elder was named Tova, and she had teeth like Emma's. She shared a secret with him. She said she was going to die but not in the usual way. He saw her turn into a bear! An animal! She transformed into a bear and then just ran off into the woods. He knew in his heart it was unnatural. She may have assumed he'd understand

and sympathize but he saw her for what she really was—abnormal and wrong. Some years later, he destroyed the last Evol born with those teeth like Emma's. He taught me the importance of our purity and he was right to do so," Tamson insisted.

Max shook his head in sadness and dismay. He took out his handkerchief to wipe his eyes. "You're wrong my friend. You are the broken one. You haven't evolved one step beyond the humans. You have destroyed all we stand for, or should stand for."

"Oh, really? Tova was reborn with predator teeth! Best to get rid of Emma now. It was a kindness not a murder!" Tamson exclaimed.

"So, what? You saved us from what? From Emma turning into an animal years from now? Big fucking deal, Tamson! Was all this really worth it? I'm done with you," Max replied.

Just then, Seth jumped in to challenge Tamson with a question, "Would you care to explain how Sara is your daughter? You turned her when she was in her twenties! Was that a part of your sick plan to ensure Evol-kind was perfect? You deprived her of motherhood by gifting her that young! You're the fucking monster!" he yelled.

Max's mouth dropped open. Sara's head fell in shame and sorrow.

Yet Tamson was unaffected. "And? I didn't break any laws. I got a human pregnant and Sara was born half Evol, so I had her gifted for the full transformation. Sue me for wanting the best for her," he said, still defending himself.

Sara came forward with tears in her eyes, her face red with anger. "No, Daddy! You did not want the best for me." She turned, speaking to the others. "He paid my Gifter to rape me! I did become a mother, *twice*, and both times he took my precious babies from my arms! My father was attempting to produce purebred Evols. It didn't work out as planned though did it, Daddy? *Did it?*" she shouted as she turned back to Tamson.

"Tamson! How could you?!" Max stammered, furiously shaking with rage.

Sara continued through her sobs, "But Evol babies are born as stone children. I watched my father toss them both into the ocean," Sara explained.

"It almost worked the second time, pumpkin. We were so close. I wanted you to be a mother and have healthy perfect children of your own. I only wanted the world for you, sweetie," Tamson pleaded with her.

"What do you mean, it almost worked the second time? Was my baby alive when you threw her into the ocean? Was she?!" Sara demanded to know. She ran toward him screaming, her hands outstretched. "You wanted your perfect race! I was a means to an end. Nothing more than your own personal experiment. You put me through hell! That's not what a father does! You're a psychopath!" Sara ranted as Max tried to hold her back from her father.

Seth stepped forward. "I'm calling the Grand Council. This is out of our hands. Forcing the gift onto your child, forcing her to have children, and now trying to murder Emma," Seth informed Tamson.

At this, Tamson got a devilish smirk on his face and expelled another secret, "I don't know why you're so high and mighty about any of this, Seth. I had both of my children gifted. You've been married to one of them for two hundred years," he said, motioning in Eric's direction.

Seth stared at Eric in shock. "No. No. Tell me that isn't true Eric. It's not true. Is he your father?" Seth asked, hoping he had misheard.

Eric walked over next to Tamson, standing by his father's side. "Yes, it's true, Seth and I'm damn proud of it. He and I are going to remake the world in perfection. You're all living in denial. Our race is in danger from freaks like Emma. We will find a way to breed a better generation of Evol. By any means necessary," he proclaimed.

Max turned to walk away. "It's too much. I have to get out of this god-forsaken mansion," he bent as he walked, as though crippled by grief.

Sara started to leave with him.

"Sara, where are you going? Are you siding with them? Your home is here with us. We are the only ones who can take care of you," Tamson spoke, his words steel.

Max and Sara stopped. She looked back at Tamson, straightened herself up and stood tall. "Some humans never change their colors. Isn't that what you told me my whole life? Well, your true colors are out in the open now! You are not my family. You and Eric can both go straight to hell!" she replied and then turned away.

Max took her hand and they walked side by side out of the dining room.

Seth stood motionless, focused on Eric. He felt an enormous sense of betrayal but also an overwhelming pain of responsibility. Seth tabulated in his mind all the red flags Eric had thrown his way, which he had chosen to ignore. More than two hundred years of Eric subtly dropping hints of who he really was but Seth had kept himself in denial. He thought about them now. All the times he recalled Eric and Sara spending weekends at Tamson's estates. He wondered how he could have been so oblivious and stupid. How had love blinded him so completely? How could he have allowed Eric to become close to his friends? To Emma and Lucas. Seth realized that it was Eric who had spied on Emma more than Sara. Eric had told his father everything. *Everything!* Their life together had not been their own. It was the pinnacle to the insidious bigotry betrayal Eric had commited.

Seth was incensed with rage and sadness. "Don't go to the villa, Eric. I'll set your bags outside. Have someone fetch them, I don't care. Don't come near me again. *Ever!* I won't be held responsible for what would happen to you," Seth angrily spat at Eric.

Eric did not respond. He and Tamson were left standing alone.

***

Max was putting his clothes in a suitcase while debating what he should do next. He picked up his cellphone to make a call he truly did not want to make. One he never imagined he would have to make. But the seriousness of everything he'd just learned warranted what he was about to do. If ever there was a time to sound the alarm, that moment was it.

Elijah answered the other end of Max's phone call. "Max, you must have found the faction otherwise you wouldn't have called me at this hour."

"Yes," Max replied. "The faction head is Tamson and his son, Eric Fuller is a member as well. And that, unfortunately, is not the worst of the news. You all need to come now! Security Guardians in particular."

"His son? Are you certain? The council and I will be at Tamson's in a matter of hours. And in full force. Don't let onto Tamson or Eric that you've called me. Tell no one!" Elijah angrily demanded and then hung up the phone.

Max didn't mention anything about Sara. He wanted to see how things would play out with Eric first. Sara had been unaware of her father's true nature up until an hour ago and he didn't want her involvement known to the council just yet. He preferred to discuss Sara's position and what she'd been through, with Elijah personally, face to face.

It suddenly occurred to him that he should retrieve the security video of the dining room before Tamson destroyed it. Max made a beeline for the video room to download the entirety of the night's events onto a thumb drive. The council would need that video. He carefully made his way back to his room to finish packing, fixed himself a drink and dead bolted his room door. He barricaded the door with a dresser he slid in front of it for extra measure. He didn't believe Tamson would hurt him but then again, he also had no idea who Tamson really was.

With the council members arriving he couldn't leave, so he settled in to relax and clear his mind while he waited. Looking up at the stars Max wondered where Lucas and Emma had vanished to.

***

Meanwhile, Seth had taken a cab back to his villa. He walked in with a flurry of emotions eating away at him, kicked off his shoes and headed to the kitchen to pour himself a large whiskey. Seth wasn't much of a drinker, but he most certainly needed it then, gulping it down.

He stomped into the bedroom, grabbed all of Eric's belongings, and tossed them out the front door. Agitated and antsy, he didn't know what to do with himself. After downing his second glass he poured yet another. As he started to take a drink, he heard a gigantic *THUD* come from the master bathroom. Seth set the glass on the counter and ran to the bathroom door.

Cautiously, he opened it slowly to find Lucas and me in the jetted tub.

I still had my evening gown on, covered in blood and slimy Shimmer. Lucas's clothes were drenched in blood from the head wound he had received at the mansion. He was unconscious.

Seth looked like he couldn't believe his eyes. We had returned and we were both alive.

I struggled to get up as I yelled at him, "Quick, help me get Lucas cleaned up and to a bed. He's freezing cold in these bloody clothes!"

Seth left the bathroom for a moment, returning with a T-shirt and shorts for Lucas. We removed his shirt and I took a warm washcloth to his face and neck. Although he was unconscious, his body still shook and shivered from the hypothermia that had set in.

Seth paused, inspecting Lucas's head. He leaned away from me with a look of fright on his face. "Emma?" he said in a scared apprehensive voice. "His head is healed. Like, completely healed. There's not even a scar! How is that possible? Where have you two been?"

"I don't have time to explain right now. We just need to get him changed into warm clothes. Help me, Seth! He'll die if we don't elevate his temperature and heartrate!" I snapped.

Seth resumed the process of getting the rest of Lucas's bloody clothes off. He also gave me the highlights of what had happened and what was said after Lucas and I disappeared. I was having trouble taking it all in. *Eric and Sara were Tamson's children?* What the hell was going on with these Evols? What had I become a member of? "Awesome, the perfect end to a perfectly fucked-up night!" I mumbled to myself sarcastically. "How in the hell did Tamson think he could kill me with an axe anyway? I'm an Evol, hello!" I asked Seth.

"You are brand-fucking-new Emma! Only eight years! I told you before, you're vulnerable for the first century until your strength builds up and that axe could've killed you! Lucas survived because he's over four centuries old," he insisted.

Once we'd gotten Lucas as dry as we were able and he was dressed, we carefully got him to the bed; covering him with as many blankets as we could find. His heartrate began picking up and his breathing felt stronger. I sat next to him for some time just stroking his hair, talking to him softly. Even though he was unconscious, I knew he could hear me. He could feel me.

Seth was pacing in the living room as he finished his then third glass of whiskey. I walked out and poured myself a glass, told him that Lucas's vital signs were perking up. I finally looked down at myself. I asked Seth to sit with Lucas while I took a shower, requesting clothes for myself too. He agreed and retrieved something for me to wear.

I went into the bathroom, shut the door and blasted music from Seth's iPod. Twenty minutes later, refreshed, wearing rolled up sweatpants and a shirt I was clearly drowning in, I was comfortable and Lucas was still asleep. His heartrate continued to get stronger and more stable. I lay down on the bed beside him, Seth on a couch across from the bed. We instantly fell asleep. It was as if we had been awake for days. Everything that transpired in the hours before had completely drained us.

We remained in a dead, dreamless sleep until Seth's phone rang some hours later. It rang and rang until he answered, abruptly sitting up straight.

"Okay," he told the person on the other end. "All right. I understand. I'll be there as soon as I can." He paused, listening. "You'll send a car for me? Okay sir, I'll be ready." Then he hung up the phone.

I was awake and ready for explanations.

"Emma, I have to go back to the mansion. You stay here with Lucas. Right here, don't leave," he instructed me.

"Good, could you grab my backpack from the guest room please? It has my identification and passport in it. Don't worry about the rest of my bags but I really need that passport. Wait, what's going on?

Did someone order you back to the mansion?" I asked.

"Yes. Elijah. That was him on the phone. He's at the mansion with a couple of the council members. He wants to speak to me," he explained.

"Who the hell is Elijah?" I asked.

"He's the oldest of us. The oldest we are aware of. He runs the Grand Council," Seth replied.

"What? There's a Grand Council? Did no one think to tell me that shit! You told me Tamson was the oldest! You lied to me!" I snapped.

Seth put his hand up to stop me from ranting further. "Emma, something bad happened at the mansion. Something terrible happened to Max. He may not make it. I have to go. Stay here and take care of Lucas," he commanded as he walked toward the front door.

Chapter 16
Red Reign

A short time later, a fancy black four door car arrived to retrieve Seth. I watched over Lucas for another hour. Even though I was exhausted I decided it was time I tried to get some food in my stomach. Lucas was slumbering peacefully and looked so much better. His body temperature was warm which had put color back into his face. He was going to be okay. Releasing a loving sigh, I hooked my phone to a small speaker to softly play music for him and I tiptoed out of the room.

I opened the villa refrigerator to find it sparse but there were eggs, tomatoes, cheese, and coffee creamer. On the counter sat two loaves of artisan bread. I felt confident I could whip up some yummy, scrambled eggs. Not long after I had begun cooking, I heard sounds coming from the room Lucas was sleeping in. I stopped chopping the tomatoes so I could listen more clearly. He was moving around. He was awake! I then heard the bathroom door shut. The shower started running. The wolfman lived!

With a relieved smile on my face, I cracked more eggs so that he could join me when he was ready. In fifteen minutes, the bread was sliced, scrambled eggs finished, and coffee brewed. I made myself a plate and sat down at the table. Lucas shuffled through the hallway and out into the kitchen area, then kissed the top of my head before making himself a plate of food. Like nothing had happened!

We sat together and ate. Neither of us said a word. As per our usual game, we pretended not to be bothered by almost losing one another. Besides, I was semi-distracted staring at my creature in the far corner of the living room. How in the fuck did that thing follow me? Was it a ghost? A demon? Its stupid creepy eyes in every corner of that mansion, were now here. It was irritating.

Seth arrived back at the villa just as we were finishing breakfast. He took his shoes off outside the door before entering. He had all my bags with him and the backpack. When he set them down, he saw Lucas was awake and fine. Seth let out a big sigh and then told us he was about to dump a lot of intense information on us. That we should prepare ourselves and listen carefully. He went to the bedroom to grab his laptop, came back and set it down on the table.

We adjusted ourselves in our seats.

"First of all, I took my shoes off outside because they are gross with blood. As the car pulled up to the mansion, I could smell blood everywhere. Then, when I stepped from the car, my shoes sank into a slippery sludge of blood. Tamson's scent filled the air. It was his, his blood," Seth told us.

Confused, I narrowed my eyes. "What do you mean, it was everywhere?" I asked.

"Emma, it rained blood on Tamson's property. I'm saying it rained full-on, thick blood only over his property and nowhere else. It had stopped raining by the time I got there," he said. "Not long after Max called the council it began to pour blood from the sky. There were also small chunks of Tamson's flesh and teeth scattered about that also fell from the sky."

"Holy shit!" Lucas exclaimed.

Seth urged us to hold tight cause there was much more. When the council members arrived, they saw all the blood and began to search the place. They couldn't find Tamson or Eric or even Max. They fanned out and one of them heard a rumbling under their feet coming from somewhere underground and a voice yelling but couldn't make out what was being said. They followed the sound to the wine cellar. They found both Sara and Max hanging from the ceiling. Upside down from their ankles like field-dressed deer.

Apparently, Eric had just ripped through Max's body from stem to stern using a small handheld sickle, still gripped tight in his hand. He positioned himself, ready for a fight. The security force Guardians that were with the council members tackled Eric to the ground. He was no match for them. It was over before it started. Max was alive but barely. They cut him down and patched up his wounds as best they could.

Lucas and I were horrified, speechless. My eyes filled with tears but I desperately tried to hold my composure. I grabbed Lucas's hand and we did not flinch from Seth's eyes or words as he continued.

"When I arrived, Max was in the foyer lying on a couch and wrapped in a blanket. He was weak but alive. They'd gotten to him just before Eric was going to pull out his organs. Max called me over to him. He slipped me this thumb drive and said it was for you, Emma. He wanted you to look at it and then destroy it." Seth held up the thumb drive.

"So, he's still alive? Will he be okay? What about Sara?" I asked in a worried voice.

"Max doesn't heal quite as fast as he used to but I believe he'll be fine. Sara was ... unfortunately, already dead. She had been gutted, hollowed out when the council members reached the cellar. There wasn't anything they could do for her. Eric murdered his own sister. She's gone. I'm sorry. She's gone," he broke the news softly.

There was no stopping my tears at that point. I rolled my body into Lucas's chest and buried my face and sobbed as he held me. I thought of all the times I had felt she was annoying or bothersome. Of how quickly I had misjudged her the first time we met. Sara had tried her best to save me. She had put herself at risk to warn me, railed against her father and did what she felt was right. Although she had lived for over four hundred years, she remained that sweet and perhaps naive twenty-two-year-old girl. She was the innocence this world needed. I would've gladly gone through the excruciating pain of regrowing my teeth again in exchange for her life back. I wanted to hit the reset button, erasing the past eight years. None of what had happened felt real. How could Eric, of all people, betray us like that? We'd loved him. We thought he was our friend and a loving husband to Seth. Oh God, Seth! What Eric did to him, for two hundred years, lying every day about who he was. We were in a nightmare.

Seth turned the laptop on and put the thumb drive in. He asked me through my heartbreak and tears if I wanted to watch it in privacy. I shook my head no. I needed them there with me. I couldn't be alone. We went through this disaster together so we would all watch whatever Max thought I should see, together. I wasn't going to hide anything from them.

Seth hit *Play*.

It was a security video facing the balcony. Tamson was alone, standing by the railing and looking out into the darkness while smoking a cigar. A rolling crackle of light danced across the sky and suddenly I appeared in the video, as if by magic. I was standing about six feet from Tamson.

He jumped, startled and angry to see me. "No! You're dead, dammit!" Tamson shouted.

"Not yet you piece of shit!" I yelled back and then I sprinted toward him.

Just as my body reached his, we both vanished and another crackle of light rolled across the sky. The balcony remained empty for maybe twenty seconds before it began raining. Blood.

Seth paused the video looking at the time stamp at the bottom of the screen. "That was about the time you said you were going to take a shower! While you were in the bathroom did you wink out or whatever the fuck it is you do, and *kill him*? You did, didn't you Emma? Dammit!" Seth barked.

I stared at him with silent defiance. When he realized I wasn't going to answer him he pressed *Play* again. The video seemed to stop but then a new video immediately began. It was Max on the video in his guest room.

"Emma, I downloaded the video footage of us all in the dining room and I will give that to Elijah. The council will need to see it; that will prove Tamson's transgressions. But this video is for your eyes only. After it started raining Tamson's blood, I went back to the security room to search the recordings. I downloaded just that portion of you and Tamson and then erased the security footage. I have to go now. I can feel Eric roaming the halls looking for me. I must keep him here in the mansion until the council arrives. Take care Emma," Max concluded.

Seth shook his head back and forth; disappointed. "This is bad. What you did is so bad, Emma!" He scolded me like I was a child.

The immense sorrow and fury of Sara's death exploded out of me. A slow rolling growl rumbled through me as I slammed my hand down on the table. The villa vibrated and searing rings of gold burst forth in my eyes. "He got what he fucking deserved!" I yelled, popping up from the table.

Lucas couldn't stop himself from remarking in childlike wonder, "Whooooa. That's cool! When did your eyes start doing that?"

Seth looked over at Lucas, perhaps realizing that he hadn't seen it the first time because he had been unconscious on the floor of the mansion, with an axe embedded in his brain. Why I had done it was clear to him. He must have known how important Lucas was to me. And to him. Losing Lucas would've been more than he could handle. I guess he knew that on some level. And also, what could have happened to me or Lucas if Tamson had been left alive. He held up his hands in a defensive posture. "Okay, I know. Calm down, Emma. Shh, Shh. What I'm trying to tell you is that Tamson's mansion is entombed by a gelatinous coagulated mass of blood. Rule number one is 'Don't get caught by the humans.' Sunrise is in like, two minutes. That blood will start to reek of death and all his neighbors will know something is wrong. How will the Evols be able to hide that, Emma?" he asked.

I sat back down, allowing the light in my eyes to fade and the villa to stop trembling. Seth was about to say something else when Lucas interrupted him. Lucas put his hand on Seth's arm and told him to listen. It started slow, one drop and then two. It became harder and louder. It was rain. Regular rain. Seth and Lucas got up and walked to the TV. Standing in the living room Lucas changed the channels with the remote looking for the news. When they found it, the weatherman was on, speaking in Spanish, but there was closed captioning along the bottom of the TV in English that read:

"Okay folks, I hope you were prepared for a storm. A surprise squall developed a short time ago off the coast of the Balearic Sea. Torrential rains will be pummeling the shoreline and the local area for possibly the next two days. Take shelter and board up windows to prevent debris from flying into homes and businesses. Remember to pick up any loose items outside, such as lawn chairs and trash cans so they don't get washed away. Please check for updates."

Lucas and Seth turned their heads to look at each other and then they both slowly twisted their bodies to look back at me. I was still sitting at the table with my hands clasped, a blank emotionless look on my face.

They thought I had made it rain somehow. Maybe I had.

When Seth was talking to me about all the blood the humans would find, I began to wish it would rain. I focused all my energy on imagining a violent, powerful rainstorm. Could I have a new ability? That was cool. "It appears our problem will be shortly diluted and washed out to sea. Can we please continue our conversation? I would like to hear what else Seth has to say," I said.

Apprehensively they walked to the table and gently sat down. Seth started again, informing us that the Grand Council would be convening a trial for Eric. Seth, Lucas, and I were all commanded to be present. The trial would be held in Jerusalem in two days' time. I asked him about the council he had kept secret from me. Who were the council members and what was their importance? I asked another question that suddenly rushed into my mind. "So, the council knows Lucas and I are alive then?" I asked.

Seth sighed before answering. He told us they did know and that we were here in the villa. It wasn't something he could keep from them. He said he didn't tell me about Elijah or the council because it was simply never something he thought I'd need to know. There was no reason to scare or worry me at the time. The council consisted of eight Evols ranging in ages from two thousand to three thousand years old. Elijah was the oldest. They only got involved in Evol affairs when there was an issue so large that it could significantly impact us as a community. They were not people to be trifled with and only a slim few of us had ever met any of them.

"Emma said Sara and Eric are Tamson's children? And that Tamson supposedly forced Sara to have a baby, twice. Is that true? Does the council know about all that?" Lucas asked Seth.

Seth explained it was, unfortunately, all true. And the council did know. He and Max went over it with them. Plus, they had the security footage of Tamson admitting it. The council members and their Guardians were at the mansion collecting all kinds of evidence. They discovered a secret room behind Tamson's office that contained his journals and research. If Tamson was not already dead; the council would have put him to death. They haven't had to execute anyone in nearly eight hundred years. What happened last night qualified them to execute any person involved in Tamson's supremacy faction.

"What about this trip thing we have to take to Jerusalem? Are we in any danger? Or am I in danger from the council?" I asked Seth.

"I don't believe any of us are in trouble. They don't know what happened to Tamson. And Lucas is a victim. You and I are considered victims as well. I think our going is to finish the process of Eric's judgment. I wouldn't worry about it," he assured me.

"Emma, will you tell us what happened to Tamson when you took him?" Lucas asked me.

I nodded, yes. "I went into the bathroom and turned on Seth's iPod. Ironically, Korn's *Freak On A Leash* was playing," I began.

Lucas smiled slightly. "Excellent song."

"I stood listening to the song play, staring at my blood-soaked gown in the mirror. Lucas's blood and I got angry, *so* angry. It came on, all of a sudden, like a wave of rage. You could have died," I said, turning to Lucas. "Then I just ... disappeared, leaving here to find Tamson. After I ran at him on the balcony we sped through a fold in space. I ... pulled him across the fold to be more correct. I knew he wouldn't survive it. His body dispersed as if each of his molecules separated simultaneously. Vaporized. I didn't know it would result in a blood rain. I accomplished what I needed to do and then ... returned to the shower," I explained.

There was silence as Seth and Lucas digested.

"That works for me!" Lucas exclaimed with a smile on his face. "Hey, what does a space fold look like?" he asked.

I took a slow breath in and leaned back. "A kaleidoscope of texture and sound. That's the closest I can describe it. It's a feeling within flat blackness that you're in between everything that's ever existed. I don't have words better than that right now," I tried to explain.

"Nice. Thank you," Lucas replied.

"Soooo, are we not going to talk about where you and Lucas went when you magically disappeared from the dining room?" Seth asked.

I shook my head.

Seth said, "Fine," and got up from the table.

Lucas and I were left to absorb all the information Seth had given us. After a few moments I wanted to know if I could see Max or when I would be able to see him? Seth told me with the storm outside now raging he'd have to get back to me on that. He was supposed to take us to the mansion at daybreak. He would make some phone calls first to verify that was still the plan. I nodded in agreement then got up to get my bags.

Lucas announced that he was going to lie on the couch and watch TV, maybe take a nap. Before doing so, he took the thumb drive out of the laptop and mashed it. He then put the pieces down the garbage disposal. Seth walked over to the window; marveling at the deluge of water pouring down. He took out his cell phone and made a call. I carried my bags to one of the bedrooms, shutting the door behind me. I felt dirty and gross again from all the crying, anger, and stress. So I ran myself a hot bubble bath and laid out some of my own clothes. I didn't want to meet the Grand Council in Seth's sweatpants and baggy T-shirt.

My body dissolved as I lowered myself into the jetted tub, closed my eyes and drifted off into a semi-sleep state while soaking in the soothing water.

Chapter 17

Unearthed

I don't recall how long I was in the tub, maybe an hour, before Seth began lightly knocking on the bathroom door to say that Elijah was coming to us. We should expect him within thirty minutes, possibly sooner. Reluctantly, I stepped out of the bathtub to blow-dry my hair and get ready for company. I wasn't nervous about meeting Elijah. In that moment, I was numb, I felt nothing of note. When you go through overwhelming amounts of trauma, sadness, and death in less than twenty-four hours, your mind stops. It can be a survival tactic your brain employs to protect your sanity. It can also be a sign that you've severely broken your mind. Which side of that coin you're on is often not discovered for some time. The best you can hope for is that you land on the side of a person who is healing. In contrast, destruction and despair lash out in unthinkable ways.

I walked into the living room to find Seth, Lucas, and two males hilariously dressed as Secret Service men. Behind them stood a third man. He was very tall and talking to the guards. He looked past them and straight at me. The six feet, six inches man made his way slowly toward us. He walked with a cane. A twisted, curling long-wooded staff embedded with small blue jewels in the knots of the wood. He stopped in front of me as I tilted my head upward to meet his gaze. His skin was velvet black, like the darkest midnight, which made his aqua-blue eyes blaze with unmatched brilliance. He was the first Evol I had met who actually qualified as an elder. His hair was white, not gray, and pulled back into a bun. *If wisdom had a face*, I thought, *his would be it.*

Elijah greeted the boys and then extended his hand to shake mine. As we touched, I felt his heart. He was a person of intense light and hope and it radiated from his soul. The polar opposite of what Tamson had been. I hadn't sensed ill intentions from Tamson in the past, however, I also didn't have anything to compare him to. After recent events, my ability to feel the difference between a threat and not, had grown by leaps and bounds.

"Pleasure to meet you Ms. Alexander. May I call you Emma?" he asked.

"You may, if I can call you Elijah?" I responded.

He smiled with agreement and continued, "I can see what all the fuss has been about. You are an intriguing creature, Emma. And I also see you have your own personal guardian. Lucky girl," he remarked as he motioned over at Lucas.

"Lucas not only took an axe in the head for you, but he is also watching my every move to ensure no harm comes to you. I'm not entirely sure you are in need of protection though. Not after I witnessed your impressive escape on Tamson's security video," Elijah commented.

We all stayed silent and stone-faced. We weren't intentionally trying to be rude, but we were done; on the verge of a mental meltdown. I focused on Elijah's voice. He didn't have an accent, at least, not a discernible one I could detect. I guessed that after three thousand years, whatever accent he had developed as a child would be long gone. I believe he could see we were waiting for him to do most of the talking. Trust had been broken and we were skeptical, to say the least.

Elijah then spoke with a solemn heavy heart, "First, I wish to offer my sincere condolences for the loss of your friend, Sara. Only three of us council members were located close enough to travel to the mansion. However, all eight of us have viewed the security video. I e-mailed it to the others. We saw everything. From the time Emma was alone in the dining room, all the way through the horrid event. Every word was captured," he paused, taking a slow breath. "It was confirmed through the video and other evidence that Tamson was a part of that disgusting hidden faction," he said.

Cautiously, I asked a possible minefield of a question, "Does anyone know what happened to Tamson? How he died?" I could feel both boys' heartrates jump. They must have thought I was mad for broaching the subject, but I wasn't going to leave anything to chance. I wanted to know up front if Tamson's death was going to be something I had to pay for.

Elijah sighed deeply, looking up as if he was searching for the right words. He then looked back at us and replied, "We don't know how he died. I couldn't find anything on the security footage. It's also beyond our comprehension as to how all that blood could belong to just one person. But it does. Normally, we would investigate any suspicious Evol death. However, under the circumstances of the monster he was, the council is ... indifferent about the details of Tamson's demise. We are content with leaving his death a mystery."

I could sense that I had terrified Lucas with my line of questioning. He felt I would be found out as Tamson's executioner and he immediately switched gears.

"Did you find all of Sara's diaries?" he asked. "There were about four hundred years of diaries in a hidden room. Believe me when I tell you, Sara was innocent. She was trapped between a rock and a hard place when she realized something was wrong with her father. She did her best," Lucas explained.

Elijah nodded. "Yes, we found the room with the pink door. We skimmed the journals and they have been boxed up as evidence. It very much appears she was innocent. She made the ultimate sacrifice," he said.

Our murmurs filled the room, allowing a kind of collaborative breath.

"On that subject," Elijah continued. "Her Gifter was taken into our custody not an hour ago. He and a few others who belonged to the faction, will be sentenced with Eric."

And with that, the room fell silent again. We were reliving the horror of Sara's death in our minds and Eric's betrayal. Speaking of which, none of us brought up Eric and Seth specifically. Poor Seth was in his own small piece of hell. We should have said something I guess but truly, in that moment, I was unconcerned. My new Evol emotions generally ran all over the palce and not always in line with what the situation dictated. I was something of an unruly toddler in those days—jump first, ask questions later, etc. How any of them dealt with me as a baby Evol, I'll never know.

Seth changed the subject. I believe he was really trying to distract me from getting upset again. He probably didn't want my rings of gold to come forth from my eyes in front of Elijah and the Guardians perceive me as a threat. That could've been a whole new level of disastrous.

"What was he talking about when he told us the story of an Evol named Tova turning into a bear?" Seth asked Elijah.

Lucas's ears immediately perked up. He and I were not in the dining room when all that had gone down and he was still unconscious here in the villa when Seth had told me about it. I hadn't mentioned it to Lucas yet. Honestly, I had pushed that small detail from my mind.

"There was an elder named Tova who disappeared over a millennia ago," answered Elijah. "She was a Gifter, *my* Gifter as a matter of fact. A fierce shield-maiden and a true Viking, long before the term 'Viking' was even created. I searched for her for a few hundred years before ... well—I don't know how much of Tamson's story is true. We may never know," Elijah finished.

Lucas looked over at me but said nothing. Even if it were true that an Evol had turned into a bear; it couldn't possibly be the same bear on his property. That would mean his bear was over a thousand years old. Bears don't live that long. It just felt like more of a coincidence. Visibly, Lucas looked like he wanted to say something, like the words about his bear were on the tip of his tongue.

"Did you want to say something, Lucas or have a question?" Elijah asked.

Lucas stammered out his question, "How is Max? Where is he?"

I had the distinct impression that Elijah eyeballed him for slightly longer than necessary, before replying calmly, "Oh, Max is doing much better. He's been asking about you three continuously. More concerned about you than himself. He will be flying to Jerusalem today with me on a private jet, which brings me to the next topic," Elijah said with both hands resting on his cane. He leaned forward quite a bit to get closer to me. "I am extending to you the rare opportunity to be a part of history. All three of you. What do you say? Will you join us in Jerusalem?" he asked.

I felt that was a cagey question. Seth had said earlier that we were commanded to attend the trial. As in, no option. It's possible he misunderstood, or it was possible Elijah was just trying to be nice about it now. Either way, I wasn't going to miss Eric's trial. Period. Besides, the three of us had already wrapped our brains around the idea of going anyway. I flashed Elijah my pointy sweet vampire smile and answered, "Oh, we will be there."

Elijah suddenly stood up straight again as some emotion seemed to wash across his face. I felt his heartbeat race a little faster and stronger. I realized he had seen something in me he recognized, someone he knew and possibly lost, or missed.

"Emma, I have not seen a smile like yours since I was a young man just newly gifted. Never allow anyone make you feel as though you don't belong. You are not the abomination Tamson called you. You're a miracle. We all are," he said, blue eyes locked on mine. He then looked around and made his final announcement to the group, "Well, it's settled. A car will pick you all up tomorrow at noon. I am leaving these two Guardians here," he gestured at the two guards still standing further back in the room. "They have been instructed to stay outside and rotate keeping watch. This is solely for your peace of mind to ensure you get a full night's rest."

We murmured our group thanks in a mixture of confusion and gratitude as Elijah looked around the villa again and spied the small back patio.

"This is some weather we've been hit with. Emma, I know it's a downpour outside but I see there is a covered patio. Would you escort me so we can have a chat of our own?" he requested.

"Umm, sure. That would be fine. Right this way," I answered.

Once outside Elijah stood, leaning on his cane, and watched the rain fall for a moment.

"Emma, I wanted a minute alone with you to ask how you're holding up? Your heartbeat has been steady this whole time. After such tragic events I would expect to feel an internal struggle. Are you okay?" he asked, concern etched into the lines on his forehead.

"I don't know yet. That would be the honest answer. I don't know," I replied.

"You know Max has shared with me some of your interesting traits and abilities. Do you have other unusual powers besides the disappearing act?" he asked.

"I might. And I might not. I'm sorry but I'm not really in a trusting mood at the moment," I offered.

"I understand and you're right to feel cautious. Evols were supposed to be above human defects. For more than four millennia we ran like clockwork. The council members don't go to the Gatherings or many events. Our presence is to be as minimal as possible. Myself and two others happened to be in Spain on sabbatical. These are dark events and ones I hoped I'd never have to be witness to," Elijah said.

"Question. After I was gifted, a folder was put in my hands. In the folder was a brief description of a committee that supposedly takes care of these things. Is the Grand Council that committee?" I asked.

"Yup, one and the same. We want to put it out there that infractions come with consequences but not explain the whole 'Grand Council' aspect of it. New Evols have enough to deal with in the beginning," he said.

"I will be glad when it's all over and taken care of. I want nothing more than to go home as quickly as I'm able. I need to put this behind me," I said.

"Right you are, Emma. The trial will be over soon and then you can go home," he replied.

Elijah sat, offering to tell me the story of how he came to be an Evol. I wasn't expecting that. In the moment I found it odd and unnecessary. However, the purpose became clear as his tale unfolded. He was raised in the Kingdom of Nobatia. One of three kingdoms that comprised what we now call the country of Sudan. More than three thousand years ago his land had been bountiful with rich soil and the crops and livestock thrived; his people thrived. Not like it is today in Sudan, a desolate wasteland. His tribe was at the hierarchical top of the surrounding tribes. Others looked to them for knowledge of medicine and farming implementation.

Upon his birth, his father and uncles wanted to drown him in the river. His eyes were icy clear blue and they thought him damaged or blind. He would be a hindrance, a bad omen. Born wrong, even evil. Maybe. His mother protected him; refusing to give in to their demands for Elijah's death. She sheltered him; keeping him close until he was strong enough to protect himself. As he grew the tribal leaders remained skeptical of him. Elijah developed a natural understanding of herbs and medicines. He could converse with the spirit realm and heal the injured. After much contemplation, the elders of his tribe made him their shaman, deeming he had been sent to the tribe as a gift and not a curse.

What they had once feared and been disgusted by, they then turned to for help with all matters. Elijah rose to become a prime member of his tribe. He married a warrior woman who also had a closeness with the ways of herbs and medicines. Together, they healed their sick and prayed over the crops. Until the day came when a savage illness swept throughout the tribe. With all his gifts, Elijah could not stop it. The pestilence consumed everyone in a matter of weeks, his wife and five children included.

The tribe was gone in the blink of a rheumy eye.

Only Elijah and one other person survived. More than 200 souls were snuffed out and he could do nothing but watch them die. After burying his family, he left. He wandered the vast grasslands and deserts for years. Keeping to himself always, not wanting the company of any human. That was when his Gifter found him. Tova had found him. She had offered him a new life, far from his home of immense pain and Elijah accepted, feeling he had nothing more to lose.

And now here he was, sitting before of me. All the history he must have witnessed over three thousand years just … blew my mind. The point he'd been trying to get across with his story was that humans would always do human things. The people of his own tribe shunned him at birth and wanted to kill him. He was born with different eyes than theirs, nothing more, and for that they would have tossed him in a river. Whether twenty thousand years ago or three thousand, or even an hour, humans remain human. Some just have a proclivity for violence toward individuality. And it will be that way for as long as humans are on this earth. Tamson did not become a monster overnight. He had always been one. Upgrading his DNA did little to change his already sullied heart and mind.

Elijah finished his story and gave me a gentle pat on the arm before making his way back inside. He waved goodbye to us all and left, heading for the airport. Oddly enough, we relaxed and collectively exhaled. Elijah's visit may have been a solitary kindness in the aftermath of the events of the previous day but we didn't speak about it. We each did a load of laundry and ordered take-out. It was our attempt at distracting ourselves with mundane things, to compartmentalize the awfulness.

The Guardians came in one at a time to eat with us and joke around. They were really quite delightful people. Dressed as they were in their *Men in Black* suits was still cracking me up. I learned they were chosen as Guardians due to how they were born as Evols. Extreme natural abilities and talents developed during their transformations. Their eyesight and strength, in particular, was well above those of your average Evol. They were basically like superheroes. About one in three hundred people gifted end up like them. They become the literal guard dogs of the Grand Council, should they so wish.

As awesome as it was to meet and get to know the Guardians, Seth was forefront in my thoughts. Settling down and putting to rest my unruly toddler emotional side brought me back to what was really important. We had spent so much time talking about blood, Tamson, and Sara's death, that the subject of Seth's husband had been left behind. I could not imagine what he was going through. To be with a person for two hundred years only to have them snatched from your life in the most brutal of ways. Eric didn't die in an accident, he hadn't divorced Seth. No, Eric had been lying to Seth for centuries and then murdered one of Seth's friends.

Eric was the product of his father's madness and we were going to see him at trial. Seth would have to see him at trial. *What would that feel like?* I wondered. How could Seth stand it? How was he so calm, wandering around the villa doing laundry? If I sensed him feeling the full weight of it, I'd be there to pick up the pieces, I vowed. Lucas and I would be there when he was ready. We would get through our terrible shared experiences of the mansion, together. For the moment we were more tired than anything else.

Once sleep took me, my wolf and I strolled through lush fields of amber vegetation. Calm warm breezes lifted my hair, making it dance in the swirling wind. I was not a spectator. I was a participant. It was me. I could feel my wolf's incredible pelt of fur as I kept one hand on his back. I could smell joy and love in the air. My lavender-skied planet to the rescue again, temporarily removing me from the harshness our world enjoyed perpetrating on its residents. A buffer zone. A respite to put my mind right again.

How or why this consistent dreamworld came to be I didn't know, nor cared but I would need the soothing nature of the visions in the future, again and again.

Chapter 18
Beneath the Wailing

Iron sharpens iron. You can't be sharp hanging around butter knife people.
—*Kimberly Jones a.k.a Real Talk Kim*

The next day we locked the villa and turned in the keys. No one would be returning to Spain after the trial. We boarded Elijah's private jet and into the sky we flew. The Guardians and the boys joked around some more to pass the time. I stared off into the clouds, not thinking of anything in particular. Just spacing out, every now and then, the thought of home would wash through my internal abyss, reminding me where I needed to be. The flight was fairly short, about twenty minutes, but it was hot. Dry hot, and my breath felt shallow in my lungs. Still, before I had time to gripe about it too much, we had landed.

There to greet us on the Hadassah Airfield airport runway in Jerusalem was Max. He looked to be healed physically. I didn't know how he was holding up mentally after the ordeal he had survived.

We piled into a pair of large Mercedes SUVs to start our journey, driving to where the trial would be held in The Hidden City. I didn't hear a peep from anyone as we drove. It was soaking in, the severity of why we were there. The streets were heavily congested. A lot of start and stop. I was having a moment because of how similar that area and drive reminded me of Bagdad, Iraq. We had never been safe in Iraq and a bit of panic welled up in me. I closed my eyes, hoping we'd get there soon before I flipped out. I'd peek every now and then but the mostly smiling faces of busy people darting around us did not lessen my anxiety.

Arriving at our destination, we exited the vehicles and my panic turned to gob smack as I stood in awe of what I was seeing. The Western Wall, otherwise known as The Wailing Wall was the last outer wall of an ancient Jewish temple. Its massive structure was constantly surrounded by tourists and Jewish people who pray to it. It was an unbelievable sight I hadn't known I'd needed to see until I was staring at it, frozen with my mouth open.

Max called over to me which unlocked my gaze of wonder. The others had started walking on without me. A slight jogging gait and I had caught up with them. We walked by the wall through a courtyard and around to the other side by way of a camouflaged passageway. What secrets that hallowed place held hadn't been revealed in thousands of years. I felt underdressed and inadequate to say the least. A Guardian held open a door for us that appeared to be built of old granite and iron. Once inside we were patted down as if at a police station. I mean, seriously? None of us needed weapons to hurt someone. We then walked through a short hallway which led to a flight of stone steps.

Descending winding stairs for what felt like an eternity, I was becoming increasingly claustrophobic. My thoughts wandered. This was a bad way to start a new adventure. It's often how horror movies begin. Where were the stairs leading us to? And why hadn't someone invested in an elevator? How the hell did Elijah make it down these steps with his cane? I wasn't sure how things would play out but I grew more concerned when I realized I would have to walk all the way up again, eventually. Yuck. Down and down, and down further still we trekked.

Finally, we reached an open area that appeared to be a large parlor-style sitting room. It did, however, also feel like a dungeon. We were directly underneath the wall. Although that room had to be at least a quarter of a mile below, I could still hear the wailing prayers of those above us. At that depth they sounded like ghostly cries. We were listening to the woes of a world within another world. Between the wailing and the reason we had been summoned, I imagined we were in some epic apocalyptic movie. Max sat down in the parlor, motioning for us to also get comfortable.

He explained how the night was going to proceed. First, he warned us that Eric's trial would be a sentencing. There'd been overwhelming indisputable evidence against him. The council had convened earlier that morning and his trial had already been completed. What we'd be witnessing in a couple of hours was the official reading of his punishment. Max told us we'd be shown to our bedrooms shortly. Dinner would be served and then at 8 p.m. we would proceed to the courtroom chamber. I remember thinking how formally he spoke to us, how official he sounded. It gave me pause. He appeared unfazed by it all. A deadness lingered in his tone.

None of us were in a chatty mood and Max could sense it. He was attempting to soothe us without disregarding the obvious seriousness of the situation. I was alarmed to think that only eight years ago, I had been happy in my remote cabin. Knowing nothing of this other world. Wondering if I'd made the right choice to not fight off Seth's kiss of evolution the second time we met. I longed for it to be over, giving myself an internal pep talk. Trying to convince myself that I would be able to live a normal life again soon. Scotland was only one day away after the stupidness of that trial was done.

Staff members came into the parlor asking us to follow them to our rooms. My room was small, sparse, and humble. Cozy and warm were the words that ran through my mind. It suited me more than the extravagant guest room at Tamson's mansion.

Elijah joined us for dinner that night and we seated ourselves at a grand circular table feeling like guests at King Arthur's Round Table. There was a medieval presence or vibe down there that enveloped the senses. The air was saturated with the scent of dust, metal, and of lost souls of the past. I hadn't yet been exposed to an environment that ancient since becoming an Evol. My body was somehow lit up with electricity and heat by the depth of history that pulsed throughout the room. I had to break the tension. "Can I ask about the stone children? Seth told Lucas and me about the things Sara said in the dining room. Is that why Evols don't have children?" I asked the group.

"Evol DNA can create life," Max began. "However, there's an issue with our advanced healing ability. The children are not actually made of stone. They have the appearance of stone or rock. During the gestation process our DNA overproduces calcium when producing bone, encasing the tiny body until the child is frozen," he explained.

"Was this already known to Tamson before he forced her to become pregnant?" I asked.

"Yes, he did know, Emma," Elijah answered. "There are records dating back thousands of years solely about the stone children. Two Evols have never been able to reproduce successfully."

I let the subject drop after that. I couldn't imagine the torture Sara must have endured, knowing she could be carrying essentially dead children. The level of betrayal she must have felt from her father's actions. To know he threw her babies, dead or not, into the sea. I couldn't wrap my head around it. How could he do that to his own daughter? He was the ultimate sadist; the Devil incarnate. And he got away with it for centuries. I began to think I may have killed him too quickly. He had deserved to die slowly and painfully. My bad.

Before we knew it, the meal was finished and we were back in the parlor, waiting. The sound of an alarm buzzed three times. Max stood to escort us to the courtroom chamber. Upon entering we saw all eight of the council members seated on the same side of a long table. We sat down in the four chairs that were setup for us just off to the right of the door. In the middle of the large room, in front of the council table, was a circular area with a kneeling bench in the center. My creature was there too. In a far corner hidden among the shadows. I had guessed that even underground it would stick with me. Every day since my transformation, my creature had stalked me, even here. *I mean, really?* What was the deal with this odd invisible stalker?

Across from where we were sitting, on the opposite side of the circle, a door opened. Eric shuffled out, closely followed by three men and one woman. They were all handcuffed and wearing leg shackles. They walked single file to the center of the circle, lining up in front of the council. Their abuses were egregious and unyieldingly destructive; to humans and Evols alike. I was curious to see how my new kind dealt with offenders such as these. What form of punishment would be handed down? Would I feel it was just?

Elijah called forth a man named Nicholas. It was Sara's Gifter. He stepped forward to the kneeling bench and Elijah read out his charges:

"Nicholas, you have been found guilty of using your Gifter ability irresponsibly by way of turning a twenty-two-year-old human. You have also been found guilty of rape, and two accounts of the commission of rape for the purpose of producing a child. Finally, you have been found guilty of conspiring with a supremacist faction," he paused briefly. "Do you deny any of these charges?"

"Regrettably, I cannot deny the charges," Nicholas replied.

"You are hereby sentenced to endure the cage. Once in the cage twelve spears will be pushed into your flesh. This is where you are condemned to stay as you slowly starve until your death," Elijah announced.

Two Guardians retrieved Nicholas, removing him from the chamber. Elijah instructed Eric to step back and the other three to step forward. The three kneeled on the bench. A council member named Sonya read out their charges. A long list of conspiracy and subversion. They each pled guilty, one by one. For their offenses they were sentenced to death by a Gifter.

Another council member stood and walked around the table. He was an elder and a Gifter. Facing the three kneeling on the bench, he raised his hands with the palms facing up, then he closed his eyes for just a moment before sharply closing both his hands into fists.

As his fists clenched, we heard the ribs in their chests crack and splinter, as if they were being crushed by a large vice. Blood erupted from their mouths as their own ribs pierced their hearts. We sensed their organs imploding with the single motion of the Gifter's hands. The three instantly fell over onto the ground, dead.

Guardians entered the room and dragged them out by their arms, like bags of trash. Two Guardians also removed the kneeling bench. I thought of how difficult it must've been for Seth to not use his Gifter ability of death on Tamson or Eric. He could've killed them both right then and there in the mansion.

Elijah instructed Eric to step forward to the middle of the circle. *They saved the best for last,* I thought wrily. And for good reason. Once Eric was in place, Elijah read out the charges:

"Eric Fuller, you have been found guilty of conspiring with a supremacist faction. Additionally, you have been found guilty of the murder of your sister, Sara and finally, for the attempted murder of Dr. Harris."

A short video appeared on the wall above the heads of the council members so Eric could clearly view it. It was a crime scene video. It was also the first time the three of us would see what had happened to Sara. Max was there, but we'd had no real idea of the horror. We braced ourselves but no preparation was enough. Sara's tiny body hung upside down from a rafter in the wine cellar. Her dress had fallen; draped over her face exposing her body. Her arms swayed slightly, stretched out with her fingertips hovering just above the stone floor. Her belly had been crudely sliced open in several directions until it was a gaping hole. Entrails, intestines, and organs dangled down. Her insides on the floor; strewn about in a puddle of blood.

It was a good thing my brain was still locked in a numb disconnected state, otherwise, my temper may have caused me to do something to Eric in front of the council that I may have regretted. Even so, my eyes began to glow and my chair vibrated. A wave of heat radiated from my body. Lucas squeezed my hand tighter, attempting to alert me to what he sensed was growing inside me. Blinding hate. The first reconnect of emotion in a day. I glanced at him in acknowledgment and tried to calm myself. The brightness of my eyes faded as I took a few deep breaths.

"Do you deny you maliciously murdered your sister, Sara? Do you deny you attempted to murder Dr. Harris?" Elijah asked Eric.

Eric proudly smirked and replied, "I do not deny any of it."

"You are hereby sentenced to be executed by way of severing," Elijah announced.

Eric's pride seem to drop off his face as he began to shake and I heard Seth whisper, "I can't be here for this." He got up, silently walking out the same door we had entered.

Sonya excused herself to follow Seth and sit with him while the execution continued. The rest of us had no desire to miss Eric's death, blood-thirsty as we were. I only hoped whatever was about to happen would be painful, prolonged, and epic. If anything, I'd be happy to see him hung upside down and gutted; as he had done to Sara. An eye for eye.

Moments later, the door opposite us opened and a massive Guardian walked through. The room immediately felt cold. The giant man had on sunglasses and coveralls. His girth and presence reminded me of Michael Myers but what he did next put him in a category above. He stepped directly in front of Eric, towering over him.

Eric's body trembled uncontrollably as he pissed on himself. The pool of urine grew larger by his feet as he desperately pleaded for his life.

Everyone stayed completely still and silent, deaf to his cries for mercy.

The executioner tore the front of Eric's shirt, exposing his torso. He then produced a large knife, cutting deep parallel lines down each side of Eric's chest as he wept. The Guardian dropped the knife and then forcibly shoved his monstrous hands into each of those cuts. He grabbed onto Eric's ribcage through the muscle tissue, his fingers interwoven between the ribs.

Eric's screams were so visceral and intense that it could only be described as otherworldly.

The sight was ... fascinating. Where did they come up with this fresh hell?

The Guardian slowly began to pull Eric's ribcage apart until his torso cracked in two. A brilliant spray of blood filled the air. The red plume hung above them like a cloud, and time itself seemed to stop. I held my breath, focused on the slow-motion shower head of blood-fly above. Inexplicably, in that moment, I could still sense a faint heartbeat in Eric.

The Guardian took his hands out of Eric's body, grasped Eric's head with both hands and twisted it clean off what was left of his body. Then he tossed the head to the ground.

No more heartbeat after that. I was so jazzed by the sight I desperately wanted to clap and shout, encore! Encore! It took a lot to stop myself from cheering. I'm not ashamed to admit that it was both the most devastating and the most awesome thing I'd ever observed. Justice had been done. I was satisfied.

The council adjourned now that the executions were complete. Max, Lucas, and I went out to check on Seth. He and Sonya were on the couch embracing each other as she was trying to comfort him. She held him and rubbed his back gently. There was no question that Seth agreed Eric's death was appropriate but to hear that screaming must have been traumatic on a level I could not comprehend. Me, on the other hand, I wanted to see it again. And again. Lucas looked pretty content as well and let out a peaceful long sigh. His obvious relief that it was over was not noticed by Seth. Evols tend not to retain a whole lot of tact, specifically the older Evols who drop much of their pleasantries. And I ... well, I was a baby Evol mess as far as emotions were concerned.

Max pulled me aside to say he and I were to meet with Elijah in the library.

We made our way toward the library through the underground maze of tunnels and I remarked how crazy huge the hidden structure was, and how neat I found it. That's when he informed me that I was standing in Elijah's home. I hadn't seen that coming, I'd just assumed it was a secret meeting place for the elders and council members. "He lives here? How long has he been beneath the wall?" I asked.

"Oh, I'd say about a thousand years now. He moved in once he became a member of the council. It's not required you move here but he just wanted to," Max replied.

"Seems like it would be a pretty cool place to live. Except for the wailing above that I can still hear, it's creepy," I commented.

"Yes, it is creepy, I agree. But you do get used to it over time. I don't think Elijah even notices it anymore," he said.

Once in the library, my mouth dropped. I was thinking it would be like a home-sized library or even maybe university size. Nope! A cavern, that's where I was standing, inside a cavern. It was huge, stadium-size huge, and filled to the brim with books. Max saw my face and explained that it was where they kept all the archives, journals, and historical documents. To be honest, I thought of Batman, then the Bat Cave. I was hoping Alfred would appear to offer a witty joke or refreshments. Crazy awesome echo too. I'm not sure Max appreciated me testing out the acoustics. Oh well, I thought it was cool.

Elijah greeted us and asked us to take a seat by his desk. "Emma, I understand the last few days have been unbelievably stressful and trying. I have no doubt you cannot wait to fly away tomorrow. I don't blame you! But Max and I wanted to speak with you apart from the others before you readied yourself for bed," he said.

"Okay, I'm all ears, gentlemen. Shoot," I replied.

Max started, "There are many creatures, beings, and entities on our planet that not even we can explain or comprehend. Many of them slip into our world during the linking process."

I obviously looked as confused as I felt. Complete with a tilted head.

Elijah continued, "The linking process is the moment a child receives its soul. Imagine a window that's opened in between the folds of space. A soul travels through the window and then the window shuts. But if an entity attaches itself to a soul, then it can trail in behind the soul and into our world," he explained.

"All right, I think I'm following you but why are you telling me this?" I asked.

"We believe your abilities are not because of your transformation, per se. Our gift unlocked what was already within you. Something attached itself to the soul your body was given at birth. The gift Seth gave you is what we believe triggered the entity to flourish!" Max exclaimed.

"Furthermore," Elijah added, "we don't know for certain what the entity is but all signs point to it as being a Lost One. I know it's just a legend or fairytale but Emma, you have so many connections with those beings," he stated.

"Oh, come on fellas. Not this again. You two do realize you're making my already significantly individual situation into some kind of circus? The very thing Tamson and his Nazi goons hated. The whole time I was human I had something unseen attached to me? That's what you're saying?" I asked.

Elijah held his hand up and replied, "You're not a freak. We're just trying to help you. We want you to be comfortable with who you are but that means we must figure out who that is. You've developed different gifts than most of us. And that's okay. But if we know which kind of entity attached itself to you then perhaps we can help you better. A Lost One is a distinct possibility," he said.

Instead of being placated, my irritation grew as my patience had worn thin. I embarked on a mini rant. I informed them that I realized after all I had been through and seen I shouldn't be discounting any possibility but it just was not true. It was a fairytale of a being they didn't even have a real name for. They didn't know what our world looked like before the so-called 'resurfacing.' They knew so little about those beings that the story written was only like a page and a half long. That wasn't even a story, I told them. "I would sooner accept that I was a stupid sparkly vampire or a pixie with jaw malformations than any of this nonsense. I just want to go home!" I snapped, ending my childish outburst.

I got up to leave and Elijah stopped me, adding one more thing, "Emma! Max and I truly hope we are wrong about this. Vampires and pixies don't possess the power to destroy the world as we know it. A Lost One would have that power," he warned.

I stormed out; mumbling as I walked back to my room. I mean, what kind of good shit were these people smoking? It was because they were old as dirt, their minds had addled! Did they think I was just going to go along with this crap? I went along with Tamson's charms and look where that got me! Look where that got all of us! So, what if I was one of those fucked-up fairytale beings? What then? Huh? No one had any answers for that shit! *How was this my life now?* I thought. I was so outta there!

I made it to my room, slamming the door behind me, wrestled on my nightgown and climbed straight into bed. Lights out and goodnight fucking John-boy. I needed sleep to find me fast. The quicker morning came, the quicker I'd be on an airplane and out of that whole nightmare.

What was supposed to be an amazing adventurous Gathering had turned into a painful, murderous, and disgusting contest of betrayals and loss. You can rest assured I wasn't planning on attending anymore Gatherings or reunions or executions ... or any other functions held by the Evols. Thanks for the party. It was swell.

Chapter 19

The Hits Just Keep on Comin'

I stepped through the door of my Scottish cottage and left the prior week's events outside. A three-day trip to one country morphed into seven days of hell dragging us across multiple countries. Now, back in the country I currently called home, I was putting the whole experience in the rearview mirror. Although I hadn't been away for very long, I had a strong compulsion to clean the house before doing anything else.

I emptied my bags straight into the washing machine, dusted and straightened up an already immaculate living room. I scrubbed the tub, shower, and toilet, scouring everything because I felt mentally dirty. What we had gone through had left a gross layer of sadness and cleaning the house was my way of fixing that.

After several hours of useless housekeeping, it occurred to me that I had been pacing. Washing away the sadness was obviously not the only reason for my obsessive anxious sterilization. Moving around the house and working pointlessly was also a warning that I needed to feed. It wasn't my time of year but my body was telling me it was time to hunt, regardless. I use the word 'hunt' loosely. The animals came to me. One perk of this mysterious craving for blood was I didn't have to work very hard to acquire it. Seems lazy, doesn't it? I didn't make the rules though.

Putting the washed clothes in the dryer I looked around, double checking that I'd cleaned everything, and making sure I was satisfied. I fixed myself a drink to bring with me to the side yard that faced the ocean where I built a fire, sitting myself down in a lawn chair to begin the normalizing process. The first step was to simply get lost looking out at the endless blue waters, breathing in deep and trying to sink into a meditative state of peace. Furthering the distance of that horrid so-called vacation was my then-priority.

Once night fell, I closed my eyes and sent out an alluring signal to any animal willing to listen. In no time at all a fawn trotted over to me. I gazed into his sweet adoring eyes while petting him. He wasn't a newborn but small enough that I could pull him up onto my lap, gangly legs and all. I caressed and cuddled the offering. When he was lulled asleep, I sank my angel teeth into his throat, cradling him as if he were a child until he was drained of blood. Then I carried the beautiful limp body to an embankment about a hundred yards from my home.

Gently, I set him on the edge of a cliff and watched as he slid down the side into the sea. Returning to the fire I realized I didn't want to drag my bloody clothes into the recently made spotless home. So I stripped right there, tossing them into the fire and sat naked, finishing my drink before heading to the shower. Mission complete. Everything was once again as it should be. As it should have been all along. A quiet life without murder or mayhem.

As the weeks passed by, I began to feel like my old self again. Seth, Lucas, and I had texted each other when we arrived back at our individual homes after leaving Jerusalem. Just to ensure we had all made it safely but, other than that, we hadn't spoken since. This wasn't due to any disagreement, I believe our silence was the product of all we'd gone through. We were still loners at heart. Too much chaos had been dumped on us in too short a time and we were resetting ourselves, regrouping. Soon enough we would be back in each other's lives again.

After six months or so, Seth called me and we had an excellent conversation. He told me that Lucas had contacted him earlier, sounding to be in good spirits. I had also recently spoken with him and we planned for the three of us to meet up. Somewhere neutral, like a vacation, a *real* vacation. Seth was on board. We met up in the Azores. A gorgeous tiny chain of islands off the coast of Morocco. We really did have a great time. Lay in the sun, swam in the warm ocean, and ate tons of food to our hearts' content. It was a simple, stress free, and normal vacation with good friends.

I even showed Seth my cool ball of light trick. He also had no clue as to what it did but was enamored by it. I asked him not to tell Max or Elijah. I wasn't ready to share all my tricks just yet. More especially since I was still unsure of what the orb did or its importance. He encouraged me to keep practicing and growing my abilities. He believed one day they could help to keep me safe, much as my power to disappear had done in the past. Overall, I felt our trip was a huge success. It reconnected each of us to the other again.

During the time we spent together, Lucas brought up the idea of getting Elijah to visit his home for the purpose of meeting Tova. Seth and I agreed that might be a neat thing to do. If nothing else, it would put the suspicious coincidence to rest. Elijah didn't know about the bear on Lucas's property and Lucas wasn't planning on telling him. He thought it would be better to make up another reason to get Elijah to his house. After Elijah arrived, he would then introduce him to the bear and see where it went from there. That was a typical 'Lucas

Plan'—don't tell anyone anything and just let the chips fall where they may.

Seven years later, Lucas informed Seth and me that Elijah was going to visit him. I know it seems like a long stretch of time between our vacation and Elijah's visit. You have to understand that once you wrap your head around the theory of indefinite life, you don't rush to do anything. Much like how humans procrastinate even though their lives are over in a flash, Evols are procrastinators too. Very Ent-like. A simple task that humans might push off for months, Evols can push off for decades. When you consider that, Lucas moved pretty fast actually. Seth and I wanted to be there. Lucas was excited we were going to be together again. Us joining him would take the pressure off to entertain an elder by himself.

During those seven years the boys and I were in constant contact. Countless video calls, emails, and a few trips to visit each other. Our bonds grew to be undeniably unbreakable. The bond with my children, however, had degraded. My attempts to reach out to them over the years were erratic. Even though I'd been trying to keep a distance, it was so hard to completely dislocate. But both had grown impatient with me. They couldn't understand why I wouldn't visit them or allow them to visit me any longer. They had aged but I had not.

It was an unfortunate side effect that Evols must pull away from their families, sooner rather than later for the benefit of all involved. We stay frozen in time for the first three hundred years or so. Not only had I not aged, but I also became younger looking by a decade.

The grip of pain hit me from time to time that I was going to lose my two remaining children. They would age out and die long before I would. I understood that I would have died if Seth hadn't shown up all that time ago, that I would've left them too early in life at the age of forty-nine but ... that suddenly felt like it would have been better; I should have died. It's the natural order of things. Parents are supposed to die first. Burying my youngest son all those years ago was where I was headed right then, with Josh and June. They would die and I would be left with the pain again. That knowledge forced me to pull away from them to begin that process. I knew they would remember me as the mother who abandoned them. That hurt the most.

Lucas and I spoke almost daily over the months leading up to Elijah's visit. Seth and I coordinated our flights to land around the same time as Elijah. That way Lucas could pick us all up at one time. No one likes making multiple trips to the airport. We were happy to see Elijah again. He was an uncommonly kind man with a wealth of knowledge unmatched. I was looking forward to staring into his aqua eyes; they fascinated me. Years earlier, I had to stop myself from staring too long in a manner that was probably creepy. He had to be used to it though by then.

The day before I was preparing to fly to America, I texted Lucas, but he didn't respond. The day passed by without a response. I texted Seth to see if he had heard from Lucas. Seth hadn't, so he also attempted to contact him but with no luck. We tried not to worry about it, figuring Lucas was just out shopping and getting his house ready for guests. The next morning neither of us heard from him still. I called Elijah who was just about to board his plane. I didn't alarm him about Lucas's radio silence, I just convinced myself everything was fine and we'd see him at the airport in a few hours.

Seth arrived first and waited for Elijah's plane to land. An hour later, my plane touched down. We met in the baggage area after

Elijah and I processed through immigration. Another hour went by and still no sign of Lucas. Eventually, we decided to rent a car so we could drive to his house. Elijah knew something was up but he didn't ask, letting us handle the situation. That was a perk of being an elder; you sat back and watched, more see than do.

When we drove up to Lucas's property, we spotted both of his dogs running free. That was when I pushed the panic button. Lucas would not have allowed those two to just roam around by themselves. Seth knocked on the door and looked through the windows. He found the spare key underneath a planter on the porch. As soon as the door opened we smelled blood. My heart began beating from my chest and we made our way to the source of the scent. In the dining room, the table was pushed all the way over to the wall and one chair was in the center of the room. Under the chair and throughout the room, the floor was thick with blood. From wall to wall a large amount of still coagulating blood.

The scent in the air was that of Lucas. Every drop of blood on the floor was his.

Seth ran off frantically through the house, calling Lucas's name, searching each room. My first thought was, *why did all the bad shit happen in dining rooms?*

Elijah solemnly turned to me. "No one would survive with that much blood loss," he said.

Seth came back to us. There were no signs that Lucas was in the house. He then went outside to the backyard, quickly walking the perimeter of the property. Lucas wasn't outside either. I didn't know what to do. None of what was happening felt real. My mind screamed, *Are you kidding me?* Another nightmare on the horizon? Was this to be the standard? Stumbling upon blood or destruction every few years? I could've stayed in the military for that.

"Seth, I'm going to call Sonya and probably end up handing the phone to you for information. Stay here a minute," Elijah instructed him.

"Shouldn't we call the cops?" I asked.

"No, Emma. We have our own investigators for Evol situations. Human police wouldn't know what to do with all this. Our investigators are located throughout the world. We should have some close by," Elijah explained. He immediately called Sonya and I heard him talking to her. "We have a suspicious death, Sonya. Send our closest investigators to my location."

He had said the word death. He said it out loud. He was that positive Lucas was somehow dead and his body missing? Was it a kidnapping? Did one of the hidden faction kill him and then dispose of his body? How could he be dead? I didn't understand. I had just spoken to him two days earlier. Everything was fine. It was fine! While my mind was going into shutdown mode Elijah handed the phone to Seth. He described the scene to Sonya and how much blood was on the floor. After a minute more he hung up the phone, handing it back to Elijah.

"Sonya is sending a team to investigate but based on the sheer amount of blood, she thinks there is zero chance Lucas is alive. It's just not physically possible, even for an Evol. We can't heal ourselves if we don't have any blood left in our bodies," Seth explained as he pointed at the blood-covered floor.

"That's easily five liters of blood, at least. I'm so sorry Emma, I'm at a loss right now. I can't think straight. This doesn't make any sense. Where's his body? There are no other unusual scents that I can pick up. He's just vanished!" Seth rambled, clearly upset.

I went to the living room and sat on the couch. Elijah continued fielding phone calls. I stared at the wall in front of me. I wasn't jumping into action, I wasn't crying. Catatonic would probably be the correct word for my state of being. Hollow, gutted, and dry.

The investigation team arrived and begun buzzing around the house. Here and there they went, combing through everything, collecting blood samples and fingerprints from around the door, the kitchen, and in the dining room. I sat like a stone statue, didn't even look at any of them. A lump of flesh with no conscience or input.

One of the investigators asked me to leave the room. I did not move. He asked two more times and then reached for my arm. I snapped my head up, piercing him with fiery rings of copper gold. The house began to vibrate ever so slightly. That stopped him and he promptly backed up. Elijah was stunned by my reaction and quickly inserted himself between the investigator and me, insisting that we go outside while the team did their work.

I followed his orders without thought and we moved to the back porch. A strong gust of wind hit me in the face the second the door opened and I caught the scent of a bear nearby. The breeze instantly pulled me from the catatonic state and my fiery eyes faded. I knew what I needed to get done. If there was nothing I could do for Lucas, then at the very least I might be able to accomplish the purpose of our visit. I truly couldn't think of anything else. *It was now or never*, I thought.

With no emotion in my voice, I made a request of Elijah. "I need you to do me a favor. I would like you to stand with me out in the yard. Okay?" I asked.

He did so with no questions asked in return. We moved twenty feet from the back porch; into the grass. He had a bit of trouble due to the recent rain and his cane kept sinking into the softened earth.

When I was satisfied we were far enough out, I stopped. We stood next to each other facing the woods. Another strong breeze came at us from behind that blew past, swirling its way into the forest. A moment later we heard the sound of a large animal's paws trampling the ground, moving fast in our direction and picking up speed.

A giant brown bear galloped out of the tree line, headed straight to where we were standing. Elijah stepped back in a panic and I grabbed his hand and told him to trust me. Reluctantly, he stood still, heart pounding. I could feel it. For a second I thought twice. I didn't want to be responsible for giving our oldest elder a heart attack.

The bear sat down not a foot from us and I reached over to scratch its shoulder. She was intensely sniffing Elijah, moving her head back and forth. Inching herself closer and closer toward him. She nudged Elijah's leg, wanting his attention.

I took Elijah's hand and reassured him it would be okay, placing it on top of the bear's head. He smiled, petting it lovingly until suddenly his expression changed. It was as if a heavy, hundred-pound emotion dropped down on him. He let go of his cane and as it fell to the ground, he put both of his hands on the bear's head. He began to laugh in disbelief and joy. He and the bear were suddenly face to face and that's when I knew. That was the moment he felt her. He saw into her soul.

"It's Tova! This is Tova, my Gifter. Oh, Emma. How is this possible?" he asked through the tears that wet his face.

No one had told Elijah about the bear or her name. That was all the proof I needed. He spoke her name, Tova. I explained to him this was the reason Lucas had wanted him to visit. Lucas met her on this property more than a hundred years ago, right after he moved into the house. Animals were highly attracted to him, so he didn't think much about it. He had just come up with the name Tova, said it just popped into his head. I told Elijah how Lucas and Tova chased each other and rolled around in the grass quite often. They were friends. And we wanted to see if there was any validity to Tamson's story about his Gifter and Tova.

Elijah was glowing and giddy like a child. Tova sat and he hugged her massive body. She wrapped one of her huge paws around him, hugging him back. If I had not seen it with my own eyes, I wouldn't have believed it.

I continued to tell him it seemed impossible she could really be the same Evol-turned-bear from so long ago. That I had wanted to test it out. I assured him she didn't really know me. She had never come for just me. I figured that if I could get him out there and she came running; the mystery would be solved. "She smelled your scent, Elijah. Tova raced to us because of you. A Viking's love is eternal," I ended.

Elijah beamed with happiness and his aqua-blue eyes danced with joyful tears. "Thank you, Emma. Thank you so very much. I can't tell you what this means to me. This is the most incredible thing I've experienced in ... over three thousand years!" As he continued to pet her, he looked to the heavens. "If this is not the definition of the word miracle, then I don't know what is," he softly uttered.

Leaving Elijah consumed by his emotions and focused on Tova in the backyard, I quietly crept away. Aimlessly it seemed, I wandered down Lucas's driveway on foot and onto the dirt road, not a thought in my head, not a direction in mind. A voracious emptiness was growing inside me; a hollow dark cloud, wrapping itself around my body and suffocating my reason. Nothing good happened when any form of extreme emotion took hold of me.

I walked and I walked, and then I walked some more.

Chapter 20
The Depths

I believe whatever doesn't kill you, simply makes you stranger.
—*The Joker - Heath Ledger*

Soft hues of purple and red swirled above me. The sky seemed to breathe and sway as more of its secret colors revealed themselves. Folding in and out; gold ran into green, orange churned into violet. I raised my body to realize I was lying in a field. I was home, the dreamy peaceful sanctuary with my black wolf asleep by my side. I rose to my feet; my body draped in a long cloak made of pale blue velvet. The wolf and I wandered through tall grass toward a hill that was beckoning me. Everything was crystal clear and bright. As if in Technicolor, the brilliance of the trees, the ground, and the flowers were almost blinding to look at. I made my way up the grassy knoll and felt a deep longing within me gradually spread throughout my body.

Atop the knoll I saw a grand golden lake not far below. An old woman was standing at the water's edge and I called to her but she didn't turn to look at me. Her body seemed to be bent with age. While walking down to her I marveled at the extraordinary, vibrant vegetation and unbelievable pureness of the air. My wolf and I came to rest next to the woman by the lake. She had long hair that nearly touched the ground in the most beautiful shades of gray, white, and copper. She wore a robe similar to mine and her face was gentle and soft, aged and weathered. When she turned to smile at me my heart melted as warmth pulsed through me. She took my hand in hers and led me into the water.

A man's voice rang out over the knoll where I had been. He was waving his arm and motioning for me to come to him. I appeared to be too far away to recognize who he was but how, with my super vision, was I not able to see him clearly? The old woman insisted I follow her into the lake. We left my wolf on the shore as we stepped forward. The water was cool but not cold and it sparkled with the dance of life. We waded, hand in hand, until we were completely submerged. I could see beneath the surface with my eyes comfortably open. As I looked back to her, she released my hand and floated away. I needed air, but when I broke the surface of the water I found I was staring at a wall, not the sky.

I realized I was lying in a bed and the ceiling was in my room, in my Scottish cottage.

A spark of panic bolted through me. Wasn't I just at Lucas's house? I was just in America. *How did I get here?* I got up to search the house. There were no travel bags, I couldn't find my backpack, and no cell phone. I turned on the news to discover it was the next day. I didn't know how I'd gotten there or where my things were. I had no phone or landline. It dawned on me that I could call Seth by using my laptop. I opened it and placed the video call.

Seth answered, "Emma! Oh, thank God! We've been looking everywhere for you. You disappeared yesterday. Where are you? We'll come get you."

"Umm, I'm sitting in my house. In Scotland. I don't know how I got here. Are you still at Lucas's?" I replied.

"Your house!!?" he exclaimed. "We are still here. I have your bags and cell phone. I can mail them to you. I'm just so glad you're okay. Have you looked in a mirror yet Emma?" he asked, oddly.

I made a weird face. "No. Why? What's wrong?"

Seth pointed his finger at the screen. "Your eyes. The irises are black. Deep black and all glittery. Like the galaxy is swirling around your pupils,"

I got up from the table, more than a little alarmed and ran to the bathroom. My eyes *were* different. Anger had been the trigger in the past that changed my eye color but I wasn't feeling any emotion at that moment. Looking at those weird space-sky orbs now, I tried but couldn't get them to fade or change back. They weren't the brilliant rings of gold I'd produced before. Now, they'd upgraded to silky black metallic diamonds with infinitesimal random specks of light. Alien ... or demon? Why not a demon? I mean, I had raked Tamson across a fold in space and made the sky rain his blood. What else could I be if not evil? Fuck it. Whatever.

I returned to the laptop. "I don't know Seth. I don't know what to tell you. They look demonic to me," I said in a flat tone.

"No, they're gorgeous, they can't be demonic," he smiled.

"The most dangerous things in all worlds are gorgeous, Seth," I replied.

He tried to sidestep the subject and move on. "What's the last thing you remember, Emma?"

I thought as hard as I could. "The last thing I remember was an incident with a local man and then I was here," I answered.

"What incident? Start from the beginning," he insisted.

I tried to take it one step at a time and detail what I could recall. I was walking on a dirt road. It started to get dark. An intense heat began to grow within me. I could see my creature following me. I focused all my anger on the creature. I wanted to know its identity. I ran toward the creature through the woods. But no matter how much ground I gained, the creature stayed the same distance from me. I remember I gave up eventually and retraced my steps back to the road. An old pickup truck had slowly driven past me and then backed up. A man was driving. He rolled down the passenger window to talk to me, asked if I needed a ride and I told him no. He continued to drive next to me as I walked and again he asked if I needed a ride. I told him again, no. "This is where things go fuzzy Seth," I said, struggling to recall.

"Okay, okay. You're doing good, what else? Go slow, step by step," Seth encouraged me.

I continued as best I could. The man pulled the truck over in front of me and got out. He had a gun in his hand. He demanded I get in but I refused and tried to walk around him. He grabbed at me, so I broke away to run. He tackled me to the ground in the ditch beside the road. He was trying to get my pants off and unbuckling his. I do clearly recall biting him hard on his arm during the struggle. He stopped and quickly got off me, covering his ears with his hands, screaming in pain. Like there was a loud sound in his head. Blood started gushing from his eyes, ears, nose, and mouth. And then I woke up here in Scotland.

Seth tried to process my words as he spoke softly, "Well, that explains the dead guy we found high in a tree next to a running pickup truck. That also answers the question of what would happen if you bit a person with your angel teeth. I will have a Guardian take care of the body and the truck. Are you okay Emma?"

"I am. I think. I'm not really sure. This is nuts, man," I replied.

"I wouldn't worry about the asshole in the pickup truck. It sounds like you were a victim of opportunity. A woman walking alone on a deserted dirt road. You did the world a favor. I'm so glad you're okay. Or at least you appear physically okay," he said.

"What's been going on there at the house? Any sign of Lucas?" I reluctantly asked.

"Emma ... Lucas's Gifter called Sonya. He felt Lucas die a couple of days ago. It wasn't fake like I did with you at Tamson's mansion. Lucas is really gone. I can't express how sorry I am. We will be here a few more days while the investigation continues," he explained.

The news hit me hard, but I suppose I had already known it was coming. I seemed to speak on automatic. I could tell from Seth's expression that he knew. "Okay. I guess I'm going to order a new phone and colored contact lenses to hide my eyes. Thank you for shipping my bags. Keep me in the loop if there are any changes or discoveries?"

Seth nodded and with that, I ended the call and closed my laptop.

The thought of living in this world without Lucas was impossible to fathom. This was different from when I lost Jake. It felt much different anyway. Possibly due to the erratical Evol emotions or because I had imagined getting to be in Lucas's life for hundreds of years. This felt worse. You're told you are technically near immortal and then Evols start dropping dead? I was confused. I went to my bedroom, shut the curtains, and collapsed on the bed. I wanted to sleep the pain away. I sank down into a new low of depression. I slept off and on. Not eating or drinking much. I would get up just long enough to pee and take a sip of water. For days I wallowed in misery. All the amazing times I had spent with Lucas replayed on an endless loop in my head. I was so angry inside. An anger stitched together with such agonizing regret. If I hadn't met and fallen in love with him, I wouldn't have been lost in this paralyzing pain. Worse was that I never professed my love. He and I didn't physically act on our attraction, but I was solidly in love with him. I thought we had all the time in the world. It felt like a waste.

All the 'I should haves' and the 'Why didn't I?' regrets in my head crushed me. A steel beam lay on my chest, I couldn't breathe; I couldn't move under the weight. I needed a pill or something to take away the knot in my chest and the ache in my soul. How was I to continue without him? Even though we had lived on different continents, we always felt close, no matter the distance. But death was a distance too far.

After the sixth day, I made the decision to get out of bed and take a shower. It was a beautiful day, uncommonly warm for that time of year in Scotland. I opened all the windows to air out the cottage and tried to force some toast into my stomach. I wasn't better by any means, I was on autopilot. My body forced me to get up, not my heart or mind.

While checking outside for post which contained my new cell phone and contacts, I heard two cars moving in my direction. I stood at the door waiting to see who it was. Two Range Rovers drove over the hill and down my driveway. Among the Guardians who got out of the vehicles were Elijah and Sonya.

Have I described Sonya to you yet? No? She couldn't be more than five feet tall with thick, raven-black braided hair. Due to the advanced age on her face, I could only assume she dyed it that color. Curiously, I hadn't detected the smell of hair dye though the first time we met in Jerusalem. She spoke very few words but gave off an incredibly strong vibe of character. Elijah looked like a giant when they stood next to each other, but she was just as intimidating as he was. She was the type of person people would steer clear of at a party.

Much like me, she appears to have resting bitch face. It didn't mean she was upset. Some of us just look that way.

"Hello my friend. We come bearing gifts. Your personal effects," Elijah announced.

I invited them inside as a Guardian put my things down in the living room. They made themselves comfortable at the kitchen table while I fixed us some tea. We sat quietly for a bit, sipping. Elijah looked much older to me than he had just days earlier. The difference in his eyes from before he arrived at Lucas's home to now sitting at my table was distressing. Lucas's death and the subsequent investigation seemed to have drained the light from his spirit. Time was catching up with him. I wondered to myself how much longer he'd be with us.

Sonya interrupted my inner thoughts as she broke the silence first. "Your eyes are spectacular! They're like two black holes swirling glittery light around your pupils. Intriguing. Although, be sure to invest in some contact lenses before going outside," she remarked.

I nodded and pointed at the box I'd brought in from outside. "Got them," I replied.

"The Lucas homestead has been cleaned and released by our investigators. The investigation into his death will be ongoing until they find the person or persons responsible," Elijah said.

"What about his two dogs? And what will become of his house? I'm sure he has no family to speak of anymore," I asked.

"His dogs will be well taken care of. An investigator took a shine to them and they to him. As far as his house goes, it's yours Emma. He had a will in his office and left it to you some years ago," he explained.

"No, I don't want it," I sharply remarked. I just couldn't imagine being in his home again. Without him in it? That wasn't going to happen in any shape or form.

Sonya took out the deed from her purse and slid it over to me along with a pen to sign for it.

"Well, think about it for a while. Maybe you'll change your mind. Or you can sell it," Elijah encouraged me.

Silence fell again. After a moment or two, I had an epiphany. The perfect solution, I thought. I motioned for the Guardian to come over to the table, wrote something out on the document and pointed to the place on the form where a witness would sign. The Guardian signed his name and then I slid the deed across the table to Elijah.

"You should have the homestead, Elijah. Tova is there. You can visit her whenever you want. I just signed over the deed to you, as you can see. It's yours now," I told him.

Elijah looked at the deed, then to Sonya and back to me, disbelief on his face. "I don't know what to say Emma. That's most generous and very kind of you. It hadn't occurred to me when or how I'd get to see Tova again. Thank you," he said with a warm smile.

We attempted idle chitchat after that but it was a struggle. Lucas weighed heavy on all our minds and Elijah, sensing I wanted to be alone again, stood up and said they needed to catch their connecting flight to Jerusalem. I walked them out to say our goodbyes. Sonya stayed by my side after the others had gone to the cars. She told me she would like to give me peace if I'd allow her to. I agreed, although I hadn't a clue what she meant.

She turned toward me and wrapped her arms around my body, hugging me. It was a prolonged hug while she whispered something to me in a language I didn't recognize, which was odd as my Evol brain knew all languages. I thought it did anyway. As she embraced me the knot in my chest relaxed and my sadness eased; the cinder blocks of pain seemed to fall from my shoulders. Sonya could remove hurt or grief, to a point. That's what she had been doing with Seth outside the courtroom chamber, I realized, during Eric's trial.

As I watched them drive away, I couldn't help but wonder if I'd ever see them again. Something about our parting felt very final. I went back into the house and unboxed my new phone and contact lenses, I cooked myself a proper dinner and tried to watch a movie. The sense of loss was still with me but I was able to function in a more normal capacity. Sonya's gift to me, I believe, helped save my life.

For the time being, it gave me a little breathing room so I could work on my emotions in a healthier way. I really could've used her touch when Jake died. I didn't know what the future held in store for me. I just had to make it from one day to the next to find out.

Chapter 21
Resurgence

The end of nine months was approaching. Nine months without Lucas. I could feel Sonya's gift of peace waning. Not that I'd been all happy and smiling before then but I was sensing the tragedy of his death creeping back in. My footsteps steadily became heavier and slower. The ability to get out of bed was failing. I had begun another descent into darkness and heartache; checking the mail was a chore, going into town to shop felt like a huge inconvenience. What small joys I got from living in my cottage soon deteriorated. Whatever had been holding me together for those nine months was about to let go.

The postman visited my cottage because I hadn't checked the mail in weeks. He was making sure I still lived there, and he had a bundle of my mail to give me. I answered the door without even putting contacts in my eyes. Not that I had done it on purpose. It wasn't until he stopped in the middle of a sentence to stare that I realized what was wrong. I looked down at the stack of mail in my hand and thanked him for the personal delivery, assuring him I would be mindful to check the mailbox in the future. Then I closed the door and hoped he would just think he was seeing things.

As I poured through the junk mail, I came across a letter from Elijah.

He had retired from the Grand Council and moved to his new home, Lucas's home. In his letter he explained that he was overdue to retire and needed an extended break from council life. The council members all moved up one rung, which had left a vacancy at the bottom. Max was offered the opening and accepted. It really wasn't a retirement, per se. You can't really retire from being an Evol but you can eventually get too old to deal with it. Elijah knew his time had come.

He wanted to live out his last days in the seclusion of the mountains, far from council dealings. It was the first time he had permanently lived anywhere else besides Jerusalem in over a thousand years. His letter spoke of peace and serenity, the love he had for his new vegetable garden, his daily visits with Tova. Although she couldn't speak words, he could feel her spirit so keenly it was just as good. One of the Guardians took a picture of Elijah and Tova together in the backyard. A copy was enclosed in the letter.

Normally, a letter such as that would've made me feel all warm and fuzzy inside. It did not. I was still spiraling down. I was happy for him but couldn't feel it nor express it. My walls were closing in on me. The heavy beam of steel had begun to press on my chest again and a desperate longing to escape to my lavender planet was bubbling constantly. Lucas's face haunted my every waking hour. Day by day it got worse. And, to add insult to injury was the video call I would receive from Seth.

"Hey Emma. How've you been? I haven't heard from you in a while?" he asked.

"So-so. Life comes and goes. What can you do, right?" I replied.

"True. True," Seth began. "Listen, there's something I want to tell you. I've debated for a long time whether I should or not, but in the end, I think it's something you should know."

"What is it?" I asked, dully.

"Lucas made me promise never to share it but I feel you should know. He had teeth like yours. He had angel teeth. Well, I believe that's what they were anyway," Seth said.

"I don't understand. His teeth were normal and he never mentioned anything about it. What do you mean, you believe they were angel teeth?" I asked, the fog lifting slightly.

Seth explained. He had me recall how Lucas's Gifter was a piece of garbage and didn't show up for Lucas until three years after he gifted him. During all that time alone, Lucas really thought he'd gone crazy. And what made it worse was that he was reborn with sharp teeth. The way Lucas described them to Seth, they sounded like mine. Anyway, within weeks of him being on his own, he used an iron filing tool to flatten them down. He just wanted to be normal again. He didn't want to keep scaring his neighbors with his smile. He had no idea he was an Evol or what he was at all.

"You're not messing with me, are you Seth? Are you being serious? What. The. Fuck? When did he tell you this?" I asked.

"Some time ago. About a hundred and fifty years ago, I believe. His Gifter didn't even know. By the time he showed up, Lucas had long since filed his teeth flat. And because his Gifter was—is an asshole, Lucas sure as hell wasn't going to tell him. When we met you and saw your teeth, I was certain he would tell you eventually," Seth said.

"Did he have anything else unusual, like feeding on animals or being able to jump through space folds?" I asked. I was both furious and confused by that point.

"He has never shared with me anything else that might've been unusual; other than his teeth," Seth replied.

"Do you think he didn't tell me because he thought I was a freak and he didn't want to be one too?" I asked as tears were forming in my eyes.

"Come on, Emma, no. Not in the least. I'm so sorry I didn't tell you sooner, but he made me promise not to tell. Now that he's gone, I thought it didn't matter," Seth said. "He loved you, Emma. Lucas truly loved you," he finished.

With tears streaming down my cheeks, I ended the video call. I didn't want to hear any more. Whatever little of Sonya's gift I had left within me was officially gone. I, once again, retreated to my bed. I stayed there for months. My emotions swung from prolonged sobbing to extreme angry outbursts and screams. How much more were we alike? Could I have learned anything from Lucas and his experiences? He loved me? Oh my God! He loved me too! Why was he dead? Why am I now cursed to live like this? Alone, with no Lucas.

As my wallowing continued, life moved on without me.

Spring became summer and summer, fall. I refused to talk to Seth or Max. Even Elijah reached out to me over text but I ignored him too. There were rare days where I would clean myself up and try to eat something. It didn't last though. In no time I'd be back in bed, drowning myself in sorrow. I escaped to my dream planet often and stayed there for days with the wolf by my side, under the lavender skies. I wanted to stay there but the woman of the golden lake sent me back time and again. Back to my empty cottage in Scotland.

One day my laptop had been pinging. A video call notification. The pinging went on for two days, every couple hours. I finally shuffled over and opened it. The failed video attempts were from Max. I really didn't want to deal with anyone, but I also just wanted him to stop calling. I returned the video call.

"Emma, thank you for getting back to me," he said. He was under The Wailing Wall in Jerusalem. I had forgotten he was now a council member.

"What's up Max? What can I help you with?" I asked, irritated.

"We recently captured the last three of the supremacy faction members. We've been interrogating them about Lucas. Although he didn't meet their idea of different, he did help you and was friends with you. We thought maybe it was the faction that killed him. None of them have admitted to anything yet," Max explained.

"I want to speak to them. How long do I have to get there before they're sentenced?" I asked, suddenly fired up.

"No, Emma. That's not going to happen. We can't take the chance that you'll lose control."

"I want to speak to them Max," I repeated.

"We cannot allow a blood rain over the Western Wall in Jerusalem! Can you grasp what the ramifications would be if that happened here? Of all the places in the world, this is the last place you'd want that to happen! The panic! We are talking worldwide catastrophe. You know how biblical humans are, they'd think the world was ending," he said anxiously.

I sat, still staring at him.

He was about to say more when suddenly, I was gone. He looked around through the laptop screen, saying my name, trying to figure out what had just happened.

Then, *POOF!* I was standing behind him, in Jerusalem.

He jumped from his chair. There I was in all my glory. Ratty old sweatpants, gross house slippers, a stained dirty T-shirt, and my way-too-long hair a tangled mess. That's what depression can look like from the outside.

"Emma! Dammit! You shouldn't be here!" he yelled.

"Either you take me to them, or I will find them my way, Max. You don't want that, do you?" Malevolence was my middle name, right then.

"Son of a bitch. Fine, let's go," he reluctantly replied.

As we walked, Max called Sonya from his cell phone. She was elsewhere under the wall but he told her I had appeared to him in his office and we were headed to the prisoners. He also informed her that she should gather as many of the Guardians as possible to meet us there. He was scared I'd do something that could expose us. Something so big humans would see it and lose their collective marbles. He briefed me that the prisoners were looking rough because they'd been tortured for days. Keep in mind, Evols heal so rapidly, the way you have to torture an Evol was ten-fold beyond anything ever perpetrated on humans.

We reached the chamber and walked through the door. Sonya, with about twelve Guardians, stood around three severely destroyed-looking Evols. Blood spatter was on the walls, the ceiling, and on the floor, full-on carnage. As I approached one of the barely alive men, he freaked. He wanted to know what I was.

"Demon!" he cried out.

I realized it was my metallic sparkly black eyes, perhaps my skin, lightly glistening with Shimmer did not help. Before long, all three of the prisoners were calling me the Devil as they tried to get out of the room. I thought that was fucking stupid, where were they trying to go?

I stood directly in front of one of them. The Guardians pulled in close; surrounding me and trying to prepare themselves for ... anything. *Must be difficult,* I thought. Without thinking about it, I conjured the purple orb of light in my hand and held it up level with the man's chest. "Look me in my eyes," I said.

He shook his head, no, and refused to look at me or the orb.

"Look at me!" I shouted, causing the chamber to rumble and sand to fall from the stone ceiling. Lights flickered as the Guardians pulled in closer.

The prisoner met my gaze, which instantly froze his body. He couldn't move or look away. The chamber became still as silence fell and I turned the orb to his chest, slowly pressing my hand forward.

The orb entered his body through his shirt and without damaging his skin. I kept my hand on his chest as the orb was still connected to the palm of my hand. Images of the man's life started to flood my mind. Birthdays, weddings, vacations, his job, his friends, etc. All his meetings with Tamson and the supremacist faction. All his dealings with any of the faction members. All his infractions against Evols and humans who did not meet their standards. I saw it all. In little less than a minute, I'd seen his complete history. I lifted my hand from his chest and the orb retreated from his body, releasing his locked gaze from my eyes.

I turned to Max and Sonya. "He didn't have anything to do with Lucas. None of them did. Lucas's name never came up, nor were any of them at his house. You can kill them now. By the way, they deserve the cage." There was more to share though. "You're missing one member. Of all the people you've captured, one is still MIA. She's a white chick with recently cut, short blonde hair. Her name is Jamie. I saw her face clearly at many of the meetings. She was the one who suggested to Tamson that he split my head in two with an axe," I added emotionlessly.

Max and Sonya looked at each other and both gasped. "Oh no

way. Could it be? We might know who that is!" Sonya exclaimed to Max.

As I was turning to exit the room, two more Guardians walked in. I stepped past them and then backed up to take a second look at one of them.

"That's her. The Guardian, that's Jamie," I said, pointing at her.

Max snapped his fingers and the other Guardians pounced on her. Jamie was able to put up quite a fight. They basically destroyed the room trying to get ahold of her as Max, Sonya, and I, just stood back watching.

Once she was subdued and shackled, I walked out. Taking a seat in the parlor outside the chamber, I felt I was done. All the faction members had been captured and I was still no closer to knowing what had happened to Lucas. For the first time in years, I craved a cigarette. Of course, I knew no one there would have any so I sat and waited until Max and Sonya emerged.

"Emma?" Sonya stepped up close to me. "How did you do that with your hand?" she asked.

"I don't know," I said. "I've been able to produce that orb for some time now but didn't know what it did. I came here to test out a theory I had and it worked." I shrugged. I was unfazed by the whole experience. Just over it.

"We could really use your talents here, Emma. What do you say? Will you help our kind get back to the peaceful open-minded people we used to be?" Max asked me.

"Help *our kind*? You want me to fix us. I didn't even want to be an Evol! I wasn't given a choice! And to be perfectly blunt about it, I'm not entirely sure I am one of *our kind*. You heard them in there. I'm a demon. The Devil, no less!" I angrily shouted at them.

"Listen, you're obviously still mourning the loss of Lucas. We understand and we are with you," Sonya said earnestly. "We will be here to help you through anything. Anything. Please don't shut us out. If you don't want to help us, that's fine. But don't shut us out."

I stood from the couch, released a sigh and told them I would talk to them later. I felt my eyes light up with silvery specks as I vanished. Returning to my cottage living room. After all that, and for some odd reason, only one thought crossed my mind. I wondered if I could jump space with luggage. I mean, if I could take stuff with me, then I wouldn't ever have to fly in an airplane again. *No more airports!* The first time it happened in my basement I had no control over it. The second time was in the mansion. I did do it myself but again, had no control over where I was going. Not directly. Subconsciously, I obviously did because we landed in Seth's villa but I now had control over where I wanted to go. To a point, anyway. Why not take luggage?

Looking down at myself I realized I was a mess. *Crackhead* came to mind. I showered and dressed in some decent clothes, braided my hair and even put on a little makeup. I made myself a sandwich and a cup of very hot, sweet tea. I suddenly felt determined and it was like energy flooding my system.

After finishing my meal, I tested out the luggage thing by putting a backpack on. My clothes made the jump so why not a backpack? Sitting on a dining room chair I closed my eyes and jumped space to see my daughter in America. It had been many years since I'd seen either of my children in person.

The backpack did not make it. That sucked.

I appeared outside her home. I stood on the opposite side of the road, sitting on a grass verge near a bus stop sign. I could have been a passenger in waiting, had anyone cared to look. I had an unobstructed view of June and her family through their big bay window. They were sitting inside, around a table, eating dinner. I didn't have to get close to see that her children, my grandbabies, were teenagers now. In that instant, my Evol eyesight was a boon. Such a beautiful family. She had done so well with her career and her children. She was now the head of her own landscaping company and her children were on track to attend just about any college they wanted to. My body filled with pride. I so badly wanted to run in through the door and hold her. It was the first time I had fled through space in a casual manner for a purpose such as this. I don't know why I hadn't done it in the past. I guess it never occurred to me to try.

My heart ached as I watched them. I could not handle visiting Josh in the same day, I knew that much for sure. It would've been too many emotions at one time. I decided it was better to visit him a few days later.

He too had grown and branched out in his life. Josh was an instructor now, teaching the next generation the subtle art of not letting nuclear powerplants fail or explode. His two boys were preparing to join the military as junior officers, doing incredibly well. Yes, my pride cup overflowed. I stayed another thirty minutes just enjoying the sight of my grandchildren and daughter. It felt like I was watching a TV show of a family I was no longer a part of. *Well, I wasn't,* I thought.

Finally, I closed my teary eyes and thought of the cottage. And just like that, I was standing in my living room again. The backpack that hadn't made the trip was still on the chair. *Dammit.* I would have to fly like everyone else. *Gross.*

Chapter 22
Evols and Vampires and Leprechauns! Oh My!

The greatest trick the Devil ever pulled
was convincing the world he didn't exist.
—Charles Baudelaire

We are going to jump ahead twenty-five years. To the year 2066. I will apprise you of what occurred during that quarter of a century. Just the highlights. First, let me do the math for you. I was given the gift when I was forty-nine years old. That was in the winter of 2022. A year later, I met, officially, Seth, Lucas, and Sara, which was after I turned fifty. Fast forward to this point, I'd been on this earth a total of ninety-three years. With my near pristine skin and long thick hair, I had the look of a young forty-year-old. Still unchanged. All my older relatives had died, my mother, father, aunts and uncles, and even most of my cousins.

June passed away from pancreatic cancer. Her children were still alive and well and my son was gray-haired and had just become a great-grandfather. I hadn't been able to be in June and Josh's presence for the last forty years. Not with their knowledge anyway. I did jump through space to be at my daughter's hospital bedside. In the middle of the night, as she was taking her last breaths, I was there. I held her hand. She felt me but didn't open her eyes again. It was peaceful. Giving birth to her had been a drawn-out, painful screaming match. And yet at her end, there was silence. Maybe because I was already aware of her illness it didn't break my heart as I imagined it would. I was grateful there was no more pain for her. It was serene.

To the question of what I'd been up to through those years. Well, shortly after I returned from my surprise visit to Jerusalem and interrogating prisoners, I wallowed some more. And some more. Until the day came that I knew I needed a change. I locked up the cottage and moved to my Italian villa in the northern countryside. In a week from thought to move completion, I just up and went.

Italy was wonderful, incredible in almost every way. The scenic views, the food, OMG the food! And the people were amazeballs. My little villa wasn't as secluded as the Scottish cottage but it was covered in the most beautiful pink flowering bougainvillea vines. The last home astride of steep mountain pass which did afford me some privacy. The villa backed up against a thick forest which gave me direct access to the 'walking' food I needed. The home itself was only one bedroom, however, there was a Murphy bed in the living room which I got a kick out of. I'd never seen one except on TV. I could've spent a lot of money on a larger, more separated home but I couldn't justify blowing that much money on a home only I lived in.

I did say it was incredible in *almost* every way. What I hadn't bothered to research before moving there was the wild animal situation. Deer? No, no. Not just deer. The wild animals up north are much larger. It was sort of like being back on my American mountain again, except the animals in Italy act as though they're on steroids. I wasn't quite prepared for the size and bullheadedness of their inhabitants.

There were Marsican brown bears, Lynx, Ibex (which are huge

rams), and wolves, just to name a few. That was good news and a happy accident since I had no clue what was in store for me. My feedings had increased over the years. What began as a once-a-year thing gradually grew to be around a quarterly event. Want to know a fun fact about Ibex? They're stubborn and strong as fuck! An Ibex would heed my siren call but somehow also fight it every step of the way. Hilarious to witness. They seemed to change their minds back and forth. Three willing steps forward and then a step backward as if they were being yanked on an invisible rope. I got a kick out of that, sorry. My strength also increased by leaps and bounds. That was useful when dealing with animals as large as them. I still needed strength to get rid of their bodies.

My new permanent metallic black eyes allowed me to see new things. The veil was becoming transparent. I hated wearing contact lenses in public but it was a necessity. However, the contacts didn't prevent me from noticing the beings that had been previously hidden. For example, there was a man in the town square. A very handsome and disgustingly charming man. He oozed confidence and arrogance. Dressed similarly to the local residents to blend in, but he wasn't from there. He was not even human. No one around him could see the true color of his eyes except for me. Oh, they were so green. Electric green with energy waves pulsing through them.

I would spy on him in an almost stalker manner. Following him through the farmers' market and to a favorite café of mine. It was there I pretended to bump into him to get his attention. He offered to buy me a coffee and we sat down at a table together. He threw at me the usual flirt techniques. I almost forgot I was trying to figure out what he really was. Before I could help myself, I commented on his stunning eyes. When it dawned on him that I could see his true eye color, everything changed. The full veil that was draped over him vanished and he suddenly appeared ancient with large droopy ears, bald, fingernails chipped and dirty, and a stench! He bolted from his chair, knocking it over, and ran out of the café. I was left sitting there with my mouth hanging open and my macchiato untouched, the other patrons staring at me.

I called Max that night.

"Hi Max. How are things under the wall these days?" I asked.

"Emma! Things have been good. Nothing crazy to speak of. We haven't spoken since you moved. How's Italy been treating you?" he replied.

"Italy is amazing. Truly great so far. But listen, I wanted to run something by you. It's about other beings on Earth's plane. What do you know?" I asked.

"There are many, we think," he replied, his manner suddenly becoming focused. "There have been Evols in the past that have recorded seeing strange things or unusual people on their travels. Why? What have you seen?" he asked excitedly.

"Well, I met a really attractive man with electric green eyes and in the moment he realized I could see them, he changed. It was like his true self was revealed. Decrepit and gross, and the smell was unbearable!" I exclaimed.

"Ah! It sounds like you saw a troll, Emma! You met an actual troll! I bet you were thinking he was a leprechaun at first, didn't you? Was he dashing with lots of charm? I bet he was. How great is this! You can see the underworld! How long has this been happening?" Max looked like he was trying to contain himself, coming undone with giddiness.

"Umm, trolls and leprechauns? You're not serious, are you? No freaking way. I've been seeing things since my eyes changed to black. It was just a few small changes, a little here and there at first in

Scotland but now there's larger changes I can't ignore," I responded.

"Oh, I'm dead serious. This is fantastic! You can help fill in some of the holes we have in our *The Book of Beings*! Don't be alarmed by the trolls, by the way. They're harmless. To us they are anyway. And for you, they don't represent any danger," he said, still beaming with excitement.

"Okay then. That's cool, I guess. I can email you the details of the troll if you like? Out of curiosity, are there hidden beings I *should* be cautious of?" I asked.

"And that's the problem Emma. We simply don't have enough information on any of them to say if they're dangerous to us or not. If I were a betting man, I'd say *you* were the most dangerous ticket in town," he replied, giggling.

That was slightly disconcerting. The giggling, I mean. "Well, if I see anything else crazy, I'll let you know. I'll email you and we can discuss updating that book of yours. Take care, Max. Say hi to Sonya for me." We exchanged parting pleasantries and I promised again to be in touch.

Trolls, huh? And yeah, I had gotten a leprechaun vibe from him. Even though he wasn't super short as humans would have you believe. He did present leprechaun if that makes sense, dripping with charm that almost had me fooled. But in truth he was a troll. That would be something I couldn't wait to share with Seth. He'd been doing good too, over the years. Better and better since Eric's death. He seemed to have made peace with the whole sordid tragedy. And of Lucas's death, well, that was a sore topic for us both, we missed our friend but Seth was planning a trip to visit me in Italy one day soon. We were still close friends and confidants.

As more years sped by, my discoveries of the shadow world around us continued to grow. I wrote to Max often about the curiosities I came across. Mostly benign creatures. Many we had no names for. They didn't match any of the descriptions in fairytale books. Neither in looks nor attitude. With my new eyes, I tried like hell to get a glimpse of my own creature. The one that stuck with me no matter where I traveled. It was somehow able to even follow me during space jumps, through the folds of time, to countries, and across oceans but I couldn't see its true identity. I kept trying though. One day I would catch it.

Oh, how I missed Lucas. The more time that passed the stronger my longing became. I would've given anything to just get one of those infamous side hugs of his. I began to forget how he smelled, my memories of him were not fading but the sense of some of his physical attributes were disappearing. Like the way his emotions and body lit up inside whenever I was near, the distinct sense of happiness that lingered after he played with Tova or his puppies. Those feelings were leaving me, slowly, until I was left only holding his ghost.

So that's what I did.

In my dreams he was real. In my dreams we could be together still. I brought my memories of him with me to my planet of lavender skies. We could be free there, in my dreams.

Toward the back end of those twenty-five years, a trip into town turned into a nightmare. I was shopping, preparing for a visit from Seth who was coming for a couple of weeks. While browsing the stores, a sudden earthquake hit. It had nothing to do with me if that's what you're thinking. It was a real earthquake. A 7.6 on the seismic scale. Some of the older shops and homes fell in on themselves, injuring locals. Nearby trees and rocks came tumbling down and I got cut off from my home. I assisted many of the injured people, my medic mentality kicking in. It was time to rally not panic.

I was setting the broken ankle of an elderly man when I felt a pull to look up, across the street. Among the rubble and chaos stood a man. Like ants, the emergency workers scurried about but he stood motionless, staring directly at me. Even with my supervision his face was inexplicably blurry. He couldn't have been more than fifty yards away, so I should've been able to see him clearly, should've been able to hear his heart beating and catch his scent. But I could not. His body looked like that of a human man. I could clearly make that out but his face was severely distorted. The elderly man brought me back to his injuries, and when I looked back to the other man, he was gone. Gone, gone.

After the dust literally settled and I had helped those I was able to, I attempted to jump space back to my home. I couldn't do that either. For the first time in my recollection, I was unable to call on my special gift to escape a situation. All roads leading to my home were barred by fallen debris. I was trapped in town. My need to return home wasn't just to leave the mess behind, it was also due to a sudden insatiable sense of craving that had developed within me. I didn't understand what was happening. I was suddenly ravenous and not a single wild animal in sight. Not even stray dogs or cats. Nothing!

One night became two, and I was still trapped and growing concerned. On the third night, I walked the desolate streets alongside the ruble and stone. Down an alleyway I noticed a woman speaking to a man. He was not a man though. My eyes detected something disturbing about him. I could sense that the woman saw him as human but I could almost see through him. He was hollow, like an apparition. He suddenly put his hand over her mouth and bit her. He tore into her neck. *What was happening? He could feed on humans? A vampire? Teeth sharp enough to tear into flesh.* My Evol nature prevented me from caring about the woman's fate in an sympathetic way. I could never feed on humans, I knew only too well what happened when I used my angel teeth. Anyway, animals tasted great, so I had no need …

The fourth night came and went and I could no longer contain my hunger. I tried. I ate every bit of Italian food I could get my hands on. As much as my stomach could hold. It wasn't enough. I was still hungry. There were still no wild animals in sight and I couldn't jump space to anywhere. I spotted an older gentleman walking alone. He appeared tipsy. I assumed he was heading home after a night at the local bar and I followed him into an ally.

There, I attacked him.

I bit down into his neck and began to drink but as I completed the first big gulp, an incredible fire-like sensation seared through me. I stopped immediately, pushing the man down.

I fell to my hands and knees, coughing up his blood.

He was holding his hands over his ears, screaming in pain from whatever sound was emanating in his head. As I convulsed and puked, he began to bleed out from everywhere. That poor guy was succumbing to my venomous fangs. In the middle of us both writhing in pain the strange man from the day of the earthquake revealed himself. He stepped from the shadows. Not the same as the creature that drank the woman's blood, he appeared to be something else. The energy I sensed coursing through him was so strong it felt like he was made of lightning itself. I lay on the ground, stunned and still choking and disoriented. The strange man began to walk toward me with a smile on his blurry face. Only feet from me and still I couldn't see him clearly.

Before he could reach me, I belted out a scream in pure terror, which caused some sort of an aftershock. The odd blurry guy stopped, and the town trembled as ripples of something oscillated through the air.

Suddenly, I found myself on the floor of Max's home, under the wall in Jerusalem. I looked up and saw that I had interrupted what looked like a romantic dinner, just Sonya and Max. I had surely spoiled it forever by my arrival, puking up blood everywhere.

They ran over to me and tried to calm me, tried to get information or some coherent answer inbetween my dry heaving. I spewed some crazy explanation, "Vamp ... vampire! And a guy made of lightning ... I don't know what happened. There. Was. An. Earthquake. A weird blurry guy ... I couldn't jump space ... I couldn't leave ... water ... please, water?" I begged.

Sonya got me a glass of water while Max picked me up off the floor. He set me on his couch and put a blanket over my shoulders. A bucket appeared. The puking of blood slowed. I sipped the water and tried to focus. Max and Sonya waited, seemingly on pins and needles. I calmed my breathing and tried again to tell them the story of what had transpired over the last few days.

They both had some interesting tidbits for me. Max started first, explaining that the thing I thought was a vampire was not exactly that. He reminded me of the story about the linking process. How sometimes an entity follows a soul through the window. That, he said, was one of those entities. They don't stay with the baby after getting into our world. They wander around on their own. They don't receive a body of flesh but can appear to be a real human, to another human. Only for brief moments. Just time enough to drain a human victim. He didn't know to what end, but it was called *vampire* in some cultures and *demon* in others. In *The Book of Beings,* it was called a Vaemon.

"So, it's a demon or spirit more so than what we think of as vampire?" I asked.

"Emma, whatever its name, it is evil. It represents only malice and hate," Sonya insisted.

"From what I can gather from your story, you cannot successfully drink human blood, which is good. However, it's also bad when stuck in the type of predicament you were."

"You said right after the earthquake you saw a blurry man. A man you were unable to sense a heartbeat from but you felt his energy when he tried to get close to you?" Max asked me.

"Yes. I felt terror as he walked closer, which is how I'm assuming I arrived here. Do you think he could've caused the earthquake? That I couldn't jump space because of him?" I replied.

"What you're describing is a being that has been around since before memory. Our records of such go back almost eight thousand years. In some of the oldest records there are passages of a being they called the Begetter. It means 'father' or 'creator' in many languages," Max explained.

"You mean, God? Jesus, Mary, and Joseph! Bull-Shit! No way!" I said through my laughter and still spitting up blood.

"No, not God. God wouldn't do the things that being has done. In every record of the slim few that have encountered him it was during something major. The Begetter, we feel, is responsible for Pompeii, Atlantis, Rapa Nui, The Indus, and so forth. Disasters on a massive scale," Sonya said.

"Clearly, you and I have read different bibles because your god is destructive as fuck," I sputtered. "Sounds to me you're just hoping the Begetter isn't God. What is he then? Why did I see him? Is he the Devil?" I asked, giggling a bit. I was probably hysterical, it wasn't funny.

"Some believe he created our unique DNA and some believe he caused the resurfacing that changed our world. If he has appeared to you, it's not for a good reason, Emma," Sonya continued. "He's a bully, a child, he enjoys toying with humans, Evols, and all creatures. His power is beyond our comprehension," she said in her most serious voice.

"Well fuck me! Dammit. Can't I make it through my first century without all this supernatural, biblical, racist factions, and leprechaun crap? Is it too much to ask?" I loudly snapped.

"You need to feed. Do you want me to have a Guardian bring you a goat? It's no trouble, seriously it's okay," Max asked, suddenly changing the subject.

"No thank you. Goats creep me out. I'm going to attempt jumping home to Italy. I will feed on something there. I appreciate you guys for taking care of me." Then, thinking I should try to lighten things before speeding off after the way I'd entered, I asked Sonya for that amazing rice dish recipe she made that we had spoken about weeks earlier—talk about off topic. Meh.

After some more small talk I hugged them both and we said our goodbyes. "Sorry I disrupted your dinner. I'll call you later. Thanks again," I told them, standing up and making embarrassed excuses to leave. Those poor guys, I had totally interrupted their Don Quixote moment.

I closed my eyes, focusing on my Italian villa. A moment or two later and I was home. Thank fuck! Being able to see the previously hidden beings around me should've been a good thing but I realized then that if I could see them, then they could see me. That was not a good thing. It may have attracted that weird blurry being to my town. Effectively destroying the lives of many who lived there with his earthquake arrival. I didn't want him to find me again. Although he hadn't technically harmed me, he did do a number on the town. I didn't want the residents to endure another visit. One meeting was one too many.

Max had mentioned that many Evols didn't believe the blurry man even existed because so few of us had seen him. He was just another fairytale. But I knew some of the deadliest things often hide in plain sight and the Begetter could be one of them.

Chapter 23
Lost in Purple

Moments after returning to my home, I ventured outside to feed. Then, later, after cleaning myself up, I lay down on the couch and turned the TV on. It wasn't long before my eyes closed and I dreamed of my happy place. The planet with lavender skies. That had become my home away from home. Lucas appeared once again. It was always a treat whenever I could drag him into my dreams. We never spoke to each other, but it didn't matter, I could look at him.

Something was different. A change. I was walking with my black wolf as I often did but this time, there were many people around. Normally I didn't come across too many, if any. Sometimes the old woman of the lake and sometimes Lucas. But no one else really. Yet this time, people stood all around. They said nothing but nodded in silent greeting as I passed them by. I spotted Lucas beyond the mass of people and made my way through the village, trying to reach him. The longer my wolf and I walked, the further away Lucas seemed to be. Like being on one of those moving walkways in airports. *Airports again.* I couldn't get closer to him. The people around me spoke to each other but I couldn't hear their conversations. I wasn't upset or panicked that I couldn't progress toward Lucas, I remained calm and relaxed. The way my emotions always had been during visits here.

Suddenly, a loud sound rang out from the sky and then it came. The sky floated down until I was standing in a purple fog! The villagers disappeared and Lucas stood alone, still far from me. Then he waved goodbye as he vanished into the fog. My wolf broke away from my side and bounded after him. The fog swallowed my wolf and he too was gone. I continued to wander but couldn't find a soul. I was lost. Lost in a purple haze that was thick and wet. Much like a mist, it stuck to my robes and skin and a feeling of urgency overcame me. I tried running to where I thought Lucas should be but purple misty clouds enveloped everything and I got nowhere.

That was the first time my dream turned on me. I kept repeating to myself that I was lost. Lost. Lost. Everyone abandoned me, leaving me to aimlessly wander in purple, drenched in the illusion keeping me frozen in time.

A faint voice in the distance called out my name, "Emma. Emma. EMMA!"

I sat up from the couch to see Seth banging on my window as he called me. I groggily wiped the sleep from my eyes and let him into the house. "Hey, how did you get here? I thought the roads were blocked off?" I asked.

"When I rented a car from the airport, they warned me about the earthquake. They said I might not be able to get to you but I thought I'd try anyway. Your roads are being cleared as we speak," he replied.

"Oh. Awesome. You can drive us to town so I can get my own car that's still there. We have to grab a few groceries too. That's what I was doing when the earthquake hit. Hey, come here. Let me hug you! It's so great to see you, Seth," I said, hugging him tight.

As we drove to town, I updated him on the curious events that had taken place over the last few days. He encouraged me to get ahold of Elijah. Since he'd been around for so long, he might be able to shed some light on the blurry creature called the Begetter. I told him I'd think about it, but I was more on the side of trying to forget. The likelihood of me coming across him—it again would be next to nil. Seth dropped the subject because he was too busy giggling about some of the other new creatures I had found. He was trying to come up with names for the ones we had no names for. Ridiculous names he thought were funny.

We made it to town and went into a grocery store. While there he saw an attractive man who seemed to know me. When the man spotted me, he left his grocery cart and sped out of the store. *Odd.* Seth asked what that was all about. I smiled and just told him not to worry about it. That man was a troll. Seth couldn't believe it. I told him yup, that was probably how the troll wanted it. He was a parasite, a charmer. He beguiled a human and then lived off their money for a while. Seth looked disappointed. I could see he was going to worry about men he met in the future, wonder if they were real or nothing more than a troll. Then again, what could be worse than Eric? I guess you're screwed either way. Some things should be just left a mystery.

Seth and I had a great visit. No sign of the Begetter. Just me and him enjoying mass amounts of tortelloni with porcini mushrooms, ribollita soups with crispy, freshly baked bread that had Seth humming in orgasm, risotti of every single flavor, cheeses to build kingdoms on, osso bucco, delectable salty bottargas, *don't get me started!* Meaty canerderli ... and wine. Much wine, laughter and peace.

He did also bring with him something that was not fun, but it was unfortunately, necessary. I was overdue to change my identity. Every eighty to one hundred years Evols must change their identities.

It would be a pain, he explained, but had to be done for me to continue owning my homes and bank accounts. And he assured me that the process got faster and easier as the centuries moved on. He showed me how to create a death certificate for myself—*nice*, and how to acquire the name of someone new. The people in my tiny circle would always call me Emma, no matter what my new legal name was, which was good to hear.

After we completed my new identity and that business was out of the way, we continued our awesome time together. One night, with a bottle of Italy's finest red Barolo wine, we reminisced about Lucas. All the good times and laughter. Seth took the opportunity to ask me about when I had vanished with Lucas at the mansion. I hadn't ever told him where we went, or anyone for that matter. At the time I was just overstressed and didn't feel I could properly explain.

"Will you tell me now where you and Lucas went after disappearing from the mansion?" he asked.

"I'll try. We originally landed on the floor of what looked to be a home. More like a shack with wooden walls and floors. I didn't recognize it but I stayed still for some time with Lucas's head in my lap," I said.

"Do you know how his head healed so perfectly?" Seth asked.

"So, after a while of us just sitting there, a man came into the shack. He seemed shocked to see us at first, then he went to a cabinet to retrieve a glass jar containing a honey-like substance. He poured the stuff onto a cloth and approached us. He held the cloth on Lucas's wound as he looked into my eyes. I trusted him but didn't know why," I replied.

"Shit, that's crazy weird, Emma," Seth said.

"After maybe five minutes, the man removed the cloth and

pointed to the door. He wanted us to leave but I couldn't carry Lucas. So he picked him up like he weighed nothing and as we passed the threshold of the shack, we were suddenly in your bathtub," I said.

"That's nuts. And that dude never spoke to you? Weird," he said, pausing. "Thank you for telling me. I've thought about that for many years now, it has always weighed heavy on my mind."

I could see he was perplexed but glad I had divulged it to him finally. I owed him. He had, after all, shared many secrets and experiences with me. It was the right time to give him the much overdue explanation. It was a release of sorts for me as well, getting it out. We moved onto other conversations throughout the night. Being his last night, we packed in as much as we could but I began to think on the Begetter again.

Weeks later, I decided I would ask Elijah about the creature or being or whatever the hell he was and gave Elijah a video call.

"Hi Emma! How nice to hear from you. How are you? What's been happening over there in Europe?" he asked.

"I'm good. Things have been going okay. I see Tova behind you in the backyard. How've you been? How's your retirement going?"

"Oh, well, let me tell you I should've done this eight hundred years ago! It's amazing. It truly is a gift and Tova has been doing great too!" Elijah exclaimed.

"I was hoping you might have some information stored in that vast brain of yours, Elijah. What do you know about the Begetter?" I popped.

"Wow. I haven't thought about that being in ages. Let me see … The last time he was spotted was about, well, over a millenium ago. He always shows himself in a blurry form. It could be he's trying to hide his face or possibly our eyes just cannot reconcile his form. The

Begetter predates us, his age is unknown. Why the interest?" he asked.

"Well, I saw him in the town below my home. He tried to approach me and I immediately blinked out. You know, I escaped in Emma fashion. Seth suggested I ask you about him," I explained.

"Oh, that's not good. Nothing positive happens when he's around. I would stay far away from him, if possible. Don't go pulling at this thread. Let's just hope he doesn't find you again," Elijah said with concern in his voice.

Hmmm, interesting. I stopped the questions about the Begetter after Elijah's warning and we chatted about everyday things. He was looking rough physically. Age had run right over him. His spirit, however, was strong. As if he hadn't already been an incredibly kind and patient man before, he had much more of that feeling about him now. His retirement and departure from the council had proven to be the best thing for him. He was in his own heaven, loving every moment of his new life and it warmed my heart to see him in his happiest place.

Time moved on. Ten more years went by. I continued to see odd creatures here and there, Max made great progress in completing *The Book of Beings* with my help. Did you know there are small beings that inhabit many cats? I realize this won't come as a shock to most folks. Cats are already super mysteriously weird creatures.

One day, I was sitting in the town square drinking coffee, just minding my own business, when a stray cat came to rest not feet from me. He was a fuzzy gray color, surrounded by a yellowish green hue. Almost a pixelated look to him, like old staticky black-and-white movies. I asked the waiter who approached me a question to clarify what I was seeing.

"What kind of cat would you call that one over there?" I asked.

"A Calico, looks like," he said. "Orange, white, and black spots, is a calico. My nonna has two."

So, it was a new creature. I couldn't see the colors of the actual cat. I was looking at something else. Something that was inside the cat. Just then, I heard a male voice in my head. It called me an idiot! I looked straight at the cat and out loud, I asked him if he had spoken. He glared at me. I mean, he actually squinted his little cat eyes and glared at me! Then he jumped up onto my table and sat in front of me. I picked up my coffee so he wouldn't knock it over. The same male voice rang out in my head again. We had a silent conversation with just our minds.

"I bet you think you're clever, don't you?" he asked.

"So, you can read my mind? That explains a lot. Does your kind have a name?" I replied.

"Nothing the likes of you would understand. I owe you nothing. Peasant!" he insisted.

Clearly, he was an arrogant asshole, cat or not but … I *was* talking to a cat in the middle of the town square. At least his attitude matched what most people think of when they see cats. Maybe I could trick him into telling his secrets. Arrogant people always feel the need to correct others, possibly this being was the same. If I angered him, he might give me some information. "You probably don't even know what you are. No smarter than a damn dog. Dog people are correct then, dogs are better. Certainly nicer," I baited.

"I am a Bullfol. We are royalty! You're the mutt here and no brighter than a sheep!" he angrily replied as he kicked over the sugar container with his back foot.

"So sorry, *Your Highness*, but what good are you really? You're just a cat. You have no power," I told him.

His little eyes lit up a brilliant blue as he replied, "I have more power than you can fathom."

"Oh, your eyes light up. That's cute. So do mine. No big deal," I told him, mockingly.

At that, he looked over to the traffic outside the town square and as if on cue, a car crashed into a building. No one was hurt but shortly afterward, a man got out of his banged-up car, and the car burst into flames.

The cat-Bullfol-asshole looked back at me smugly. My, my, this creature had some skills. Bullfols have the power to speed objects up maybe? He accelerated the car which caused the gentleman to lose control and then sped up the ignition of the fuel that was on the ground. If a leprechaun could speed up good luck, then a Bullfol could speed up bad. I wasn't entirely sure but that was the direction I headed with what little information I'd gained. "Impressive. Why cats? Why inhabit cats?" I asked.

"Cats are agile, small, and people are suckers. They take care of us, spoil us. As they should!" he explained. Then he jumped down, walking away with his tail in the air showing me his ass.

Bullfols were in *The Book of Beings*, but it wasn't known where they hid or how powerful they were. Now I guess we knew. Unfortunately, I was unable to find out what their true form was, when not inhabiting a cat. But the information I did get was most useful. Maybe I'd get the chance to trick another one into sharing that last secret of what they really looked like. Just so you know, they're *not* royalty according to *The Book of Beings*. Not sure where they came up with that. Their power is upper middle of the pack of beings, as recorded thus far.

Also, during this timeframe, I agreed to be on call to the Grand

Council if my purple orb talent was in need. They did utilize me twice to extract information from potentially corrupt persons. Luckily for those individuals they had nothing nefarious to hide.

I'd begun to make peace with who or what I was. Of course, I didn't know what that was exactly, but the question no longer bothered me. Max still tried to convince me I could be a Lost One and the more my talents developed, the stronger his convictions got. He was insufferable on the subject. I would agree that I was lost but not a Lost One.

My dreams had not returned to the strange solace they'd been before the purple fog fell. Each time, now, it was different. Me, alone, surrounded by purple mist. I wasn't sure it was my home any longer. My dream planet had always been my way of escape from stress, from everything.

Another five years flew by and I had been trying to get ahold of Seth for many days. After I grew more worried, I placed a call to Max, jumping straight in. "Hey, question, have you heard from Seth lately? I can't seem to get ahold of him," I asked.

"We were going to call you. Seth is missing. We don't know what happened. Investigators traveled to his home. There wasn't any blood and no signs of a struggle, but there was also no luggage and some of his clothes were gone. We thought he maybe took a trip but we haven't been able to confirm that," Max said.

"Have you contacted his Gifter?" I asked in panic mode.

"Yes. We called his Gifter and he hasn't heard from him. He also hasn't sensed Seth's death. He hasn't sensed anything out of the ordinary. So, at least we know Seth is alive. We just don't know where he could be," Max explained.

"What can I do to help? There has to be something?" I replied.

"Not really Emma. We've issued a Be On The Look Out bulletin to all Evol agencies worldwide. All that can be done, has been. I'm sorry I didn't call you but I didn't want you to worry until we had more information," he said.

It felt like Lucas all over again.

Another of my friends had gone missing. At least he wasn't dead, but Seth was my moral compass, which was of paramount importance when trying to control an entity such as I was. Immediately, I began texting him several times a day, demanding he call me back. I even flew to his home and went through his stuff, looking for clues. He had just vanished. He had packed his bags, it seemed and just vanished. I didn't buy it.

His Gifter and I spoke often, trying to put the pieces together. There had been zero reasons why Seth would be out of contact. None that we could come up with.

The last thing Seth had done was meet with his most recent new Evol. Someone he'd created a year and a half earlier. But that was months ago when he was helping that new Evol member come to grips with his new life. I traveled to the new Evol's home to question him. Not something he was prepared for. Just think of what his reaction would've been if I hadn't been wearing my contacts. I imagined he'd have started screaming the word demon as so many had done in the past. I spared him that. Besides, my teeth were alarming enough. I needed him focused on the details of Seth's visit. Nothing he described to me was out of the normal routine.

Once I returned home, my mind became unhinged. I had so few in my circle of ride or die friends. And that circle appeared to be dissolving. I reveled in my alone time, always had, but the thought of being left completely alone again was unbearable. I became angry. There was a pit in my stomach that felt perpetually hollow. I ripped through damn near half the animal population in just a year's time. Gorging myself silly and needlessly. Nothing would fill the hollow pit in my stomach. I had lost too much already; I wasn't prepared to lose more.

Turning my attentions to a recent trick I discovered, I began fucking with the weather. It may have not been a new trick. I might've done it once before. The surprise squall that appeared after the bloodbath I had dumped over the Tamson mansion, for example. I still cannot say if I had a hand in the so-called miracle that washed away the blood. Either way, I'd officially begun my practice of harnessing the winds and water currents. You could call it a supernatural bender, so to speak.

Over the next five years I would call on the skies to unleash its secrets, on a whim. Lightning storms, the likes of which the local residents had never witnessed before, came. Hail and torrential rains flooded the valleys. Each month or two my anger would well up again and I'd find new ways to release it. Crop growth and livestock took a hit. Tourism crawled to a halt due to the extreme weather patterns. The humans around me suffered but they didn't know the reason. Their only saving grace, you could say, was that I didn't know how to start plagues. Not that I would have. I don't believe I would have anyway.

But I wasn't quite finished. Lashing out like a two-year-old in a temper tantrum, I killed three trolls in town. Slaughtered them for no other reason. I convinced myself they wouldn't be missed. Who would care? They were just hustlers and leeches feeding off the world. It didn't make me feel better though. All it did was bring down detectives and cops to scour the town for clues of the killer. They, of course, had no idea those people were trolls. They appeared to be humans, dead humans now, so it had to be investigated.

And that meant I needed to leave.

I moved myself back to Scotland. Back to my little cottage by the sea. I allowed myself to slip into madness, maybe, in a direction I didn't want to be in. I hurt people and creatures that had done nothing wrong to me. That wasn't in my nature. I was unsure if it had to do with Seth's disappearance or if I was becoming something else. Maybe whatever was inside me was changing. Maybe I really was a demon. Or an alien and beginning my plan to take over the world. Wouldn't that be something? Lost. I was lost and losing more of my mind every day.

Sonya would call weekly to check in on me. Some calls I would pick up and some not. I wanted to hear from Seth. Getting a call from anyone else was a disappointment. I needed him to come and see me and pull me out of the hell I had created for myself. I would've made it rain blood again to save him were he in peril. But nobody had seen him. No one knew what had happened to him. No words. No clues. Silence.

Chapter 24
Passing into Legend

Just over twenty more years piled on and still no Seth. His Gifter hadn't gotten that weird internal death notification but, with his absence being so extended, it felt as though he were dead. Speaking of dying, my last remaining child passed away. Josh was privileged to peacefully die of old age, surrounded by his children, grandchildren and friends. All my children were gone. My great grand babies only knew me as the woman who abandoned her family some seventy-five years ago. I was no more than a forgotten shadow to them.

I once again devolved into that shut-in I had been many years ago.

The cottage I had taken so much pride in was now a mess of disrepair and filth. Day after day, month into month, year after year, I would wake and I would sit then sleep, wake, sit and sleep. I hadn't slipped down the rabbit hole, I had thrown myself down it. Screw everyone and everything! The only chore I would complete with any consistency was to check the mail. And that was only to prevent a mail carrier from having to knock on my door. After returning from my weekly trips to the mailbox, I'd toss the mail on the kitchen island and forget about it.

Only shopping for food every six months or so. I'd been sustaining myself with animal blood. Not because I needed to but because I didn't want to drive into town. Cereal and blood were the extent of my diet. That was all my brain could handle. If or when I ran out of milk, I'd eat cereal dry rather than drive to the store right away. Just the worst form of grouchy hoarder person who yelled at everyone. I hated the world. Fuck this. Fuck that. Miserable mess. My life.

While fixing myself one of those bowls of cereal one morning a letter caught my eye within the overflowing stack of mail. It wasn't junk, it was a handwritten envelope. Reluctantly, I pulled it from the pile. It was from Sonya. She might be the last remaining entity on earth who still wrote letters.

Dearest Emma,

It is with a heavy heart that I write this letter. Our sweet Elijah has passed from this world.

You should know that when last I spoke with him, just a month earlier, he was as happy and as content as I'd ever heard him. It seemed as though we'd never lose him but he slipped away. He was such a gentle creature. As he was tending to his beloved garden the Guardians heard his heart stop. When they reached him, the great bear Tova emerged from the forest, frantic and swiping at them before she lay down next to Elijah. The Guardians let them be while they made calls to notify us of Elijah's death. When they returned, they attempted to remove Elijah from Tova's embrace, assuming she was sleeping, only to realize she had died next to him. It was quite a bit of work but a grave large enough for both Elijah and Tova was dug, in a clearing behind the property, surrounded by nature and love.

They are now truly together again in the hereafter.

With love,

Sonya

Slowly, I sank onto a chair and wept. Evols don't have funerals nor memorials. They feel it's a slap in the face toward humans whose lives are so brief. We're given extraordinarily long lives which meant second, third, and fourth, chances to improve ourselves. Humans don't have that luxury of time. When we pass away it is final and peaceful. No funeral required. Elijah had been walking our world for over three thousand years. He, of all people, wouldn't have wanted a somber and downcast memorial. If the Evols did anything in remembrance it was a celebration of life.

Scanning my cluttered and dusty home, I thought of Elijah. He wouldn't have wanted this for me. If he were with me, he'd be giving me a pep talk and trying to pull me from my self-destructive pity party. He'd lost countless loved ones from his life and had always continued to move forward.

I stood and opened a window. Then I opened another. Beginning with the kitchen, I washed the dishes. That was all I accomplished then but it was a start. The following day I worked on the living room and piles of laundry. And the day after I cleaned a little more. By the end of the week, my cottage had become livable again.

Within a month's time I had also painted many of the walls and hired workers to fix the roof. Creeping along, little by little, I made a valiant effort to get my life back on track. I drove to town to do some real shopping, I restocked my home and prepared myself actual meals; not cereal. The color in my face returned as my body felt healthier. It didn't happen overnight, but I did finally pull myself from that pity party. Even my dreams increasingly got better. The purple haze lifted, leaving me looking up at a beautiful sky swirling with shades of red, gold, and lavender.

Upon checking the mail one morning, I saw that I had received a wedding invitation. From Max and Sonya. The ceremony was to be held in Dubai in front of the magnificent Burj Khalifa skyscraper. And the reception at the famous Burj Al Arab, a lavish seven-star hotel. I knew they were becoming romantically involved but was unaware of how serious their relationship was. Against their wishes I had been avoiding them. Not because of anything they did wrong; just me being sad me. The wedding was in two months. I had sworn I wouldn't attend anymore Evol events after the mansion debacle but their wedding was different. I knew I couldn't miss it. I'd never forgive myself.

I continued to put my best foot forward during my recovery. Wanting to be in good spirits for their wedding, I researched Dubai, particularly the two locations where the wedding proceedings would be held. While booking my hotel room at the Burj Al Arab, shockwaves went through me when I was told the price of a room. Like, *holy shit!* Who the hell affords that? Oh, I had the funds but I was also a bit of a miser. Considering I had traveled nowhere in more than twenty years, I booked a room, a great room. It was high time I started to live a little. An excitement built within me, something I hadn't allowed myself to feel in a long time.

Shortly after arriving at the hotel, I met up with Max and Sonya in the lobby. They were surprised to see me to say the least. Even though I had RSVP'd, a small part of them had obviously secretly thought I wouldn't show. After all, I was MIA for more than two decades. Hiding in my cottage and wrapped in a cocoon of despair and heartbreak—my usual self-loathing issues. They were genuinely ecstatic to see me. Max and Sonya ran up and hugged me simultaneously, one on each side, like a hug sandwich. All smiles and joy. That was to be the tone of the wedding. Nothing less was acceptable.

That night many of the guests gathered in the hotel conference room to engage in pre-wedding drinks and frivolities. Sonya opened the evening with a toast to the late Elijah. He was one of a kind; an irreplaceable being of pure light and love and an outstanding leader and stellar friend. He had gladly shared his knowledge with all who required it, holding nothing back for himself. Generous to a fault and stronger than the mightiest of beasts. There wasn't a dry eye in the room as we raised our glasses to: Elijah.

The next morning, we traveled to where the wedding would be held. Guest chairs had been arranged in typical fashion just outside the Burj Khalifa entrance facing the megastructure. The breathtaking marvel was in the shape of a spiral reaching to the heavens at the staggering height of 2,722 feet. As we sat listening to the ceremony, I reminisced of my time with the people who were not in attendance. Seth, Lucas, Sara and, of course, Elijah. They all should've been there. Elijah had good reason, he died naturally and at an astronomical age. The others, however, were snatched from us in unnatural ways. Seth had mysteriously disappeared. Lucas and Sara murdered. It felt so unfair and wrong.

Anyway, Max and Sonya had written their own vows which were spectacularly simple and right. You couldn't help but key in on their radiant souls that seemed already linked. The minister completed the ceremony before asking them to seal their love with the all-important kiss. After which, Max and Sonya turned to us in the audience, now man and wife, holding hands, and beaming from ear to ear. Everyone clapped, cheered, and whistled.

And that's when the party stopped, and hell began.

I recall this next part in extreme slow motion. Frame by frame.

As I clapped, the hair on the back of my neck rose and my focus was pulled over my shoulder. On the far right of the chairs stood the Begetter. He was glaring at Max and Sonya. I looked back at Max just as he too spotted him. Max looked at me. We both looked back at the Begetter who tilted his head upward above Max and Sonya, toward the spire of the building. He raised one of his hands. He was about to snap his fingers. We knew in an instant he was going to destroy it.

I blinked out, reappearing directly behind him. In the palm of my left hand was the purple orb. Without thinking, I shoved it into his spine a millisecond before the snap of his fingers.

An agonizingly painful high-pitched squeal sounded in my head. My hand flew backward, separating the orb from his body. Like a bullet from a gun, the Begetter shot straight up into the sky. A bright light trailed behind him as if he were a shooting star. His escape caused me to fall forward to the ground. I was awake but paralyzed. Although I couldn't move, I felt a massive amount of electricity coursing through my body. I lay on my back motionless, helpless. Guests rushed over to me as Max and Sonya pushed them aside, trying to reach me.

"We need to get everyone inside. Come on Emma, we'll carry you," Max said, panic-stricken.

"NO! NO! He's coming back! I saw it. All of us need to get to the hotel, far away from here. Leave the chairs and belongings. He has to think we're in that building. He's going to take it down regardless! MOVE! NOW!" I shouted with militant urgency.

Max instructed a Guardian to pick me up while everyone else ran to their cars and taxies. Across town we fled, honking horns and swerving through traffic; arriving at the Burj Al Arab Jumeirah Hotel just as the massive spiraled Burj Khalifa building cracked apart. With a deafening roaring sound that rivaled the World Trade Center Towers explosion,

500,000 tons of twisted steel, concrete, and glass began to rain down on the city block. We watched in horror as a vast cloud of debris rose up, blotting out the sun. Screams of terror and disbelief echoed in unison from the surrounding residents. We felt every cry of pain from every person in a ten-mile radius. Dubai had fractured. Blood, body parts, and death would be their new lives for the months to come.

We were damn near debilitated by the sounds and smells of the cataclysmic disaster. Max, Sonya, and a Guardian whisked me to my room as the sirens in Dubai began squalling. Many of the guests traveled back out into the sand-filled darkness to help where they could. The hotel went into shutdown mode. Lights flashed in the hallways. Announcements were made over the intercoms. After I was set on the bed, Sonya grabbed a lock of my long hair bringing it forward to show me. My once brownish blonde hair had turned to streaks of gray, white, and copper. My eyes were not just their usual metallic black but also neon rings of deep purple ran around the outer edge.

As the feeling in my limbs slowly recovered, I began to wince with pain. Every bone in my left hand had been shattered. My body was trying to heal itself, leaving my hand in a decrepit-looking state. The Guardian with us had experience in such cases. He told Max to hold me down and then he straightened each bone, re-breaking them and setting them into their proper places.

Sonya covered my mouth as I screamed. Once it was done, the Guardian held my hand still while my body healed the bones correctly. My brain was swimming. The electrical shock that asshole being gave me felt like it had fried the wires in my head. After my heartrate began to slow down and the pain in my hand lessened, Max started in with the questions.

"Did you push your orb into him? I couldn't see from where I was standing. What made you do that? Tell us what you saw Emma. What was in the Begetter?" he demanded.

"I don't know exactly. When I reappeared behind him the orb was already in my hand. So, I just did it. With the others I've used the orb on, their memories start from the beginning and move forward. His moved backward. I saw what he was then presently planning and then his timeline went in reverse. Once I dug into him, he fled. If the rest of his memories are inside me, they're locked away because I can't remember anything else," I explained.

"You must come back with us to Jerusalem. You will be safer underground, Emma," Sonya said.

"I can't. I may not remember all that was in his head but he's not happy with me. Your underground city won't save me, nor will it protect you. He just slaughtered thousands of people during your wedding in broad daylight. We need to separate," I replied.

"We need to stay together. We're stronger together," Max said, jumping in.

"Oh really? Two hundred Evols out there today plus eighteen superhero Guardians and he still accomplished his mission. Whatever kind of mindblowing freak he is, we can safely assume that he can fuck us collectively with one snap of his fingers!" I argued back.

My bone-setting Guardian spoke up, "She's right sir. None of the Guardians even detected his entry into the atmosphere. When Emma sneaks in and out of our underground home in that special way she does, we get a tingling of sorts. Her entry triggers our senses. But with the Begetter there was nothing. No warning. Zero trigger."

"All right, all right. For now, we will plan to separate. Just until we can come up with a better solution. Agreed?" Max asked as he looked around the room.

"I'm so sorry Max, Sonya. I never would have wished to bring such ... misery to your wedding day, I—"

Sonya shushed me before I could say more, giving me a tight hug, reassuring me they didn't blame me.

Then I jumped through space to my home in Scotland. I was furious inside. A raging inferno. Why did I think going to an Evol event would be okay? With my track record I should've thrown their invitation in the trash. I hadn't wanted to bring pain on them or anyone else. Was I just attracting asshole beings and monsters? Was it me? "Out-fucking-standing!" I yelled in my living room to no one. There was always a problem, it seemed.

I kept to myself for the next four months. Radio silence. I didn't fall back into depression but instead worked on a plan to evade that fucker. There had to be a way to get him to stop. I just didn't know what that was. I didn't know how to contact him or where to look for him. If I didn't know his routine, then I couldn't evade him. I attempted finding him in open space, no luck. If nothing else, it forced me to practice my jumping techniques and that's how I found the time portals. I did not enter them, however. I wasn't ready. I didn't know where I'd end up or if I would be able to get back. But my abilities did expand one-hundred-fold throughout those four months. The best defense is a good offense.

Sonya video called me on the fifth month. She had texted 911 to me first indicating I had to answer the video call. "Emma, good news. We matched up our archive sightings of him with catastrophes worldwide. We found incidences where hundreds of Evols perished at the same time in major disasters. The Begetter has done this at least three times in our history. Think of it as a cruel method of population control. Dubai's disaster had nothing to do with you. It had to do with all of us," she explained.

"Okay? That's good news? Cause it doesn't sound like it," I replied.

"Don't you see? The Begetter wasn't at our wedding for you. He may have been curious about you that time in Italy but you didn't draw him to us. Because you were at our wedding is the reason we all survived," Sonya said.

"Forgive me if I don't feel like accepting medals right now. I would rather know what he wants from us. Does he hate us? Is he challenged by us? Or is he just the ultimate douche bag?" I said, outraged.

"I believe it's the latter. Call it boredom or sport, the Begetter is just occupying his existence by playing games and snuffing out his lessers. We are nothing more than ants in his farm, Emma," Sonya replied.

In my heart of hearts, I knew she was right. Knowing that he most likely hadn't been there for just me eased the guilt that gripped me. It did, on some weird level, make me feel better about attending the wedding. On the other side of the coin was the bad news. There was an all-powerful nut job freak out there, somewhere in our universe who enjoyed destroying us on a whim. He had wiped 4,231 souls from this earth with just the raise of his hand. And that was just one event of many he'd perpetrated. *How did you deal with that type of creature?* I wondered. How could I stop a being that strong? And which of his memories were still locked inside my brain?

Fear of the unknown IS a valid fear.

Chapter 25
I Wasn't Alone

Over the next several years I would jump to Jerusalem on a regular basis. Max, Sonya, and I pored over the vast archives in search of information on the Begetter. With the number of times I hurled myself through space, my skin became permanently shiny. I didn't need to produce a lot of Shimmer to make jumps anymore. Perhaps those first couple of times it had happened it had been unwillingly and it had been necessary to damn near drown me in Shimmer. But by this point, I had it under control and required very little to accomplish a jump.

I would laugh at myself when looking at my reflection in the mirror. The sparkly sheen on my skin along with my vampire fangs reminded me of the one thing I didn't want to become during my transformation. You know, those diamond skinned vampires from the popular movies in the '00s? Well, that was exactly how things were looking. The more I jumped, the sparklier my skin became. *So ridiculous,* I thought.

Once, during a visit to Jerusalem, a Guardian walked by me and remarked that I looked like Bella—from *that* vampire movie. *Ugh.*

I answered that I thought it was more like *Bite Your Tongue or I will Rip Your Heart From Your Chest*. Right? Wasn't that it *that* movie?

My hair was another issue. The Evols loved it but I wasn't so keen on the change. I tried to dye it several times with no success. Each time I would leave the hair dye on longer and each time there was zero change. The color refused to hold. With my white-copper streaked blondish hair, fangs, and glittery skin, I resembled some made-up creature at a Halloween party. Not to mention my eyes, the neon purple rings had faded, thank God, and I was back to metallic black shimmering pools. The others didn't mind my appearance. They were no longer afraid of me since the wedding tragedy. If anything, they were gravitating toward me. Fascinated by me. A freak no more, I was their savior from the disaster of the Burj Khalifa building.

It was an odd sensation and a very uncomfortable one at that. I tried not to stay long whenever I visited Max and Sonya. Word would get around and Evols began flocking to the archives. Speaking of which, we hadn't made much progress in locating more information on the Begetter. Almost eight thousand years of records and very little about him was in them. However, on one of the shelves I found a small box that had been pushed out of sight behind the other records. It was dirty and fragile. Sealed shut with a wax substance.

While going through that box, I came upon what looked like super old archive-style entries written on papyrus. There wasn't anything about the Begetter but there was something about me, in a roundabout way. The entries were written by a woman in the first person, detailing her struggles and questions as an Evol. It was painful for me to read as so many of her accounts paralleled mine. Much like witnessing a bad accident; I couldn't look away from it though. I read it aloud to Max and Sonya.

She spoke about the year she had become sick. So sick there were many times she believed she would die or may have already. The day she awoke with what she described as predatory teeth. And how she began to feed on animals, raw with no cooking. She drank their blood, unwilling, but she felt, physically, that she had no choice. Remarks about how she didn't fit in with others she had encountered. Possibly, she was talking about other Evols. There was a brief description of a being that trailed her every move. She never got a good look at it though, and referred to it as her Shadow Friend.

Then, the day she realized she was a Gifter which further separated her from the rest. Drawn to people who lived alone, she would kiss them and then leave. Later she would learn that those people became Evols too. She was fairly confused for her first hundred years, it seemed. She also described how her feedings increased and how she caressed the animals before killing them. She would give thanks for their offering of themselves. Over the years, the ritualistic killings became constant, around every turn of the moon. Alarmingly, to me, she spoke about strange dreams or visions. Dreams of a land with unusual skies that fluctuated and flowed. Atypical colors that swirled over her head as she walked through foreign vegetation. The similarities were too similar not to be the same.

In her words, she called that place Valhalla. In her Valhalla there was a bear that followed her, walked next to her, and seemingly knew her. There were passages chronicling her eye color changes. She had to hide herself more and more—I assumed that was due to contact lenses not being invented yet. I couldn't imagine how isolated she must have felt. I was isolated in my changes too, but at least I had the benefit of technology to help hide some of my freakiness.

"Oh Emma, she sounds a lot like you. That's so crazy. She had something following her around too. What do you call yours? The creature? What else does she talk about?" Sonya asked.

"Guys, I think this is Tova. As in, Elijah's bear, Tova. In her human form," I remarked in awe. I continued translating. I have to say, being able to read almost every language made going through the archives easier. That just came with the territory of our DNA but I'm getting off track. Many of her next entries spoke about a more recent charge of hers. A human she had gifted our DNA, turning them Evol. Many decades after his transformation, they became inseparable. She described him as an uncommonly tall man with silky skin as dark as obsidian. His eyes were the color of gleaming Nordic glaciers and his heart was open and uncorrupt. She was in love with him. She went onto describe the moment she knew he was one-half of her beating heart.

"It is Tova! I'm holding Tova's words in my hands," I exclaimed. "And her and Elijah were in love! This explains the way he looked at me the first time he saw my teeth!" I almost shouted. "I must have reminded him of her!"

"No wonder Elijah was so quick to move in Lucas's home. He was able to live out his last days with his lost half," Max remarked.

I went back to reading the last page of papyrus. Tova had written down a warning or foreboding. Once her dreams consumed more of her days than her waking life; she knew something was about to change. Her bear and the strange land she called Valhalla was all she could think about. She realized it would be her fate to transform into a bear. She had figured it out. The bear would take over and she would no longer exist. She left Elijah because she felt it coming. She didn't know how to tell him, so she simply disappeared. She knew his heart would break either way. But she was going to share her transformation with another Gifter because she trusted him to tell her tale. "Oh, it's Tamson's Gifter she's talking about. Shame he turned out to be an asshole," I commented.

"Do you have dreams Emma? Dreams or visions of the world she described?" Sonya asked.

"Nope. Nothing like that," I answered.

"Well, at least that's good news. You won't be turning into any kind of animal then," she replied.

I lied to her. I lied to them both. My visits to the planet with lavender skies was the one thing I hadn't shared with anyone, not even Lucas. I lied because I didn't want them to question me about my visions, if that's what they were. A large black wolf stuck with me in my dreams. Was I going to change into a wolf one day? Was that to be my fate? Wandering forests for a thousand years as Tova had done in her bear form? Would I be trapped in a wolf's body cursed to live an unnaturally long life? It was too much to wrap my brain around in that moment, sitting with them. So, I lied.

Changing gears, Max began digging through the boxes Elijah had left behind before he moved to America. Lots of paperwork and journals Elijah told Max might be useful overtime. Max hadn't yet touched any of them before that day. He'd been putting it off. He missed his friend. It's a difficult task, rummaging through belongings of those who have left us. I could see the reminiscence in his eyes as he unpacked. While Max was perusing Elijah's journals, Sonya and I continued to look for more documents on the Begetter.

Max stopped us for a moment. "Listen to this. A journal entry dated in the year 631. 'I haven't been able to locate Tova. There has been no word or sightings. I fear the Begetter may have taken her.'"

"Wait, why would Elijah think the Begetter took Tova?" I asked.

"According to his journals, he was working on a theory that the recent missing Evols were due to acts of the Begetter. Just before the time frame Tova disappeared, there was a rash of Evol vanishings. No explanations as to why or how. They were just gone one day," Max explained.

"Do you think that's what happened to Seth? He just vanished. Maybe that piece of shit super jerk took him!" Sonya said.

She took the words right out of my mouth, I thought. But, "Yeah, I don't think so. I mean, his bags were missing along with some of his clothes. I can't imagine that asshole letting Seth pack a bag before making him vanish," I replied.

"True, the Begetter is more of a poof-you're-gone type of monster," Sonya agreed.

"You know, I'm just thinking Seth did go on a trip and then something bad happened to him. It's been what, thirty-five years now? Even if his Gifter didn't get the notification, Seth is gone," I told them.

"I think you're right. And the Begetter could have snagged him as soon as he went on that trip. Those stupid missing bags and clothes is why we held out hope for so long. This is a cruel world with mean creatures floating around," Sonya replied.

I could feel the craving for animal blood nagging at me. Since I had still not developed a taste for goat, I told Sonya and Max it was time to call it a day. They agreed and that we'd meet up again in the months that followed.

After returning to my cottage, I went outside to build a fire and watch the sunset. So many new discoveries had occurred in such a short time. I needed silence; from all those who lived under the wall in Jerusalem and from my own brain. As the sun began to melt into the sea, I lulled myself into a trance. The state of calmness that enabled me to call upon the animal sacrifices I required to survive.

That night I escaped to my home away from home. My happy place.

I was no longer sure my dreams were in fact dreams. Tova's eerily similar dream accounts had given me pause. Maybe they were actual visions of where I belonged. Or possibly a planet I had been time traveling to unknowingly. Those were just guesses and amusements. They had to be dreams because my precious Lucas would often be among the other inhabitants. He'd become a permanent fixture on my purple planet and it was the only way I could clearly see him and be next to him. Although we didn't speak or touch, he was still a part of my home away from home. My sanity depended on it.

Over the next decade, we had gotten no further in discovering the Begetter's true nature or identity. Luckily, there had also not been any more unexplained catastrophes either. The year was 2123 and I was about to turn one hundred fifty years old. Max and Sonya were itching to throw a party of some kind. The Evols hadn't held a Gathering since the mansion massacre. Reunions and celebrations had fallen to the wayside. Apart from their wedding, and we know how *that* turned out, there hadn't been many Evols willing to gather in one place again. I didn't blame them. But since the Begetter appeared to have moved on from torturing us, Sonya wanted to have a small function to celebrate my birthday.

I hadn't recognized my birthday in more than a hundred years. Even before I was an Evol, there were several birthdays missed. No one around me to celebrate with. Birthdays were just another day like any other. And once I was gifted my Evol life, they became nonexistent. What's the point if you could live for three thousand years? That's just too much cake and candles. I refused their offer. I just couldn't do it. I had no desire to be in a crowd. I would've been paranoid that something bad would happen again. I told them to carry on with their plans without me, this time. If they wanted to have a get together then they should. Selfishly, I had it in my mind that if their party went well in my absence then I would attend the next function.

They did have their party and held it on my birthday. I stayed home, happy as a clam, curled up on the couch watching movies and eating junk food. There was something cathartic about it. It felt really good to be doing something I would've normally been doing in my human life. No hocus pocus, no space jumping, no dusty archives, and no new discoveries. Sonya texted me pictures and short videos of the festivities. Video clips of people wishing me a happy birthday. Video clips of Max drunk and giggly. That was the rarest of sights, he wasn't a heavy drinker in the least. What I was enjoying was the new technology of video calls that had become holograms. Full 4D images popped up from a tablet of sorts. That was both mindblowing and creepy. And side note, I'm sorry to break it to you but there still weren't flying cars as all the 1950s movies used to suggest. Anyway, It looked like a great party. They even had a cake with my name on it. I appreciated them immensely but even after watching the videos I was still glad I hadn't attended.

Life moved along in the usual fashion. Nothing horrific happened. My eyes were bothersome though. One would think that covering up black eyes wouldn't be too difficult. Wrong. I was wearing the darkest brown contacts with the newest iris typing technology I could find but the light would still break through along the edges. It was the sparkly galaxy-like specks that made them near impossible to hide. When I'd switch to the more solid-colored contacts my eyes really looked like movie monster craziness. So, those were out of the question.

I didn't stress over it too often. It wasn't like I had a job to get to daily, but I did enjoy going grocery shopping without people staring. I resorted to wearing sunglasses when in town, in addition to also wearing contacts. Yeah, that didn't look suspicious. The recluse woman who rarely came to town. The one with the weird multicolored long hair, sunglasses indoors, and who never smiled to hide her fangs. The local folks were fine with that, *not*!

That was one of the perks of hanging out with Evols, they accepted me as is. It took them a while but they did eventually see me for me and not for my freaky eyes or scary teeth. I knew the very moment they made their peace with how I looked. It was the moment they were more surprised by my swearing than my appearance. They had been so focused on my exterior they hadn't realized how belligerent I could get. All that finally changed. *Why are those four letter words so cringeworthy to others?* In any case, I didn't feel weird or uncomfortable around any of them anymore. That was pretty great.

Life was going well until the night an unwanted visitor entered my dream. I was with my wolf among the people of the purple planet village. We were by the lake of gold and silver. Just existing together and breathing in the intoxicating air. Feeling our hearts beat as one. It was a beautiful, peaceful dream. Then, out of nowhere, something turned in the air, suddenly. A rolling, earth-moving, thunderous sound emanated throughout the valley.

For the first time, dark clouds began approaching. My wolf growled, his hackles raised. Never had I experienced him upset before. Then, looking in the direction of the storm, I saw him. He was standing just beyond the people, beneath the black shroud of violence that had rapidly moved in.

It was the Begetter. Through his blurry image I could feel him glaring at me.

With a slight grin on his faceless face, he held up one hand and snapped his fingers and all the good in my world disappeared. The people vanished. My wolf vanished. The lavender sky was swallowed by storm clouds, the golden lake dried up to a desolate dustbowl complete with dead and rotting fish. Lush fields and forests ignited into a raging inferno and darkness fell around me. I was encased within a dense black fog that burned my lungs with each breath.

Another clash of thunder and my eyes sprang open, relief sweeping over me as I realized I was safe in bed. It was shortlived. Panic set in next. I thought the Begetter might've destroyed something or someone. I looked outside but all appeared to be fine. I turned on the local news; nothing nefarious had occurred. The world news was the same; all clear. I called Sonya to check on the status of the Evols. She had nothing of concern to tell me. Everything was well and good.

You might guess she found my call odd but by then, Sonya had grown accustomed to my quick in and out calls and questions. It had just been a nightmare and to be expected was what I would begin to assume. After all, he did put us through hell; a few nightmares of him were normal. I chalked it up to bad memories. PTSD from the wedding maybe. We were researching him too much and it had seeped into my brain.

Three months passed and still nothing horrible transpired. No real-life sightings of the douche bag Begetter either. The coast was clear. However, it was also about that time I realized I hadn't been dreaming, at all! Before his appearance in that last dream, I had many dreams of all kinds. Of my children during the happy days of our youth. Of holidays and birthdays with them and the grandchildren. Exhilarating times of military triumphs. Good memories spent with Seth and Sara. And of course, my visions of the lavender-skied planet, the only place I was free to conjure the memory of Lucas. They had all halted. No dreams or nightmares. Zip. Zero. Nada.

He stole them from me, my dreams. With the snap of his fingers, he had exacted his punishment. The Begetter entered my safe haven and washed it all away. Retribution for me preventing him from killing us at the wedding.

I attempted jumping into open space to find those time portals. The idea was to return to the day he entered my dream. I hoped to somehow reverse it. I didn't know how to do such a thing but that was something to figure out once in the portal. Guess what? I was unable to find any of them. Who or what the fuck was this guy? Did he destroy the time portals, or had he just hidden them from me?

I could only keep my fingers crossed that the anti-dream curse would lift. I waited and waited; I tried staying optimistic but alas, my dreams did not return. Year after year with no soothing means of welcome escape from humans. Who by the way, were killing each other again. Wars had begun to pop up here and there, sending the world into hysterics.

Besides keeping to myself in that quaint little cottage, my only other way to achieve bliss was to dream. But my home away from home had been stripped from me. Along with my sanity.

The Begetter had accomplished what he wanted; I was becoming emotionally unbalanced.

Chapter 26

Answers in Whispers

Maybe this world is another planet's hell.
—Aldous Huxley

By the human calendar, it was the year 2165. I was one hundred ninety-two years old. Spending the last forty-two years, three months, and five days dreamlessly miserable, I'd had enough. Over it all. What was the purpose of my existence? What was the purpose of any of our existences? Why would I continue to hang around this place? I was ready to admit I might be a Lost One but to what end? Even if I were, so what? The information didn't help me. It didn't change what I had been enduring all these years. It didn't bring back my loved ones and friends. Useless. I felt useless and I was perfectly lost!

Humans were in the middle of WWIV. Destroying what was left of Earth and each other. Honestly, I was surprised it had taken that long for them to enter yet another world war. Once again, their struggles were interfering with Evol lives. Many had to flee their homes from the countries that were warring. Some didn't make it out in time and were forced to fight or die. Our instant healing ability sounds like a bonus in war, it wasn't. Yeah, we survive but the humans saw crazy shit they shouldn't. It drew too much attention. Shot six times, no problem, just give me a minute and I'll be fine. That doesn't fly with humans. A few Evols had to fake their deaths during battles just so they could escape. Wars; just humans being human.

Technology had grown beyond our control. Artificial Intelligence began killing people by way of technical errors. Three jumbo jets plummeted to the ground on the same day in North America. The cause was due to AI and its inability to distinguish the importance of human lives. You can program AI to do many amazing things but emotions still wasn't one of them. The ability to value human life *is* an emotional choice and one many humans didn't even possess.

The AI onboard those planes sensed a mechanical issue but instead of forcing the planes to land; it went into self-destruct mode. Did humans remove AI from other airplanes after that? Nope!

The ongoing issue with humans was that the further they advanced, the further away from common sense they got. The more our world changed, the more it stayed the same. Arguing over invisible lines and killing each other over religion and skin color. They were just unable to get past the barbaric instincts of their ancestors. I had hated watching the never-ending carnage unfold before my new life began and now, I hated it more. What was the point of what they were doing? It was a hamster wheel. They were not on a journey to better themselves or each other. One generation to the next; on the wheel to nowhere.

I still missed Lucas so much I could hardly breathe at times. Couldn't get over the fact that he had been reborn with teeth like mine. I still didn't know what that meant. Had he been like me? Did he know how special he was? I wondered where he'd gone after he died. Was there a heaven somewhere and was he in it? Would I get to see him again? Without dreams to distract myself I slipped into these answerless questions. Was I going to become a wolf? If my calculations were correct, Tova was about three thousand years old when she transformed into a bear. Did I really want to be here for three thousand more years before running off into the forest? Would there even be a forest to run off into by then? Not at the rate the humans were destroying everything in sight.

All the tragedies that occurred before I became an Evol and all the horrors that unfolded afterward. Useless. More useless pain and heartache. I hadn't spiraled into depression as I'd been known to do in the past. Instead, I had grown perpetually angry but ... clearer minded. I felt it was time to end it. I had seen the world, completed my bucket list, and accomplished all I wanted. If I could do nothing to protect humans from themselves then I would remove myself from the equation. I hadn't yet figured out how, but it was time I released myself from our planet of disappointment and terror. One hundred ninety-two years had been more purgatory than I could stand. To quote a line from *The Hitchhiker's Guide to the Galaxy*; 'So long and thanks for all the fish.'

I decided to visit with Max and Sonya one last time. Not that they knew it would be the last. We came together to have a family style dinner beneath The Wailing Wall, complete with all the Guardians. A lighthearted, forget the world, outstanding meal. Love and laughter filled the whole dining room; if only for that one night. A much-needed break from the warring humans above us. A time to reconnect with each other and strengthen the bonds that brought us together in the first place. Although they were unaware; they had given me the most perfect sendoff I could've asked for. Not much had changed under the wall. I believed that's what I liked about it. The world above was so loud and fast moving but the hidden city below was calm, slow creeping like a shallow stream.

Once back in my Scottish cottage, I began the arduous process of closing up shop. I left my Italian villa to Max and Sonya. My precious Scotland home would remain in my name on the off chance I was unable to accomplish my mission. By the way, I finally picked up that boulder next to the cottage. It was awesome! Anyway, I wasn't going to stay there. I felt it would be poetic to kill myself in the place where it all began. My cabin home atop the solace mountain I so loved still. It was there I first escaped from the world around me and it would be there I'd permanently escape from Earth itself.

I didn't want to morph into the beast I knew I was inside. To be lost in the wilderness, having no memories of love, of my children, grandchildren, friends, or of real, amazing food! Cheeseburgers and french fries. Chocolate milkshakes and ice cream. Or true Sicilian pasta and clams with the best tomato sauce ever to exist. To be robbed of all those things would be the saddest of crimes. I couldn't go on as I was and I couldn't wait out the wars of humans. No matter how old I lived to be, it wouldn't be long enough to outlive their desire for destruction. So, I took my last flight to America. The last time I'd have to deal with gross people in an airport.

Once I arrived at my cabin home, a flood of nostalgia rushed over me. Making it all the more palpable was the winter snow falling. The first time I met Seth, Lucas, and Sara. Waking up next to a dead moose and seeing Lucas's adoring eyes hold me within his gaze. That home was the last time I had been able to video chat with my children. The last time I had heard the tiny voices of my grandchildren. My sweet cat Vader was there, lovingly trying to comfort me. It was the place of many amazing transformations, both physical and spiritual. It felt right to be ending it there.

I had to get creative to pull off a suicide with a body that healed itself instantly. I was finally old enough that not even a henchman's axe would be able to kill me. So, hanging myself wouldn't work. My physical strength had grown such that my neck muscles wouldn't have given into a rope. Guns were useless. Shooting myself in the head wouldn't work. I'd just be knocked out for a time until the wound healed. And obviously I wouldn't be able to drown myself. It took some careful thinking, but the answer came to me eventually. I would bleed myself out. Slicing my wrists or throat wouldn't work, they'd just heal. I had to find a way to keep a vein or artery open. A lightbulb illuminated. An intravenous catheter a.k.a. IV tubing and set up. You recall, I had been a medic in another life. Medic till I died.

I purchased what was needed from a local medical supply store and then took one last look at my mountain on the drive back. I placed a large bucket on the back porch next to my rocking chair, got comfortable and implemented my plan. I inserted the IV needle into my arm, removed the needle, leaving the catheter in place, and connected the tubing. The catheter would prevent my body from healing the wound. It would allow the blood to flow. Out. I cut the long tubing down to about a foot in length and dangled it over the bucket. I may have been killing myself, but I was still a neat freak. I didn't want anyone to find me in a huge mess of blood all over the place. Speaking of, my Gifter was missing so no one would know I had died for some time. I'm sure the Evols would find a way to cover up my death, hiding it from the humans.

My grand plan was to sit quietly, watch the falling snow, and bleed out. It wasn't a great plan because of how long it could take but

I knew it would work. I sat there for maybe twenty minutes, slowly growing sleepier and more relaxed. Closing my eyes off and on as if I were willing myself to die faster.

As my heartbeat softened, I realized my creature in the distance had been getting closer. It was walking toward me out of the woods. *Oh my God,* I thought, was I finally going to set eyes on it? Would at least one answer to all my answerless questions be settled? What a gift that would be. A mystery solved.

It slowly moved closer and closer from out of the shadows. Approaching in an almost ghostly manner, footsteps not quite touching the ground. As it came into the dim porch light, I saw it. No fucking way! *It was me!* She was nearly translucent but it WAS me! Totally me. So creepy weird. Was I hallucinating? Was my brain shutting down due to the blood loss? *It had to be*, I thought. Maybe I had already died and didn't know it. This whole damn time my creature was actually me? Well, that was kind of a letdown. Lame!

As I stood in front of myself, I smiled at me with a peaceful grin.

"What are you?" I asked.

"Simply put," I replied. "I am what you humans call a soul. I am your soul."

"You have been my creature all this time? But why? How?" I asked myself.

"First, I don't like your name for me, 'creature.' And second, the night you accepted the Evol gift, I was ripped from you. Shoved out by something else. An entity much stronger and older than any of us. Unfortunately, I am bound to stay with you for as long as your body lives," I explained.

"That's a relief. I thought maybe you were the Devil following me," I sarcastically replied. I tell you, talking to yourself as a separate entity at the end of the world *is* a mind-bender.

"That thing, you call the Devil, has no power. There are much worse beings out there. How did you think that man, Seth, was death? Death doesn't even have a name! I've lingered between worlds for the last one hundred and forty-three years because you fell for something so stupid! You were forty-nine years old when he came to you out of nowhere; you weren't smart enough to know that was a bad thing?" I snapped at me.

Okay. Well, I knew for sure at that point she was my soul because even in her ethereal state she was a sarcastic bitch. Super freaky talking to what was essentially me. And I really didn't care for her—my tone. I would keep calling her 'creature' just to piss her off! I moved past the moment, feeling my body weaken further. I needed to know one thing before I died. Since she had showed herself, she had to answer one more question. I couldn't allow the opportunity to pass by. "What—" I began.

She interrupted me. "Let me guess. What are you? Is there really a god? What does heaven look like? Blah. Blah. Blah. Humans all ask the same questions," she said, being condescending and rolling her eyes.

"No, you stupid cunt! What is the Begetter? Where did he come from? What is his purpose?" I asked. I'd saved my pissy for my final moments.

That set her back on her heels. It gave her pause and she just stared at me for what felt like an eternity. I was lethargic and lightheaded as my blood continued to drip into the bucket.

"I'm not allowed to tell you anything about that. Shh, just let your body die and I'll get to go home. You won't care about these questions once it's over," she whispered.

The nerve! I was sinking fast but still stubborn, so I asked again.

And again, she refused to tell me. With what little strength I had left, I reached for the IV tube in my arm. I threatened her that if she didn't tell me then I would rip the line out. She would never go home. She began to panic but could also feel I was as close to death as one could get.

Reluctantly, she bent down to me, placing one hand atop my head. I instantly felt a sharp searing pain like an aneurysm had popped in my brain. An unbearable blinding migraine ran through my head then was gone. She unlocked all the information I had gained from the Begetter the day I pushed the purple orb inside him. It had been in there the entire time, just chained up and sealed.

Within seconds, millions of years exploded like a grenade in my mind. Everything he had done was suddenly there. All my questions about him were answered. Many of my questions about myself, about this world, and about life itself; all answered! My heart raced, expelling blood from my body faster. Learning who he really was angered me and I shouted at her, "What the fuck? What. The. Actual. Fuck!"

She paused and then smiled. "Now you know but it's almost over. It doesn't matter anymore. Relax and slide into silence," she softly said.

Since when had my soul become such an asshole? A white-hot rage was building. Change of plans. I wasn't leaving here just yet after all. Closing my eyes, I hoped to pull off what should've been impossible by then. Engaging my siren song; calling out to the forest offerings.

My creature stood; waiting for me to die, not knowing what I was up to. Which was odd, she was my soul, all things considered. My heartbeat slowed to just two beats per minute. Then, there, I heard it, the crunching of snow as a great stag emerged from the woods.

Soul Emma turned to see it and realized what might be happening. She begged me to stop but I would not.

I had briefly considered drinking from my own blood bucket as I was at death's door, however, what a fucking mess that would have been! Plus, lifting the bucket in my weakened condition just wouldn't have happened. The stag walked directly through other me's translucent body and lay down on the deck in front of me. I ripped out the IV with what must have been my last heartbeat and flung myself forward, onto my savior. I drained the stag dry, collapsed on the animal with no strength left in my body. If it hadn't been for his own heartbeat moving blood into my mouth, I don't think I would've made it. Lined up behind him were three more offerings. As I fed, I witnessed my soul retreat into the woods, hearing her sobs of betrayal. She wouldn't forgive me for this, but I had spent enough time with her to know she couldn't harm me either. So, I didn't care.

After I'd drunk my fill and my arm was healed, I staggered inside collapsing on the bed where I slept off and on for three days. Once recovered, I began planning my next move. I had a powerful being to stop and no idea how to do it exactly. But come hell or high water, I would ensure he got what he deserved.

Since I was no longer going to die, I called a local realtor. I gave him license to sell my cabin home on my behalf. I didn't believe I would ever see it again. There might be a few Evols upset with me for what I had planned so I didn't tell any of them. I began this new life on my own and I would be changing the fate of everyone, also on my own, alone.

There was so much do. My concentration was limited and degraded. Way too many events and thoughts crammed in my head. Opening the flood gates of the Begetter's memories had sent me into a drunken-like stupor. I'd detail out my mission one minute, then stare off into the distance the next. What if I couldn't think clearly enough to even get out the door? I would be stuck there for God knew how long, starting and restarting. Should I tell Max or Sonya? Maybe they could help keep me on track? No, I couldn't. I didn't want them involved. I didn't want anyone else to get hurt. Lists. I made lots of lists to keep my thoughts in line. First on the docket was to get the realtor to the house. Just get that accomplished and move on from there.

Days later, as I packed my clothes, I heard a knock at the door. I assumed it was the realtor come to take pictures of the house and walked through the kitchen to the door and opened it. What I saw just about floored me to hell.

I stood stunned and frozen. Forcing myself to grasp who I was looking at. It was impossible. Perhaps my dreams had returned and I was just *in* a dream. He couldn't be here. But he was.

Lucas. It was Lucas standing on my porch!

I couldn't get the screen door open fast enough. Leaping into his open arms, we held each other, tight. The safest I had ever felt in my life was in that moment. After several minutes of the strongest best hug, we put our foreheads together. We were breathing as one. At the same time, we tilted our heads up, slowly pressing our lips to one another's. That kind of deep breathtaking kiss everyone longs for. The explosion of life itself. A kiss that forces your heart to beat in unison with theirs. We finally stopped and went back to the forehead-to-forehead position again to catch our breath. The words peaceful and whole are just not strong enough to describe what was happening inside me.

While still reveling in that outstanding moment, Lucas spoke, "Now, let's go kill that son of a bitch." I swiftly looked up at him, puzzled. He grinned, ran his fingers through my hair, and down my cheek. "My creature shared some secrets with me too," he told me.

I put my hands on both sides of his face and lovingly kissed him again before I replied, "Let's do this!" I turned to go back inside the house; excited to finish packing.

He held my hand, stopping me from going inside just yet. "Wait, wait. I brought someone with me. I hope it's okay?" he said.

I moved my head to the side to look around him and there, in the driveway, was a man sitting in the driver's seat of a truck. Seth! And he was gleefully waving at me through the truck window. I thought my heart would burst from my chest with the arrival of Lucas *and* Seth. If I'd had any doubts before about whether I would be able to complete my mission, those doubts had vanished. I grinned from ear to ear and excitedly waved back at Seth in an almost bouncing childlike manner.

Lucas and I went into the house to get my bags. As we entered, he grabbed my waist and pulled me toward him, kissing me again. Oh, I just hoped I wasn't dreaming. I begged the universe for it to be real. I pulled in close to hear his heartbeat again. It was real. "Where have you been all this time?" I asked him as I clung to his body.

"Our home," he replied.

"*Our* home? I don't understand. What do you mean *our home*?" I asked.

"Yup, our home. Our beautiful home with the lavender skies. It's real Emma. You've been time traveling, not dreaming. I was there too. AND, I have been keeping company with that obstinate giant black wolf of yours. He misses you by the way," he answered.

"Why didn't you talk to me or I to you, during those times? Why couldn't I speak?" I asked.

He grimaced a bit, sad that we had lost so much time. "It's difficult to describe, babe but I promise as soon as we have a moment to catch our breaths, I will tell you everything I know," he replied.

In disbelief and extreme joy, I could barely contain my next question, "Where is our home?"

"It's right here. It's not on another planet. It's always been here and we're going to get it back. Just as soon as we destroy that psychopath, the Begetter," he replied.

"I'm in. I am so, so in!" I answered.

"Listen, that thing we are about to go after has the power to vanish one or both of us. Because of that, I have to tell you something right now. I don't want to waste any more time," Lucas said. And then he took a deep breath, focusing all his energy on me. "I missed you so much, Emma. What happened to me and my absence was *not* my doing. All I desperately wanted was to find my way back to you. I'm so sorry for everything you must have gone through. With all that I am, I love you sweetheart," he said.

"I love you Lucas, with all that I am. We're in this together. No matter what," I replied as tears streamed down my face.

"No matter what," he said, lovingly echoing back with confidence.

And with that, we fell into another amazing kiss. I have no words for all that I was feeling in that moment. An explosion of answers to so many of my questions had been resolved in a matter of days and now this. I suddenly interrupted our embrace with another question, "What about Seth? He's been missing. How did you find him?" I asked.

"Well, that's a long story too. And we will tell you all about it once we're on the road," Lucas said, smiling.

Just then, we heard three loud truck horn blasts and Seth's voice telling us to *stop canoodling*! Lucas and I laughed, embracing once more. Lucas yelled out the door for Seth to come in for a minute and make himself useful.

Seth ran up the stairs, bursting into the house. He grabbed me, picking me up off my feet in a twirling hug. He was obviously on board with whatever crazy mission we were all about to embark on. "Oh, love the hair, Emma. Very chic, these white and copper highlights. Is this in vogue now?"

"You realize I should be cussing a blue streak and kicking your ass for leaving us. But I'm so happy to see you. Just so happy," I told him with my arms wrapped tight around his neck.

"And you realize I was waiting outside to see if it was going to rain blood. If your reunion with Lucas didn't go well, I would've been squealing tires outta here!" Seth laughed.

"Okay you two, we have to get Emma's stuff and ourselves out the door," Lucas instructed.

Together, we were setting out to takedown one of the most powerful beings ever. Luckily for us, my creature had unlocked the Begetter's persona, secrets, and tricks that had been tucked away in my mind. We were not heading into battle unarmed. This was not the end of my journey. However, this is where you, Dear Reader, and I part ways. For now.

I will leave you with one final message:

To Whoever Reads This,
Human or Evol, Earth is not yours. This world was never yours.
May this serve as your eviction notice, effective immediately.

We're taking our home back.
Sincerely,
Emma Jane Alexander—no longer lost.

Embrace the odd shapes and murky spaces, for those too are you.
　　　　　—*Brandy Hunter*

www.ingramcontent.com/pod-product-compliance
Lightning Source LLC
LaVergne TN
LVHW041753060526
838201LV00046B/982